ASCENDING
The Regonia Chronicles: Book Three

By Elexis Bell

Eager to stay up to date on the latest dark fiction from Elexis Bell?

Sign up for her newsletter on her website.

www.elexisbell.com

Chapter One
Novay

Reginald

Olivia's suicide attempt hangs over me, wearing me down, dragging out my steps as Rone and I step into my room. She follows me in, as she's taken to doing, and I swallow.

Taking a deep breath, I shake my head. But still, I see Olivia with those bottles, chasing pills with poison, going limp.

Has anything good come of what I did?

"The man that would've come here, the girl that came instead of Olivia..." I say, voice a hollow shell. "What happened to them?"

Rone's chest rises with a deep breath. "The man's name is Johnathan Croon. He's the Minister of Human Affairs. He isn't happy, but he's channeling it into productive work, trying to make life better for those still on Termana. And now, if the tribunal we saw is anything to go by, he's trying to make amends with the Regonians."

I sigh, grateful that someone in power back home isn't a corrupt lunatic.

"And the girl?"

My heart shudders. I can only hope she isn't enduring experiments like mine.

A wistful smile tugs at one corner of Rone's lips. "Elizabeth Croon is happy here. Her best friend had been taken the week before. She ended up in a group experiment with her. They share a communal living space with 23 other people their age."

She sighs, and the happiness falls from her face. "Not all who were taken are as lonely as you've been, as Croon would've been."

Finally, I move, taking a few steps and sitting on my bed. Rone turns to follow me, and I stare at her feet as she crosses the distance between us.

Croon isn't as miserable as he could've been. I wouldn't wish these experiments on anyone.

And his daughter found happiness.

"At least *something* positive came out of this," I mumble.

Rone comes up short, stopping just a few steps away from me. Her arms wrap around her waist, and the movement draws my gaze up from the floor.

A frown carves lines in her face, scrunching her brows together. A single tear shimmers on the edge of her lashes, and she refuses to meet my gaze.

"I thought…" She clears her throat, swallows hard. "Isn't *this* something positive?"

"Oh, Rone, that came out wrong." My heart twists in my chest, and I rise to my feet, wrapping my arms around her. With a hand on her short hair, I tuck her head against my shoulder.

What am I doing? Why didn't I think about it?

"I'm sorry," I whisper, pressing a kiss to the side of her head. "This *is* something positive, believe me. I'm glad *this* happened."

And I am.

I wish there had been an easier way to meet her, to be with her. But if I had to go through all this, I'm glad I at least get to be with her.

A tiny sniffle shakes her frame, tearing at my heart. She shakes her head. In a broken voice, she says, "Logically, I knew what you meant. But… Why did it still hurt?"

"Because feelings don't care about logic," I say.

Planting another kiss on the top of her head, I try to focus on this moment, this brief interval of warmth. Needing some sort of refuge, I recount the positive things of the day.

Olivia is alive. That man in the ship, the man that was with her in her message… He saved her.

My throat tightens, constricting around a sob as the image of my daughter lifeless in her pilot's seat floats through my mind. I shove the image away, replacing it with her message and forcing myself to stick to the positive things.

She's alive.

I'm here with Rone.

Most of the Regonians are safe.

And Eva…

I sigh.

Eva has been dealt with.

I hate the relief that floods through me at that last thought, but knowing she won't hurt anyone else calms me. I just hope Johnathan Croon can handle cleaning up her mess.

Chapter Two

Venice Space Research Station

Tenna

My fingers drum against my leg as Krona and I stand in the hangar, waiting. Through the tiny airlock window, we watch SCCS Sparrow fly in, bringing our friends, our new family, to take their place with us.

Calm down.

They haven't agreed to the ceremony. Who's to say they will?

But hope blossoms within me, desperate to welcome them into Daen Tribe. Even if the ceremony would be stunted by the limitations of the Human planet, such as it is, and space stations.

My heart expands a million times over, bursting with a joyous idea.

We could do it on Regonia when we go back!

They could come down with us. They could come to our keep.

I smile, practically vibrating with the overwhelming energy spreading through me at the thought of them going home with us. Thoughts of their imminent return to the Human world threaten to squash my hopes, quickly followed by thoughts of the war we're about to enter.

But for the time being, I allow myself a moment of happiness, exalting in the possibilities.

The hangar door locks into place, and air rushes in with a great gust. Anticipation builds within me as the ship's hatch lowers. Olivia and Ricardo descend with hands joined, and I squeeze Krona's hand.

"Finally!" I exclaim.

Krona chuckles, but I know he echoes my sentiment.

The Guard with red hair, one of the few Humans here, clears her throat. "I can open that if you step back from it," she says, smile evident in her voice.

Krona and I do as she bids, stepping clear of the airlock door. It rises before us, and we rush through, breaking into a sprint with smiles plastered over our faces. Laughter echoes through the hangar as Olivia and Ricardo barrel toward us, infected by our joy.

We check our paces, careful not to slam into them and break their bones. Pinning them between us, we hug them tight, giggling all the while.

Chapter Three
Venice Space Research Station

Olivia

Ricardo clutches my hand as Tenna and Krona lead us through the station to our new shared quarters. We squeeze through halls packed to the brim with Regonians.

Living, breathing Regonians.

They smile and laugh. They weep. They sing. Their energy fills the place, lending the barren metal walls a bit of color and emotion.

Despite the sadness in some of their voices, despite the loss I know they've suffered, their presence makes me smile.

Mom didn't get them all.

My shoulders rise and fall with a sigh of relief.

We approach the outer ring, typically the residential section, but it's different. At the end of the hall, where movies and documentaries once played on opaque glass, a curtain hangs, blocking the window alcove from the rest of the hall.

Beyond it, strange sounds shift as voices move from one pitch to another, shaking and rolling.

My pace slows, and I furrow my brows. Shaking my head in confusion, I ask, "What's going on behind the curtain?"

But dread doesn't fill me as it would amongst Humans. Curiosity slips through me, instead.

Sighing, Tenna speaks, but she does so in her mother tongue. "Loo artur ris daet mains ris loo UllaCoomlar. Loo taeban taen loo ark."

My implant translates, "They fall short of the sounds of their Lost Ones. They will seek until they find."

Turning around, Tenna says, "Sorry. I haven't used much of your language here."

I should probably learn their language, especially if I'm going to stay here. That should keep me occupied for a while.

I glow at the prospect of something new to learn, something that could provide a challenge. And then it strikes me just how quickly she learned to speak our language, how quickly Krona learned it. She switches back to it so easily and speaks without any hint of an accent.

I guess I always took it for granted, but… How smart are they?

How closely descended from the Drennar are the Regonians?

I shudder at the parallels between my idle curiosity and my mother's heinous experiments. Yet, I have to wonder if the idea behind her work was sound.

She just went about finding out in the worst possible way.

Maybe I can do it better, without killing or kidnapping or destroying lives. I could just ask them questions.

I look around at the hall, at the people who've suffered so much at Human hands and yet willingly entered into an alliance for the betterment of both our people. Silently, I vow to learn as much as I can from them.

As much as they'll let me learn.

Krona tugs at Tenna's hand, and they turn, heading into the outer ring. Every door stands open in the residential section, but those seeking sounds sit apart, cordoned off in small groups. I meet Ricardo's eyes, and we follow. I fight my curiosity, keeping my eyes from straying to the edges of curtains as we pass.

But questions fill my head.

Why do they search for a sound for a loved one? Why haven't they found it yet?

Has everyone else here found them?

My heart races, and a smile tugs at my lips. I glance around, taking in every face, every garment, every gesture. Excitement bubbles up within me, building and budding.

We reach an older couple, hair streaked through with the palest blue and faces wrinkled. Tenna and Krona stop before them, and sad smiles play over their lips. Tenna inclines her head, resting her forehead against those of the older Regonians. They rest palms against cheeks, embracing each other. Krona stands behind her with hands on her shoulders.

Tenna makes a soft, cooing purr, and I tip my head to the side. The older couple answers with a high trill.

Ricardo leans toward me and mouths, "What's happening?"

I shrug, mind swirling with a maelstrom of questions.

Tenna repeats the high trill, and the older couple answers with Tenna's purred coo.

My translator comes up empty, failing to offer even a guess at a translation. When they separate, I transform my face into a study of polite calm, trying to be respectful. But my mind strains at its confines.

Who were they? What were those sounds?

Oh god... Were those the sounds of... What did Tenna call them? Their Lost Ones?

My heart shrinks from the prospect.

Who did Tenna lose?

We move down the hall, passing more curtained off areas with sounds dancing behind them. With each one, the desire to witness the strange ceremony beyond the curtain grows stronger, but I refuse to indulge myself, to trespass upon something so clearly private.

The doors along the hall get further and further apart as we reach the family section, but still, all are open. The cry of a baby reaches out from one doorway. Intimate whispers waft from another.

An inner door slides shut within that apartment, closing the whispers off. I blush, instantly understanding the significance of that particular closed door.

But my mind never stops working, piecing together what is and isn't private amongst Regonians, which aspects of life are a part of the community and which are kept personal.

Tenna and Krona meander through a doorway that looks exactly like every other one we've passed. Somehow, I expected their quarters to have some embellishment on the outside, or perhaps I thought they'd be located in a commune so they'd have more space.

Does their position not elevate them? Do they have the same housing situation as all their subjects on Regonia, as well? Or is this just out of necessity?

Ricardo releases my hand, touching the small of my back as we pass through the door and into the living room. I stare at the cushions, all settled on the floor rather than on the couch or chairs. I tip my head to the side, taking in the stacked furniture frames in one corner.

Do they prefer to sit on the floor? There were cultures on Earth that preferred that.

Tenna turns, chuckling at my expression. "They're too small for us."

I nod, accepting the practical answer, and we move to the bedroom we'll be sharing with Krona and Tenna. My tapestries hang from a bar down the center, allowing both sides an even view of the window.

A smile spreads my lips wide.

Standing just on their side of the tapestry partition, Krona and Tenna beam down at us. Their hands link, and they exchange a glance full of nervous excitement.

"I hope you like it," Krona says. Becoming slightly more serious, he adds, "And if you ever want to talk, you can just slide these out of the way."

He demonstrates, pushing one of the tapestries toward the window.

I glance at the blankets spread out on the floor behind them, then back out at the living room where two voices speak Regonian. The songs in the hall beyond drift toward us on breezes of laughter and occasional sobs.

"I'll take you up on that," I say. Looking at Tenna, I smile and add, "I think it's time you made good on that promise to tell me some stories."

She laughs and readily agrees.

Chapter Four
Venice Space Research Station

Krona

Tenna and I pass through halls crowded with our people, listening to the sounds they utter. I do my best to commit each one to memory, determined to help them honor their Lost Ones. We venture to a conference room tucked within the security department with Ricardo and Olivia following close behind.

Once inside, Olivia hails the Survival Coalition. She and Ricardo settle into chairs, but Tenna and I sit on a bench we moved in here to accommodate us. In a heartbeat, Johnathan Croon appears on a large screen before us, despite our early appearance.

"It'll just be me today," he says, running a hand through silver strands. "In all the commotion, a few things have fallen behind. The others are attending to their duties."

"I'm sure we can manage," I say, secretly grateful not to have to speak with that idiot, Ulric.

We move through pleasantries quickly, knowing exactly what's at stake and how much lies undone. With brown eyes crinkling, Croon says, "We have some good news, finally. Our largest ship has passed all inspections, and it's been cleared to transport you all to Regonia."

I sigh, relieved, and hope floods through me. I need to run, need to see my home, feel the grass whispering against my thighs. Tenna squeezes my hand, and I turn to her, face split wide with a smile.

Light dances within her eyes, and a smile bursts over her features. "We're going home…" she says, and the words are a caress, easing the tension from my body.

Tears prick at the corners of my eyes. Putting a hand to her cheek, I pull her close, leaning our foreheads together.

"We're going home," I echo, tasting the sweetness of that promise. My mind fills with the reaction our people will have at this news, and a tear slips free of my eyes. My throat tightens, and my heart expands in my chest.

I try not to think of the state our home might be in after our absence, try not to wonder just how long it's been. That's a problem for another time.

Right now, I repeat the promise, telling myself over and over that we're going home.

Tenna touches my cheek, palm soft and warm against my skin. I open my eyes, staring into mossy green. A smile passes between us, and we turn to face Croon once more.

His expression mirrors ours, but he wipes his tears away. We let ours shimmer in the too-bright lights.

Pulling in a deep breath, Croon goes on. "Olivia, Ricardo," he says. "Since the two of you are the most familiar with our Regonian allies, we'd like you to be our official ambassadors. Of course, this means you'll have to go with them to Regonia. If that isn't amenable to you, we can find someone—"

"It's amenable. Please, don't find someone else," Olivia interrupts.

Ricardo chuckles.

"I mean… I want to go," she amends. "Ricardo, you don't have to if you don't want to."

"Are you kidding?" he says with a laugh. "Of course, I want to go."

"Then, it's settled," Croon says. "There are a few other matters to attend to first, though. We've found some recruits for you to train in the maintenance of Atlantis, Olivia. We'll be in touch later today, setting up schedules for you to work with them. And then, there's the matter of the new tech the two of you will need."

I tip my head to the side, wondering why they need new tech for this. A spike of lingering mistrust lances through me, but I contain it.

"What new tech?" Olivia asks.

"Ah, yes. I suppose you don't know yet," Croon answers. "The air on Regonia is actually toxic to Humans. It contains a molecule called alonarium which, if inhaled, causes an intense and very aggressive form of lung cancer."

The man sighs, then continues, "One hour of exposure results in death within a month. Two hours of exposure causes death within a week.

Five hours… Well, the test subjects apparently only lasted a day.”

“Test subjects?” Olivia mutters, voice strangled by emotion. Her jaw falls open, and she stares at Croon’s image on the screen with vacant eyes.

Ricardo puts an arm around her, pulling her to him.

My stomach plummets at the thought of Eva Dobovich’s depravity. Tenna’s fingers curl into claws, gripping my hand tight.

“It would seem that there were a few,” Croon says. He clears his throat, changes subject. “If the Drennar have made use of the element in question, it’s no wonder they’re so advanced. It’s a marvel. The smallest electrical current can manipulate its shape, its texture, its color, temperature, density. Some of the research done on it is showing some very promising applications. We just can’t breathe it.”

“So how did they survive long enough to capture us?” Tenna asks, voice carefully measured.

"Tech," Croon answers simply. "They made filters and installed them in helmets, initially."

Remembering that Croon knows little of our ways, I say, "Helmets won't work if you plan for Olivia and Ricardo to approach Taron Tribe with us. Hiding your face in battle or in diplomacy shows cowardice and uncertainty in your choices, in Daen Tribe and Taron. If any Humans accompany us up the mountain, and they should since Relnoc and Dresde will want to know who they're aligning their tribe with, if Humans go and hide their faces, the alliance will never happen."

Croon nods slowly, considering my words. "Then, I guess we're lucky they developed a more refined version," he says.

"I'm not sure why they were planning a return trip, but they were. They had the filters installed in their throats directly. We retrieved them before the…" His eyes dart to Olivia and Ricardo before he continues with, "execution. We've been making more ever since, and nearly have enough to equip everyone that will need to go to Regonia and all that will go to Novay. Just in case the same element is present in the air there."

I nod, but shock flows through me at the turn I've taken, accepting a form of tech that's so… invasive. I fall quiet, lost to my thoughts.

With the important matters handled, the meeting draws to a close. The screen turns transparent once more, allowing a view of space, and I stare blankly at the stars beyond. Olivia and Ricardo speak in whispers, but their conversation washes over me in blurs and static.

They rise from their chairs, and Tenna pulls me up. But my feet drag, weighed down by the realization of what I've just lobbied for.

They have to have the filters if they're to go to Regonia. They have to have the tech.

We reach the door, but I pause, not quite ready to pass beyond it, to rejoin our people. "Never in my life did I expect to endorse star-sickness," I whisper to Tenna.

She puts a hand on my chest, stepping close. "Nor did I," she says, shaking her head. "But then, I never could've foreseen any of this."

I shake my head, turning to stare out at daet Skon ris Soons. The Realm of Stars. It opens up beyond the window, and I search the white dots of light for home.

Tenna puts her arm around me, leaning her head on my shoulder. I pull her close, drawing strength from her warmth.

"Is this the right choice for us?" I ask.

"It's the only choice we have," she whispers.

Chapter Five
Venice Space Research Station

Olivia

Careful to keep my voice low, I whisper my excitement to Ricardo. His eyes shine in the dim lighting I always set my quarters to. I glance at the tapestries separating us from Krona and Tenna, trying not to disturb them, but I'm practically bouncing on the bed.

"We're going to see Regonia!" I exclaim in a whisper-shout. "We can learn so much from them, from their world. We're already learning a ton from the alonarium. I asked Croon for access to the notes the labs were compiling, and oh my god! It's like some sort of wonder particle."

Ricardo chuckles, but the same excitement burns in his eyes. The corners of his lips turn up in a perpetual smile.

"We can learn *so much*. And we can do it better, we can do it *right*. Not how my mom did it. We can work *with* them and fix so much." I let my head fall back, pulling in a deep breath.

"When can we set off?" Ricardo asks.

"Just a few days. Maybe a week." Meeting Ricardo's gaze, I take his hand in mine. "We have to get the filters, and I have to train the recruits on Atlantis. It'll be pretty rigorous, but hopefully they learn quickly."

I shake my head, incredulous at how much of a turn my life is taking.

My mother betrayed us all and tried to condemn me to death. Our last conversation plays through my head, making me wonder what would've happened if I'd reached out sooner.

But I know better.

I tried.

So often, I tried.

And the parent I spent so much time wishing for… is alive. I have to share him with the rest of humanity, but he's alive and I can reach for him, finally.

And now, I'm going to a different planet. I'll get to see a new world with new people and new plants and new animals.

I don't know if it's the anti-depressants finally kicking in or my sessions with Cait working some sort of magic. Maybe it's the excitement of finally not being bored or the closure with my mom, finally hearing her apologize and tell me she loves me. Maybe it's the lack of alcohol or maybe it's Ricardo's warmth and acceptance. Maybe it's Tenna and Krona.

Maybe it's everything, all at once.

But it hits me that I actually feel… better.

My smile widens, and my shoulders lift with a deep breath. A single lock of hair slips free, hanging before my eyes.

Ricardo reaches out, tucking it behind my ear. He lets his hand linger, and a heavy silence fills our part of the room. "It's nice to see you smile."

I blush, dropping my gaze. But my eyes only find his lips.

Beyond the barely open door, out in the living area, someone stirs. A soft coo purrs from the lips of Tenna's sister, Kala. I recognize the sound as the one that Tenna made with the elderly couple. The sound I've since learned represents her brother, lost to my mother's treachery.

"She's thinking of their brother, Efsi," I whisper, and the name is a lament. "But they carry on. Even here, even with so many gone, even with their entire life called into question… They carry on."

The marvel of Daen Tribe spreads out in my mind, enveloping everything.

"This is who they are," Ricardo says. "Krona had it right after we woke everyone up. The Drennar didn't do the work to build their tribe. *They* did. Whether the part the Drennar played is a lie or not, this is who they are."

We lay back in our bed, *our* bed, arms wrapped around each other. A sweet, tender silence falls over us, and I listen to his heart, feel his chest move with each breath.

"None of this would've been possible without you," he says. "You know that, right?"

I pull back, staring into amber eyes. They seem to glow in the warm light.

But someone else would've fixed all this. Someone else would've found out what they were doing.

Someone would've gotten her files, somehow.

But for the first time, I realize that no one else would've thought to check in on my mother, even with Ricardo bringing forth evidence. Her status as Minister put her out of reach of prying eyes and suspicion. The sudden appearance of another alien would've been turned in to the Ministers of Research and Defense, both of whom were in on it.

And I'm not sure anyone else *could* have gotten into her files.

My brows furrow as I put the pieces together in my head.

Maybe I actually did something good.

Tears prick at the corners of my eyes, but not tears of sorrow, as has been my wont lately.

Maybe I actually am... good enough.

Is that even possible?

A soft moan passes over the tapestries, barely reaching my ears. My mouth falls open, and I freeze.

Ricardo's eyes sparkle with astonishment, and he whispers, "Was that…?" He rolls onto his back, head turning to face the tapestries.

I prop myself on my elbow and strain my ears. My hand rests on Ricardo's chest.

And sure enough, another muffled moan slips past the heavy fabrics separating us from entangled Regonians.

I stare down at Ricardo and mouth, "Oh my god!"

Silent laughter shakes him. I collapse atop him, burying my face in his hair to muffle the sound of my own giggles.

Whispering against his ear, I say, "Are they really…?"

Shushing me, he fights the laughter that threatens to rumble through him.

"Should we leave?" I ask, forcing quiet words out between rasps of silent mirth.

Ricardo gestures to the end of the tapestries, parted just before the door. "They'll see us," he mouths. Pressing his mouth to my ear, he whispers, "I don't want to interrupt. They deserve to… finish."

I roll onto my back and clap a hand over my mouth. But a single laugh escapes me.

Rolling toward me, Ricardo shushes me again. "Stop, they'll hear!" he whispers, shoulders still shaking. He glances at the tapestries, as if they might part at any moment with one of our friends peeking through to ask us to quiet down.

The image breaks something loose within me, and I laugh harder, barely maintaining my silence. Tears roll down my cheeks. Ricardo leans in close, and my helpless sobs of laughter infect him.

***

Four of the most promising tech geeks we have to offer stare out at me from the screen, blocking out the stars beyond the window. I do a quick sweep of their personal computers and their work devices, getting a feel for the kind of technology they're used to working with.

For the most part, they prefer only the newest, top of the line tech. But one of them, a young man maybe three years my junior with rich brown skin, prefers a real keyboard. I give him a wistful smile, then open my laptop and tap in a few passwords.

The sound of the keystrokes draws his gaze from the screens spread out before him, and his jaw falls open. "Really?" he asks. "I thought I was the only person who liked real keyboards."

"Definitely not," I answer.

On any day in my past, I would've jumped at the chance to talk about these beautiful relics, these masterpieces of days gone by. I would've loved to gush over the exquisite beauty of typing, the feeling of being connected to the device in a way no implant can ever provide.

But we only have so much time.

And much more exciting things linger on the horizon.

We exchange names, and I familiarize them with the basics. "All our data is still present," I say. "All the security footage, all the credit information, payroll, food orders, music preferences, it's all still there."

They nod, having ascertained as much for themselves.

"The old security protocols are still in place as a fail-safe," I tell them, knowing they'll have found that much to be true, as well. "But all of that has been heavily encrypted and hidden away. The Drennar still get information from us, just nothing that's completely accurate."

From the top left of the screen, a woman in her mid-forties, Ksenia Ribald, asks, "What do you mean, they still get information from us? I thought the point of your program was to keep them from getting anything?"

"Anything important," I correct. "To them, our security appears…" I search for a word to explain it fully, then tip my head to the side and say, "broken."

I pull up an example of some footage from a café on Termana and display it on their screens. The static claws at my ears, amplified by the various devices of the tech team as it echoes back to me.

In a corner of my screen, I watch the image shift in waves with streaks of color shot through the otherwise black and white video. The audio crackles loudly with a word or two coming through every now and then.

Black splotches roam freely over the screen, slowly spreading to encompass more and more of the image. Finally, they meet, consuming the whole café, and I pull it from their screens.

"That's what the Drennar see right now?" the keyboard fan, Sekani Willis, asks.

I nod. "This is the shield. This is half of Atlantis. If they lost all contact, if they stopped receiving any information from us at all, they might've come to investigate. It would've tipped them off immediately. But when I put this program into effect, I fed them the fact that I was unleashing something."

I made them believe I was a failure.

Easy enough to do.

"This," I say, referencing the broken footage, "is meant to make them think it backfired. I plugged in the emergency shut down procedures for all the stations so they'd think all airlocks were inaccessible. I supplied them with a catastrophe to watch, filtered through static and broken audio."

"Slowly," I go on, "the footage from the stations is being weeded out. They know how much food we have on each station. They know how long each can survive without shipments from Termana. They'll assume that those on the stations died."

They'll assume I got everyone killed.

I take a deep breath, accepting the blame I know I'll bear in their minds.

"What about all the transactions between the stations and Termana? Do they just not see any of those? Are they hidden, too?" This question booms from the man in the top right corner of my screen.

His dark skin shines in the lights of his room, and I wonder how he can stand it so bright. The other three, I notice, have their lights dimmed almost as low as mine.

"That's where Atlantis starts to get interesting," I say.

I begin explaining the algorithm that rips chunks from the data, scrambling sections, pasting bits of footage from one day into the footage of the next day, blacking out entire days. I tell them how it monitors all conversation, research, and messages for sensitive words, key phrases relating to our security and our upcoming trip to Regonia and Novay, then scrubs those sections from the version the Drennar see.

"On the stations, it pulls bits and pieces from old movies and shows, filling in long, dark stretches with the sounds of panic befitting a dying station."

"But isn't a scramble like this too simple to keep them out if they actually try?" Sekani asks.

"This is just the distraction, the shield. We're still in the first half of the program," I say.

"Atlantis has a rather… complicated underbelly. That's what'll keep them out if they try anything."

I hope.

For the next few hours, we dive deeper into Atlantis. And for the first time, I don't have to stop and explain myself over and over. They understand the things I say. They even put a couple pieces together for themselves.

Briefly, I wonder if maybe I wouldn't have hated working with them if I'd let the Coalition push me into the fields they wanted me in.

But I know it wouldn't have been like this.

I might not have worked with these people in particular. Atlantis would have been rushed. It would've been launched before it was ready, and the Drennar would have seen right through it. They would have broken it and rendered it completely useless.

Suddenly, I see all the days that I struggled with it through a new light. All the times I hit a wall and blew off steam at The Little Elephant take on new importance.

It wasn't procrastination.

It was making sure it got done right.

I take a deep breath, smiling hesitantly.

Maybe I did something good.

Chapter Six
Reginald

Novay

For what must be the millionth time, I watch Olivia's message, letting it play on the backs of my eyelids. I watch the man who saved my daughter's life comfort her as tears fall over her cheeks. She chokes on her words, and he tightens his embrace.

She inhales deeply, and I wait on bated breath for her to speak. I count the breaths, the blinks, desperate to hear her first word. Her eyes lift to the camera, almost like she's looking right at me, and I know it's coming.

My heart hammers in my chest, reaching forward through the video, but I don't skip ahead.

Another deep breath lifts her shoulders. Her eyes fall to her lap, and she shakes her head.

"Dad…" she breathes, and my lungs catch.

Again, I'm hit with the desire to back the video up, to watch her greet me for the first time in twelve years. And I nearly do.

"I'm sorry," she says. "I'm not what I should've become. I drink too much, and I hurt people—"

"You're not hurting anyone," the man sitting with her interrupts. "You saved over 4,000 lives." He plants a gentle kiss on the top of her head and says, "Cut yourself some slack."

Tears fall in earnest, shimmering on her face. But each one slices through me.

She nods slowly and takes a deep breath.

"I just… I have so much to tell you. So much to ask. I just… have to get it all out there. Like Cait said."

Yet again, I wish I knew who Cait was, but Olivia speaks again, banishing that thought to some far-off corner of my mind.

"I miss you," she says, voice small and trembling. Her next words choke her. "I thought they killed you."

The man kisses the top of her head, letting his lips linger.

Please take care of her.

"Mom is… a monster. But I guess you already know that since you watched the attack on Odyssey. She's gone now."

She winces and turns to face the man that saved her. "Do you think he saw…?" She covers her mouth, crying fervently.

His dark hair tickles her face as he wraps his arms tighter around her.

The first time I watched this, I had no idea what she meant, but now… Her suicide attempt flashes through my mind. Despair floods me, and I hate that I couldn't be there for her.

Slowly, she calms down. Turning to face the camera, she says, "I can't… I'm sorry. I have to just…" She draws in a deep breath and wipes the tears from her face. "There's a lot I have to ask you, but first, I need to know. That Drennar you were with, can we trust her? If we can, I have a lot more questions, but I can't risk any of them if we can't trust her."

Gulping back a breath, she says, "Let me know if we can but… Please, send more messages, either way." She looks up at the camera, meeting my gaze across space and time. "I love you, Dad."

I pull in a deep breath.

I love you too…

A tear rolls over my cheek.

The door to the hall opens, startling me. I glance up, and Rone strolls through. She smiles at me, then sees the tear.

"Are you watching it again?"

I nod.

She comes to sit with me, settling quietly on my bed. I take her hand in mine, but her free hand fidgets nervously on her lap. "What are you going to tell her?"

"I don't know yet," I say.

Rone nods, but her hand falls slack within my own. Her wings rustle behind us.

"What's wrong?"

She doesn't answer, so I tip her head to the side to meet her gaze. "What is it?"

"It just hurts more than I expected. It makes sense, but it hurts so much more than it should."

My brows knit themselves together. "What does?"

"That you don't know if…" She trails off, gaze faltering before mine. Staring down at my chest, she says, "I get it. I'm still a Drennar, emotional or not. I'm your enemy. It makes sense for you not to know if you can trust me."

My heart clenches, and my lungs constrict.

"Oh, Rone…" I pull her into my arms, cradling her head against my shoulder. "That isn't what I'm not sure of. I just don't know if I should tell her that they showed me, that I… saw her when she tried to…" I can't finish the sentence.

And Rone doesn't make me.

Clearing my throat, I tell her, "I trust you." As the words cross my lips, I realize exactly how true they are. "And you're certainly not my enemy."

Chapter Seven
Venice Space Research Station

Tenna

The noises of my people fill the air beyond the open doorway. Joyous songs mingle with the sounds of those we've lost. Laughter and tears collide, sometimes bursting from the same person.

Sitting in the cafeteria, they wait. For us. For news.

Krona squeezes my hand, and I turn to smile at him. Finally, we can face our people with good news. It's been too long in the making.

How long have we been here?

How much time have we lost back home?

I turn around and ask Olivia, hoping she has an answer for me, or that she can find one. My gaze meets Krona's, and his brows crease. He leans his forehead against mine, placing a hand on the back of my neck. His fingers wrap in my hair, and I breathe him in.

Have we missed the harvest? Will the Vyrtons still have good grazing in their pastures?

Did Roon Tribe steal them away?

Pulling back, I take a deep breath. Krona and I stare at our tribe crammed into the cafeteria. Children sit on the laps of their parents. Many sit cross-legged on tables. They lean against each other, whispering and smiling and weeping together.

At the table nearest the door, a young girl plays with her mother's shimmering blue hair, attempting an intricate braid, the braid her mother will wear the day after giving birth to the baby she carries.

A smile plays on the corners of my lips.

But Olivia sighs deeply.

My head snaps toward her, heart plummeting. Krona steps closer, putting a hand on my back as we wait for whatever words will try to crush us next.

"What is it?" Ricardo asks.

Olivia glances up at us, but she scrunches her eyes closed soon after, shaking her head. "They didn't wake you two immediately. They ran tests beforehand, keeping you unconscious for about a month. With that, the travel, the time that's passed since they woke you, and the time-dilation…"

She trails off, but her words don't make sense. My lungs falter, but I force words past my lips. "Time-dilation? What do you mean?"

"Time works differently in space. Gravity does weird things to time. There's not much gravity in space, though the gravity on Termana and the stations is… close to that of Regonia."

"What?" Krona asks.

"I can explain more later," Olivia says. "But… Your bodies have aged about six months. On Regonia… A little over a year has passed."

The metal walls around me seem to close in. My knees go weak, and I stand only through sheer force of will.

My people are watching.

I can't collapse in front of them. I can't worry them like that.

But… We lost over a year.

I put a hand to my chest, feeling the way my heart falters.

Krona sucks in a breath.

Even if Roon didn't come for them, the Vyrtons likely ran off. Our crops…

My lungs shrivel within me.

Our crops withered with the snows, wasted. And nothing was planted when the second moon rose. What stands there now? Barren fields? Wild grass?

Will we have no food when we return?

"What time of year is it there? How many moons have risen?" Krona asks.

Olivia crinkles her brow, but only for an instant. A distant look creeps over her features as she dives into the Net once more, filtering through information for us. "Three moons are in the sky. But, by the time we get you all back there, a fourth will be visible."

My mouth falls open.

"We'll get there just in time to harvest empty fields…" I mutter. "The snows will come."

Olivia pales before me.

"Will Daen Tribe be okay?" Ricardo asks.

I turn to Krona, shaking my head. Our eyes meet, strained with anxiety. He runs a hand over the bottom half of his face, smudging it around.

"We can't go into the snows with no food…" I whisper.

He shakes his head, glancing at the crowd in the cafeteria. Two thirds of our Tribe packed into a space meant for half as many Humans. Shoulders bump together, and limbs intertwine.

4,000 mouths to feed. 4,000 bellies to rumble through the snows.

"We can't stay here, either," Krona says. "Not like this. And they won't want to split across multiple stations."

"No…" I say, hating even the thought of splitting our Tribe over the Human realm.

Beside me, Olivia clears her throat.

A message flashes on my Link, and Krona's lights up in time with my own. My translator reads the message to me, and I smile at her.

This beautiful Human.

I pull her to me, whispering for Ricardo to come along, too. Krona and I wrap them in a hug, uttering our gratitude.

Before us, the crowd takes notice. A few heads turn to face us, falling silent, and I know our time has come. "We must finish this later," I say, releasing them.

We step through the door, ready to address our people. Silence descends over the room as we enter. We step onto a small bench, and all heads turn toward us. A glance over my shoulder finds Olivia and Ricardo standing just inside the door, hands linked, waiting.

Before I turn to face my people, I hold Krona's gaze. He inclines his head, telling me that he's ready. I incline my own in answer.

Swallowing, pulling in a deep breath, I look out over the families and friends and warriors before me. Their eyes shine with worry and excitement.

I place a hand over my heart, letting it hammer against my palm for a moment so that I may feel the force of my life. A few in the crowd do so, as well.

"There is much to discuss today," I begin.

A few more place hands over hearts.

"The ship to return home will be ready next week," I say, but the expression on my face warns off the celebration I wish I could let them have. "It has been a long time since we were there. Our crops have died with the snows and the solitary moon. When the second moon rose, nothing was planted…"

Faces fall before me. Small flurries of movement draw my eyes as hands twine together here and there.

"The third moon rose, and no one brought water from the river," I shake my head. "I can't say whether the fields sat empty or if grass and Salvo plants moved in to ruin the dirt, can't say if the unharvested crops seeded themselves anew. But by the time we move through the Realm of

Stars to reach our home, the fourth moon will have risen, likely with nothing to harvest."

More hands join together before me. Faces turn, and our people search each other's gazes. My heart clenches with their pain.

Krona squeezes my hand, drawing my attention. His free hand comes to rest over his heart. I pull in another deep breath and nod.

"All our moons, save the first, will hide away soon after our return. The snows will come, and they'll find us with no crops preserved."

I run my thumb over the back of Krona's hand, drawing his attention. He meets my gaze, and I implore him to continue for me. My voice will crack if I speak another word, shattering in a throat thick with emotion.

"Until just a moment ago, we had three options. Go back and suffer through the snows, scavenging whatever food we can find. Ask to stay here, cramped into beds too small for our frames with no way to maintain our strength or prowess for coming battles. Or ask to be split up over two stations," he says.

A murmur of unease runs through the crowd, and I know we were right. They won't split up amongst stars and Humans.

"Olivia," he says, gesturing to her, "has spoken with the Survival Coalition on our behalf and secured food for us, to be sent to Regonia when we leave. It will have to be loaded up, which will push our departure back another day. It's enough to get through the snows, if we're careful. If nothing else goes wrong. If all our warriors leave to confront the Drennar, leaving everyone else on Regonia. It's all the Human race has to spare, all their emergency reserves."

He pauses, letting them absorb the risk humanity is taking to make this right. Then, he continues, "Though attacks during the snows are rare and the fear of star-sickness might serve to keep Roon Tribe and the Vaerkin at bay, with all our warriors in the Realm of Stars, those on Regonia will be left exposed."

All across the sea of faces, unease floats like a film. It reaches for me, but I squeeze Krona's hand, holding onto my faith in him, in us.

"Any warriors not making the trek up the mountain to see Taron Tribe will be tasked with training those who will stay behind, as well as can be managed in such a short time. Though the path we walk will be fraught with danger, we cannot rightfully keep you here amongst the stars when our home is within reach. Not after everything we've been through."

The little girl in front of us opens her mouth to speak but seems to think better of it.

Crouching down, I ask her, "What is it?"

She glances nervously at her mother, dislodging strands of pale blue about her face with the movement, but she steps forward. "Will there be enough food for the new baby? I can share if I need to."

I put a hand to her cheek, smiling at her generosity. "We'll make sure you and the new baby have enough food. You won't have to share. You need your food, so you can grow up strong."

"But the baby needs to grow up strong, too," she says.

I nod, and my smile widens. I glance at her mother, taking in the tattoos that adorn her arms and legs. "Are you as good at tracking and hunting as your mother?"

The girl lights up, nodding vehemently as she pushes her sleeve up to show me her tattoo. Two diagonal rings encircle her upper arm, forming an "X" where they cross over one another on the front of her arm.

Shock drops my jaw.

"You've already earned your mark?" I ask, incredulous. "You can't be more than twelve. You must be a very good tracker."

She glows, and her dark grey cheeks warm with a touch of pink.

"There will be enough food for you and the new baby, especially with trackers like you."

"Thank you," she says, sticking her chest out and lifting her chin. A soft blush still warms her cheeks, but she squares her shoulders. Dark green eyes sparkle, shining impossibly bright.

She rushes back to her mother's side, bouncing up and down. "Did you hear that, Mama? Kinera said I'm a good tracker!"

Her mother hugs her tight, kissing the top of her head. "I heard, dear one," she whispers.

I stand, taking Krona's hand in mine.

The little girl turns back around and says, "So we get to go home?"

Somehow, my smile spreads even wider. Choked by emotion, I nod. Then, I clear my throat and say, "We're going home."

All around, the cafeteria erupts in cheers.

Chapter Eight
Venice Space Research Station

Krona

Doctor Sullivan approaches, calm as ever. The bright lights shine on his dark skin, highlighting every crinkle in his face as he smiles at Olivia.

But my stomach ties itself in knots.

This isn't what I imagined star-sickness to be. Genial smiles and confidence, surgery and intention.

No disease or mutation.

No slow, looming death.

In this case, it actually prevents death.

But all the old fears of the stars tangle in my belly, trudging up childhood memories of burning rocks falling from the Realm of Stars, and entire fields being barricaded to keep the disease from reaching us. The panic that followed, the fear of catching the dreaded star-sickness, it all comes back to me, permeating my skin and pulling up goosebumps.

Yet, Olivia smiles at Dr. Sullivan, and excitement plays in her eyes. Beside her, Ricardo squeezes her hand, and they gaze at each other with warmth.

I glance at the Link in my arm, the solid piece of tech that hasn't spread to take over my entire body as it would have if it were truly star-sickness.

How much did the Drennar alter themselves to appear diseased?

Legends of gills and extra limbs float through my head. Tales of bodies without limbs which slithered unnaturally over the ground on armored bellies slide through my imagination, and the thought of clear skulls rattles me. I remember cringing as a child hearing my grandparents tell stories of the lights visible within the brains of the Drennar.

But how much was exaggerated with time? My grandparents weren't yet born when the Drennar dumped us off on Regonia. Many generations separated even them from our ancestors.

Were those mutations really there? Were they less severe?

Or were they tech?

The image of the Drennar with Olivia's father, with wings and strange things moving in her eyes, comes to mind. But she looked the same in subsequent messages. No further mutations. No visible sickness.

"We're ready for you, Olivia," Dr. Sullivan says, deep voice rumbling in my chest.

She kisses Ricardo on the cheek, then turns to face Tenna and me. Our anxiety must show clearly on our faces because she says, "I'll be fine, guys. I'll be back in no time. Then, you won't be as worried when Ricardo goes in."

I crease my brows and purse my lips, because I know I'll worry just the same.

She follows Dr. Sullivan, disappearing into a small room in the back of the hospital. As the door shuts, stealing her from view, my heart accelerates, beating my lungs into submission. My breath comes in stutters and starts.

Because I know.

I've learned enough of the mess they call tech to know it's not much better than star-sickness. The gleaming blades of metal, barely able to cut our flesh, slice through human skin and muscle like water. Fingers probe unceremoniously in bodies of flesh and bone, leaving behind chunks of cold metal, wired and Linked and programmed in.

An image of shining silver, sharp and eager to bite, poised over Olivia's neck takes root in my mind, and a shudder runs through me. Tenna's hand goes along for the ride as my arm jerks with the sudden movement. Her free hand comes to rest on my wrist, offering comfort, but when I glance at her, the same fears lurk in her eyes.

Somehow, seeing her grapple with this makes me more nervous. She's been inundated with the tech here far longer than I have. Her blocked memory kept the fear of it at bay when she first woke. But the fear is there now, rooted within her, creasing her brows and pressing her lips into a thin line.

"Are there windows into her room?" Tenna asks.

Ricardo looks up from his Link and leans forward, peering around me. "What?"

She repeats herself.

"No. They'll all be screens now, showing her vitals. Why?"

"I just need to see her. I need to know she's okay," Tenna says. "It has to be better than I'm imagining."

The need to see, to know that Olivia's neck hasn't been carved open, flayed like some poor beast, grips me.

"Is there any way we can see?" I ask, voice filled with urgency.

"Do you really want to?" Ricardo asks. "There's bound to be some blood." He pauses, as if considering this. "I suppose warriors don't shy away from blood, do they?"

I shake my head as millions of images of blood on long grass or spilled over rocky earth near the base of the mountains flash through my mind.

"Well, all surgeries are recorded. We can't afford any slip-ups. Injuries or broken tech aren't tolerated. I can Link you into it. Olivia showed me how," Ricardo says, beaming with pride.

He glances down at his Link for half a breath, and instantly, my own Link glows. Tenna's Link lights up as well, and she lifts her arm, propping it on the armrest between us. The screen glows to life, showing the room Olivia disappeared into just moments ago.

Perched directly over Olivia's unconscious form, the camera watches Dr. Sullivan tip her chin up. A nurse hands him a sharp blade, and the light catches on it, glinting maliciously. My stomach clenches.

With a hand poised carefully over her exposed neck, he slices through skin easily, marking a tiny X in two precise moves. Blood seeps from the cuts, and I lean closer to Tenna's arm, straining to see, begging the camera to move closer.

Tenna leans forward as well, and the image on her Link enlarges the cuts on Olivia's neck, nearly filling the screen with them. Two nurses reach in with gleaming tools, pulling the flaps of the X back in a grotesque mockery of life.

I recoil but never tear my eyes away. Even now, even pulled open like this, it isn't as bad as I feared. The insides of her throat lay bare, but only a small portion, no bigger than her thumbnail.

Dr. Sullivan's hand moves in, blocking the camera's view for just a moment as he makes another incision, this one a mere pinprick. Blood flows when he pulls his hand away. A square of fabric dabs it away, and then his gloved hands come back into focus, this time holding a tiny piece of black metal.

No bigger than the heart of a Bellona flower, the little disc affixes to the tiny hole in the interior of Olivia's throat. My Link provides the word 'trachea', but I ignore it. Dr. Sullivan pokes a needle into the side of it, engaging a mechanism within, and four prongs reach out from the thing, attaching themselves to her flesh.

Withdrawing for only a moment, Dr. Sullivan comes back with a little X-shaped cap that he fixes over the device. A tiny hose hangs from one arm of the X, and he snakes it deeper into her neck, somewhere behind the trachea.

The sight of his tweezers and that hose disappearing into her body sends chills down my spine, but he withdraws quickly, having done whatever he set out to do.

My Link tells me the hose deposits compressed balls of alonarium into the esophagus, sending them down to be neutralized in Olivia's stomach. But the whole process weighs heavily on me, regardless of its necessity.

As Dr. Sullivan closes up the cuts on my friend's neck, doubt settles over me.

Will that thing really keep them alive?

I'm supposed to trust her life to that small, insignificant thing?

Chapter Nine
Novay

Rone

A message comes through, and excitement explodes within me, tingling and fluttery. A smile erupts over my face. But when I look up from my pedestal at the perfect rows of Drennar in the Facility Center, tension builds. Dipping my head, I try to conceal my fervor, my desperation to run to Reginald and show him this message.

They'll only analyze me if they see me smile. They'll scan me and expect me to explain the sudden bout of emotion.

And I can't explain this to them.

I fidget beneath the weight of my secret, my little betrayal. But I know I'll show Reginald. I know I'll let him send another message, treasonous as it may be.

Mirroring the cold efficiency of the Drennar I once considered peers, I dismiss my pedestal, then I do something they never would, abandoning my experiments. I step away from the cruelty on that faraway planet, letting the network gather data in my absence.

They'll all just assume I'm going to the remote station or setting something up for another experiment.

I pass Lustran on my way out, and he meets my eyes, cocking his head inquisitively. I let slip the barest hint of a smile, and he matches it.

He sends a shielded message, a thing we shouldn't do, shouldn't have needed to do, shouldn't *be able* to do, holding my gaze all the while.

It reads, "Olivia?"

My smile grows just a touch wider.

His eyes sparkle, crinkling around the edges. Another shielded message, "Let me know how it goes."

A bubble of excitement rolls through me, and I struggle to conceal it. But Lustran sees the smile lurking behind my sucked in lips, sees the light in my eyes and my barely too-quick step.

He drops his gaze back to his pedestal, but his eyes still shine with a smile.

All around us, Drennar stand motionless, eyes unfocused, completely missing the world around them, the *worlds* around them.

But Lustran and I see them.

Free of the Facility Center, I pick up my pace, hurrying along the hallway with giddy glances over my shoulder. My wings flutter, and a giggle escapes me.

I cover the distance between the Center and the Human section of the facility quickly, checking my pace as I approach the airlock separating us. I slide the cool mask of logic back on, cloaking myself as I venture within sight of other Drennar. A few linger near the airlock, analyzing each other.

Without a second glance, without even a first glance, I glide past them. They never look at me, registering only another drone in the hive.

Stepping into the airlock, I wait, as still and patient as I can manage, while the filters work their magic, sucking the alonarium from the air. As soon as the door opens to the Human sector, I want to run, want to sprint to Reginald's room.

He should be waking soon, and I want to show him this message from Olivia immediately.

But I measure my steps, controlling every movement, every sway of my arms, comparing them to the swings and strides of my days before emotion and correcting as necessary. Time yawns before me as I make my way through one hall, then another. My heart aches in my chest, even as hope builds in my stomach.

He'll be so excited!

I fight off a smile. But another thought strikes me.

What if... the message has bad news?

And suddenly, I'm measuring my steps, forcing myself not to slow down. The urge to open the message, to check and make sure it won't hurt him, overwhelms me.

No. I can't do that.

He should see it first.

Spurring myself forward, my excitement tempered by fear, I move at an efficient pace. For comfort, I draw my attention inward, focusing on even steps and the arc of my arms, calculating for perfect counterbalance. I measure each swing, each bend in my elbows and knees. I optimize the placement of my feet, maintaining the perfect angle for force absorption.

But it doesn't stop my mind from wandering, from conjuring hideous scenarios that might plague Olivia's life.

For a millisecond, I fear she may have been taken, fear that my relationship with Reginald and his outburst when he thought Olivia dead might break the deal he made 12 years ago.

My heart skips a beat at the prospect, and I can't fathom how I hadn't thought of that. But a quick scan of the Humans contained in this sector and aboard the ship bringing the last collected 'subjects' eases my mind.

She hasn't been taken.

But that doesn't mean she isn't suffering.

At the wall to Reginald's room, I hesitate in the hall, but only for a second. As with so many other things, I need to know. So, I signal the alonarium, and it parts for me.

Reginald lies in bed with my blanket tucked around him, curled up on his side despite the large bed. His eyes flutter, barely perceptible, as I enter the room. The wall pieces itself back together behind me, and I take a seat on the edge of the bed.

I put a gentle hand on his arm and whisper, "Reginald…"

He takes only three and a half heartbeats to wake, rolling onto his back to stretch. His eyes roam over me, and a smile lights up his face.

"Good morning," he says, propping himself up on one elbow.

I lean in, taking it as an invitation, and plant a tender kiss on his lips. His hands find me, one sliding onto my leg and the other caressing my neck. Shivers run down my spine, and heat pools within me.

But now isn't the time.

I pull back from the hunger in his kiss, just enough to speak.

"You have a message," I whisper against his lips.

Reginald pulls back, staring into my eyes, excitement clear on his face. "Wait, really?"

And though my body riots, wishing I'd waited to tell him until after he could have soothed the ache within, I smile.

Chapter Ten
Novay

Reginald

My mind whirls, boggled by the risk humanity is about to take, by the request for aid that they've made. Something has to be done. The vast chasm separating our technology from that of the Drennar yawns before me, dwarfing my race and threatening to swallow my daughter.

How could we ever compare in a war? How could we ever stand a chance?

And then, I realize that *this* is exactly how. The only way, really.

I turn from the wall to glance at Rone and find her brows furrowed and her wings fluttering restlessly behind her. She stares at the floor, and the blue striations in her eyes shift and spin with the calculations she undoubtedly works through, even now.

Is she figuring up our chances of survival?

I swallow, paling before the odds.

But I have to ask.

"Rone…" I begin.

She looks at me, eyes soft, the blue motionless within the green. She waits for me to continue, but my hands tremble in my lap and my mouth goes dry.

Pulling in a deep breath, I try to speak, but no words pass my lips. My eyes fall to the floor for just a moment, staring at our feet, so close together, but…

Will this be the thing that breaks us?

The Drennar finding out about us didn't pull her away from me. But… will humanity?

My heart falters, threatening to suck my chest in on itself. But Olivia fills my mind. Her courage, her smile. Her suicide attempt.

I squeeze my eyes shut, smearing one hand over my face as if to scrub the image away. Steepling my hands against my lips, I know.

Even if it drives Rone away… I have to ask.

Kneeling before her, I scoop her hands up and hold them tight. The cold floor presses uncomfortably against my knees, but our eyes meet.

"Rone, I have no right to ask this of you, I know that. But I have to. I can't abandon Olivia again."

A wave of agony hits like a punch to the gut, and the air rushes from me. Tears well up in my eyes, and my throat tightens. I drop my gaze to our hands, clutched tight on Rone's knees, cradled atop the smooth fabric of her pants.

But she pulls one hand free.

She touches my cheek, caresses my jaw. Tipping my chin up so that I'll meet her gaze, she whispers, "You didn't abandon her."

And the world crumbles within me. My heart shivers, frigid with guilt.

"I left her. I…" The lump in my throat chokes me.

"No," Rone says. She scoots forward, sliding off the bed to kneel before me, *with* me. "You spared her. You didn't abandon her."

"I wasn't there," I insist. "All this time, she needed someone, and I wasn't there."

And this time, Rone doesn't correct me. She rests her head against mine, gazing into my eyes earnestly. A shimmer of tears hovers on her lashes.

My hands find her neck, sliding up into her hair.

"I need to try, Rone. I have to do this. But I need your help. I can't do this myself, and I know, *I know* it isn't right for me to ask this of you. But please, help me save my daughter. Help me save my home," I beg. "I know what it means for you to do this."

And then, I falter, just a bit. My stomach plummets at the thought of her saying no, at the idea of losing her because she couldn't fathom betraying her people for me…

Because I know I'm asking a lot of someone who only recently got emotions, of someone who's never had to make a decision on this scale.

So, I add, "I know it means betraying everything, but please… Just think about it. Don't answer me, now. Take some time if you need to. I… I need to think through all of this. I'm sure you do, too."

"Okay," she says, nodding. Her hair flutters about her face. "I'll think about it." The blue within her eyes shifts with calculations again, and I know she's already considering my request.

She pulls me against her, and I hold onto her for dear life, one hand sprawled on her back and the other tangled in her hair.

Olivia's life, humanity, my own life… It all hangs in the balance, completely dependent upon her.

My insides clench, churning anxiously.

Rone pulls back and wipes my tears away. "I'll be back soon," she says.

Rising, she tugs me to my feet. Our lips meet in a desperate kiss, and she goes. The wall hisses closed behind her, leaving me alone and utterly helpless.

Pacing, I beat the floor into submission with too many footsteps for this room to contain. They reverberate off the walls, pummeling me, and I can't listen to them anymore.

I plop down onto my bed, bracing my elbows on my knees and dropping my head into my hands.

Chapter Eleven

Venice Space Research Station

Olivia

Beyond the window, space sprawls out, and stars sparkle. They grant me clarity, or something close to it. The darkness before me dwarfs that within, but still, I wonder.

Am I even me, now?

The antidepressant seems to be working, taking the edge off, helping me cope. I haven't been clinging to bottles just to sleep or bordering on suicide every other second. I've actually felt happy. I've been hopeful, looking forward to things and making plans.

But…

Shouldn't I be more upset over participating in a war? Shouldn't I be upset over Mom's death?

The fear of ending up like her, cold and uncaring, seeps in, rattling me to my core. I lift my hand, spreading it against the glass. The chill of space oozes through, reaching into me.

Am I just like her?

Did she stop caring? Did she take a pill or throw back a shot to deal with losing Dad and just… stop being who she was before?

I recoil at the excuse I'm offering my mother, the pardon dying quickly. I stare out at the blackness, counting the stars that fit between my fingers.

But a solid weight builds within me, weighing me down. The gravity of what she did to the people of Bolivia Station, to the Regonians, settles on my shoulders. The agony of growing up without affection, of watching her choose to leave me alone at home every day gnaws at me, a familiar ache that I never should've had to get used to.

If only there was some alcohol on Venice…

But Ricardo's face flashes through my mind, half remembered and blurry as he ran through the halls carrying me from Sparrow.

Guilt rises within me, and I pound my fist against the window. "No!"

No more alcohol.

I can't. I can't be that person now.

For half a breath, I consider calling Cait. My Link takes the command, but I freeze.

I need to be stronger. I need to be better.

I can't bother her about everything.

This is my life, and I just have to fucking deal with it.

I terminate the call and turn from the window. Leaning against the wall beside it, I slide down, curling into a ball in the floor of our room. I cross my arms on my knees, dropping my head atop them.

But my Link flashes with an incoming call.

Cait.

I sigh and consider rejecting it, letting her get back to her life. I consider being a goddamn adult and dealing with my problems on my own.

When my Link stops flashing, I breathe a sigh that's equal parts relief and despair. But it begins again, and something breaks within me.

So, this time, I answer.

But I don't look at my Link. I set the call to play only in my mind, not wanting anyone else to hear what she might say.

In case she condemns me for being weak, for calling her outside of normal appointment times.

"Olivia," she begins, words soft in my mind, "I'm so glad you called. I was just thinking about you."

Tears rise, unbidden. They pour from my eyes, trickling over my wrists. A sob racks my frame, and I know, *I know* she hears it.

"Olivia?" she asks, voice tinged with concern. "Are you alright?"

But she must know.

She has to know I only called because I'm too weak, too broken, to be a person on my own.

Even with *the antidepressants.*

"Take all the time you need," she says. "I'll listen whenever you're ready."

Sobs shake me, cracking my voice as I whisper, "I'm sorry. I shouldn't have bothered you. This isn't your problem."

But I don't end the call, desperate not to be alone.

"You're not bothering me, dear," Cait says. "I want to help."

A hoarse cry rips through me, drowning out what she says next. Humiliated, I force myself to ask, "What did you say?"

"I just asked what was wrong."

And it all pours out of me, choked and broken by gasping breaths.

"I just… don't know what to do. I don't know how not to be her. I can't check in to see what she's doing. I don't have to clean up her messes."

Another wracking cough. Several sniffles.

"I don't know what she'd do, so I don't know what I shouldn't do. I don't want to be her. And I'm not even sad that she's gone. Shouldn't I be sad? She was my mom. She was shitty, but she was my mom, and I don't even miss her."

I fall silent, crumbling before this admission.

"Family or not," Cait says, "she mistreated you. You tried to build a relationship with her, many times, over the years, but she never reached back. The two of you weren't close. Not missing someone you barely knew, let alone someone who wronged you, doesn't make you a bad person."

Silence falls on Cait's end as I break into pieces. My hands ball into fists, and tears flow freely.

"I should be sad, though. I shouldn't be so…"

Excited. Happy.

"What?" Cait prompts.

"I shouldn't be happy," I say. "My mom is dead. I turned her in and got her killed. I shouldn't be happy that I get to go to a new planet."

I shouldn't have survived…

"Who am I, now? What do I even do?"

"It's okay to be scared," Cait says, seeing past the words to what lies beneath. "You've been struggling for so long that it's become a way of life. But depression isn't you. Trauma isn't you. Alcohol and guilt aren't you. Those are just things that get in your way. They've been holding you back for a long time, and now you're stepping past them."

I weep, shoulders shaking with the effort.

"Do those things feel safe? Just because you know what to expect from them?"

And I know she's right. I know what to expect when I drink. I know what to expect from fights with Mom.

In the smallest voice possible, I creak an admission, "Yes."

And then, I curl into myself because these things *shouldn't* feel safe.

"It's natural to be afraid," Cait tells me. "Change can be overwhelming, even if it's for the better. Opportunities, even good ones, can be frightening. And now, without your mother to hold you back and keep you busy and give you something to fight against, you have opportunities. But it also means you have choices, choices you didn't have before."

My lips purse, and my face scrunches up as a fresh wave of tears cascades from my eyes. "What do I do though? Can you please just tell me what to do? Because I don't know."

"That's the most beautiful part of this, Olivia. You get to live, now."

I smudge my hands over my face, scrubbing at the tears. My elbows dig into my knees, and I press my palms against my eyes. Strands of hair catch in the tear tracks, sticking to my face.

"When are you going to Regonia?" Cait asks. "From what Tenna's told me, it sounds beautiful. I'm a bit jealous."

"I don't remember when we're leaving…" I croak. "A couple days?"

"I hope you'll send me pictures when you get there."

I agree, grabbing onto the conversational life raft. "What has Tenna told you about Regonia?"

Already, the tears slow. They still come, but in trickles and surges rather than in buckets. She starts to tell me about the mountains overlooking the plains Daen Tribe calls home. She tells me of Taron Tribe, their allies that live in the mountains.

But the door to our room opens, and I glimpse Ricardo through my slotted fingers.

"Olivia?" he asks, voice urgent and pleading. "What's wrong?" He sets a drink on the table near the door, deserting it as he rushes across the room.

Taking a seat next to me, he wraps an arm around me, pulling me in close. His lips find the top of my head, and a fresh bout of tears gushes forth.

Now, he'll *be worried about me too.*

"Hi, Ricardo," I squeak.

"Do I need to let you go?" Cait asks.

"Yeah," I tell her. Then, "Thank you. For everything."

"There's no need to thank me. I'm happy to talk to you."

Chapter Twelve
Novay

Rone

I know my answer. It buzzes around in my head, incessant and burning away at me. It makes my fingers curl in on themselves, makes my skin itch to move.

But Reginald insisted that I think about it.

My feet pound the floor, moving just a bit too fast, just a bit too frantic. My world splinters as I walk, dividing within me as the world I've known all my life tries desperately to contain the emotions bursting within me. Order strains against chaos, and the easy efficiency of the Drennar fights to suppress the rebellion of humanity.

But the inner turmoil is nothing more than a backdrop, a soundtrack.

My decision is made.

Who knew betrayal could be so easy?

Not a single pang of guilt strikes me.

My feet carry me through several halls, moving at a speed just conspicuous enough to draw the notice of everyone I pass. But they aren't the ones I seek. I scan the Facility, just to make sure I surmised his location correctly.

At the wall that stands between us, I reach out, placing a hand upon the alonarium. I take a deep breath, filling my lungs and considering one last time.

The unfeeling stares of Drennar, their cold efficacy, flickers through my mind. A safe and peaceful option that ensures my survival.

Yet, the struggles of the Humans, of Daen Tribe, flash before my eyes. The pain Reginald has endured shoots through me, searing and all too fresh.

And I know my heart is unchanged.

I signal the wall to part, letting it slide away beneath my palm, feeling the cold edge of it as it moves beneath my skin. Lustran sits before me, cross-legged on the floor with his wings tucked neatly against his back. The wall before him showcases a Human television program called Friends, one we've all taken to watching.

A man shouts about watching a tape, then plays a recording of himself putting on lipstick and storms out of the room.

Lustran laughs, and I breathe a sigh of relief. The modifications within his brain blink, visible through the clear plate replacing most of his skull.

"Lustran?" I say.

He pauses the show and turns to look at me. A smile lights his eyes, a lingering effect of the show that disappears when he takes in my expression.

"Yes, Rone?"

"May we have words?"

Rising to his feet, he lets the wall shift seamlessly into the plain grey of alonarium. All four arms swing at his sides, and his wings curl against his back. His brows furrow as he approaches, and he tips his head to the side.

"Of course," he answers.

I take a deep breath to steady myself before blocking all recordings of our quarters. Scanning our immediate surroundings, I find no one within earshot.

Gathering up all our late-night conversations about cruelty and Human ethics for courage, I take a deep breath and say, "It's time to plan a rebellion."

Chapter Thirteen

Odyssey Space Research Station

Olivia

I dock Sparrow on Odyssey half an hour early. Considering Dr. Sullivan's concerns about running late, I know he won't be ready yet. I glance at my empty co-pilot seat, wishing someone had been able to come with me so I'd have someone to talk to.

But Tenna and Krona were busy with their tribemates, planning for the return to Regonia, and Ricardo was meeting with a few Soldiers and Guards that arrived from Washington Station this morning.

My stomach flips at the prospect of meeting them later this evening, knowing that some of them are good friends with Ricardo. My nerves tie themselves into knots at the prospect of making a bad first impression.

How much do they already know about me?

My insides freeze, and restless tension builds within me. Suddenly, I can't sit still, need to move. I push myself up from the pilot's chair and leave Sparrow. My feet march me right out of the hangar and through the airlock.

Do they know about the drinking? My suicide attempt? Do they know how many people I've let down? Do they know I'm still in counseling?

I try to concentrate on the feel of my feet hitting the cold metal floor, the way my arms swing at my sides, all the while reminding myself that Cait has told me, many times, that I haven't been in counseling that long, at least not this time around, that this sort of thing can take years to deal with and it's barely been the blink of an eye.

But my mind spirals, plumbing the darkest depths of self-deprecation.

Because if Ricardo's friends know anything about me, they won't like me, won't want me anywhere near him.

I can't even blame them.

If I were in their shoes, if one of my friends was getting involved with some mental case like me…

I'd steer him away, too.

My throat grows tight, and my stomach turns uneasily. My scalp prickles as waves of nausea sweep through me.

I glance up, desperate for a bathroom just in case I get sick. Sweat beads on my forehead, trickles over my spine as an uncomfortable heat spreads through me. My vision condenses to a tunnel, and all I see is what's immediately in front of me.

But it's enough.

The Little Elephant waits, dark interior pulsing with rhythmic lights, even at this early hour. A few patrons, likely just off the night shift, sit at the bar or dance on the open dance floor.

Dread builds within me as I realize the path my feet took out of habit, and I hate how deeply ingrained this place is within me. My mouth dries out, and the prickling of my scalp intensifies.

But it only makes me wish for a drink, for anything to ease the panic attack that I know is coming, is already here.

Behind the bar, Maria looks up, belly swollen with the twins. She smiles when she catches my eye, but I can't return the gesture.

The lights, the music, the longing for a drink… It all overwhelms me, and I sprint for the bathroom.

I'm such a shitty friend…

I haven't messaged her back in days, haven't seen her since I tried to…

My knees threaten to buckle as I push through the bathroom door, finally leaving the flashing lights behind. The door swings shut behind me, and the music dulls. It echoes through the walls, disorienting me further.

I step to the sink, lean over it.

My breath comes in short, shallow gasps, and my mind berates me. Even now, after everything, I still wanted a drink. My feet led me straight here.

How many times have I been here? How often did I come here for it to just be where I go?

"I'm so fucking weak!" I growl, but it comes out on a gasp.

My lungs contort within me, struggling to draw breath. They spasm, hacking my poor windpipe to bits as the hyperventilation starts.

A deep rumble moves within me, and my back arches as I puke into the sink.

And suddenly, soft hands find my back. A gentle voice whispers, "Oh, Olivia…"

Maria…

No, please don't let her see me like this.

Tears stream down my face, and I scrunch my eyes closed against the sight of the vomit before me.

Maria sweeps the few loose strands of my hair back out of my face.

"I'm fine," I gasp. "I'm just being stupid. Please, just… You don't have to worry."

But my lungs chop my words to pieces, only letting a few out between great, gulping breaths.

"Olivia, come here," Maria urges, pulling me away from the sink.

I cover my face, desperate to hide, to keep her from seeing how broken I am. Because I can't hide behind the alcohol now.

Another sob racks my body, and Maria touches my hands, gently pulling them away.

"Olivia, look at me, honey. I need you to do something for me," she says.

A morbid laugh bubbles up within me at the prospect of her needing me, of *anyone* needing me, for anything.

"I need you to tell me five things you see," she whispers.

"Why?" I sob. "What does it matter?"

"I just need you to do this, please."

Can I really deny her such a simple thing?

I guess if I were just a little shittier, I could.

"You," I begin, but my tears obscure my vision. I wipe them away, and she puts tender hands on my shoulders. "I see the door behind you—"

My lungs spasm, cutting me off. A deep blush spreads over me, but I keep going.

"I see the door frame, and the 'Wash your damn hands' sign. I see your earrings."

"Good," Maria says. "Now, I need you to tell me four things you hear."

"My crying…" I say, hating the words, hating how small they sound.

"Okay, that's one. Let's have three more."

Madness threatens to reach up from the depths once more, but I force myself to keep going, to indulge Maria's strange request.

"The music. My heartbeat. You."

"Good. Now, I need three things you feel."

"Why, though?" I whimper. Tears start to form, but Maria shakes her head.

"I just need to know."

"My mouth is dry. Does that count?"

Maria smiles and nods. "Two more."

"Your hands," I whisper, settling into the gentle touch of her palms against my cheeks. "My nails digging into my palms."

"Two things that you smell."

"Vomit," I say, wrinkling my nose. "I'm sorry… I'll clean it."

Tears prick at the corners of my eyes, but this time, they don't fall.

"It's fine," Maria says. Gorgeous brown eyes sparkling with mirth, she adds, "I'm pretty used to cleaning up vomit. I run a bar."

A laugh escapes me.

"One more thing that you smell."

Pulling in a deep breath, I savor the flowery smell that fills me. "Your shampoo. It smells really good."

"Thanks," she says. "It's new. The smell of the old one made me nauseous. Gotta love the side effects of pregnancy."

She pulls one hand from my face and retrieves something from her pocket. Offering me a stick of gum, she says, "Chew this."

And I do.

A burst of mint cleanses the vomit from my mouth.

"I figured I'd better wait to ask you to name something you taste until after you had that." She laughs, and I follow suit.

"Mint," I say, looking down at the floor. I shake my head and laugh again.

"Do you feel better?" Maria asks.

I nod, offering up a sheepish, "Thank you."

"No problem. It's not the first time I've found someone having a panic attack. They're pretty common, actually. So," she says, "don't you dare feel bad or embarrassed about this."

She tips my head up and issues me a knowing look. "Now, what brought this on?" She pulls a stool out from under the sink, patting it for me to sit down.

I fall onto the chair, weak and shaky. "I'm just… ashamed. And I didn't even mean to come here. It's just… built into me now."

Tears form, unbidden. But my breathing doesn't ramble, doesn't shake. It merely hitches and hiccups.

I unravel before my friend, crying into my hands as she cleans up after me. But she doesn't judge me as I feared. She doesn't mock me.

She listens, unwavering, often saving me from descents back into panic.

And guilt builds within me, leering at me within my mind, desperate to make me ache.

But I know better than to bottle it now. I can hear Cait's voice, urging me to open up, to speak my mind.

"I'm sorry," I whisper. Then, before Maria can tell me not to apologize for this episode, I hurry onward. "I should've come to see you sooner. I just…"

I shake my head, fumbling through a million excuses.

But none of them are good enough.

And I know that.

"I felt like I let you down. I was so ashamed, and I couldn't face you. I didn't have the energy to face you after what I did, and I just…"

I hid.

Like a coward.

"I know I should've come to see you. I should've checked in on you and the twins. I should've at least sent you a message…" My words catch in my throat, but I force them out. "I'm kind of a shitty friend."

"No, you're not. Not only are you dealing with all this, but you're training people on the workings of some hyper advanced security system and planning to leave the planet with thousands of people in tow. I'd say that counts as having a lot going on," she says with a chuckle. "I'd be a shitty friend if I got mad at you for that."

I laugh, but it comes out small. "I don't think you could ever be a shitty friend, even if you tried."

In the mirror, she tosses me a look as if to say, "Is that a challenge?" Maria stows the cleaning supplies away, washes her hands, and turns to face me.

"As for Ricardo's friends, I don't think you need to worry. I'm sure they'll love you. He's probably already talking you up."

"I don't know about that…" I whisper, but I rise to my feet. "I have to go, though." I hate the words as I say them. Because they aren't enough. They aren't even close.

Maria nods, as if somehow she already knew this. Pulling me into a hug, she says, "Be careful. Message me when you feel up to it." Her arms tighten around me, and her long, dark curls whisper against my cheek.

I want to hug her tight, to hold on for dear life, but I don't want to squish the babies.

"And please," she goes on, "be kind to yourself."

My breathing hitches, but I hold myself together. "I love you," I whisper into her hair.

"Tell Matteo bye for me. Take care of these little babies."

"Of course," she says. "I love you too."

Chapter Fourteen
Venice Space Research Station

Tenna

I stare at the screen before me, watching Croon analyze some last-minute data. His eyes refocus as he transfers his attention from the data to me.

Eyes sparkling with concern and curiosity, he says, "Are you sure you want to be awake for the journey? It won't be quick. And we have enough cryobeds."

I sigh, regretting the repetition of this conversation, but I know he means well.

"I won't ask my people to forfeit any more of their lives or to place so much trust in the Human Soldiers aboard the ship. We know those going with are good people, but our Tribe… Their faith in Humanity is tenuous at best." I pause, letting my words sink in, before adding, "We'll be awake."

Croon nods, understanding our reservations. A sad smile lifts his lips in an apology as he nods.

Then, I move to a point Krona and I discussed with our highest-ranking warriors, the Ullavenans and Ullavekyns, just this morning.

"It would be better if your people were conscious, as well," I say. "We need to build the trust necessary to go into battle together. My people aren't accustomed to putting their lives in the hands of your Soldiers, and the experiences they've had thus far haven't given them much reason to do so."

Beside me, Krona squeezes my hand, urging me to be firm on this.

On the screen, Croon purses his lips, considering. A few strands of his silvery hair fall loose about his face.

"It may not work out as well as you think…" he muses. "Space travel, especially the take-off and landing, require certain levels of physical training. It isn't as bad as it was when we first started leaving Earth. We have technology that dampens most of the effects, but…"

He pauses, looking at the ship behind him, taking in the cryobeds and crates of food being hauled aboard.

"Regonians seem to be far more resilient than we are, but even you may feel sick at the beginning and end of the trip. It isn't quite like the little jolt when going from one station to another. Getting up to the speed necessary…"

My stomach turns, and I wonder just how bad this may get. My mind fills with images of my people suffering even further at the hands of Human technology, and I recoil from the thought.

But in this case, there's little choice.

He turns back to face us, meeting our gazes from down on Termana. "Our Soldiers have never been subjected to such things and aren't as hardy as you. We may consider waking them after you get up to speed, but before then, I fear seeing them sickened would be detrimental to the cause."

I nod, considering this.

The Humans don't seem to understand our perception of strength in its many forms. Their view of it is so limited, hindering their interactions with us.

I start to say as much, but someone on the screen, someone in the hangar on Termana, knocks over a stack of empty cryobeds, sending them toppling and crashing behind Croon.

He swears under his breath, turning from us. His hair shimmers as he shakes his head, eyeing the metallic carnage of sensitive instruments strewn about the hangar floor.

Turning to face us, he says, "I have to go. I'll contact you again this afternoon."

Krona and I nod, and the screen goes blank. I pull in a deep breath, lamenting Humanity's skewed perceptions.

Beside me, Krona says, "We'll just have to test their mettle on Regonia. If they can't earn our people's trust on the ship, they'll have to do it there. One way or another, it has to be done before we go to Novay."

"Shall we go inform Kala and the others?" I ask, rising to my feet.

Krona stands, placing a gentle hand on the small of my back. "I suppose so. I don't think she'll like it though."

I chuckle. "Not at all."

***

Kala sits in the cafeteria, waiting for us with dark, grey eyes pinched tight. Her partner, Melnara, stands behind her, rubbing her back gently. Her smooth white hair falls forward, tickling my sister's neck.

But my sister stares uneasily at her fidgeting hands.

"Kala," I say, prying her attention from whatever emotion holds her prisoner.

She issues a soft, cooing purr, and I know she thinks of Efsi. My heart clenches at his sound, at the memories of him that flood my mind.

I whisper his sound, letting my tongue trill over its soft lilt. My shoulders lift in a deep sigh, but I stand a bit straighter, grateful to have remembered him.

I'll carry him with me in this meeting. I'll feel his presence, weigh the opinions he might have shared with us.

His perspective can help guide us, even now.

Kala lets out a breath and meets my gaze. She nods, rising from her chair to face Melnara. They embrace, then lean their foreheads together.

I reach for Krona's hand, smiling at the tenderness before me. When Kala and Melnara part, the latter makes to return to our quarters.

Krona calls her name, stopping her. "We need the Ullavekyns, as well."

Alarm flickers in her grey-green eyes, mirrored in my sister's dark gaze.

"Nothing happened," I say. "We merely need to inform everyone of some things. Your help would be appreciated."

She breathes a deep sigh before rushing to assemble the other warriors of her rank.

In no time, we sit in the meeting room, gathered before the screen that Croon occupied mere moments ago. But there are gaps in our ranks.

Efsi's position alongside Kala as Ullavena lies vacant. And he isn't the only Lost One. Two of our Ullavekyns, Rysenia and Skelvan, were lost to the Awakening.

We join hands and utter their sounds, starting with Efsi's gentle, trilling coo. Then, we whisper a deep rumble for Rysenia. A soft, sudden exultation calls Skelvan's presence into our hearts and minds. Again, my insides twist at the loss, but I know with their sounds on my lips, I'll heed their voices.

Sitting with the remnants of our highest-ranking warriors, with five bodies where there should have been eight, I try to be glad that we lost no one else. But my mind drifts over the losses within each rank, then the losses within the non-warriors of our tribe.

Efsi, one of our two Ullavenans. Rysenia and Skelvan, two of four Ullavekyns. Seven of our sixteen Ullavesans. Twenty of the Ninety-Six Ullaveuns. Our entry rank, the Ullavetrans, faced the most losses of all our warriors. Five hundred of the nearly two thousand warriors at that rank.

And the civilian casualties were far worse.

I close my eyes, aching over the losses.

"Tenna?" Krona's low voice, full of concern, tugs at my heart.

I seek him out, eyes meeting his. Lines carve themselves between his eyebrows, and I lean my forehead against his.

"We can't go on like this," I whisper. "Our grief must find a voice. We can't wait until the funeral on Regonia."

"But what can we do?" Kala asks.

With a last caress of Krona's cheek, I turn to face our inner circle. We've never lost so many at one time, even after our most ferocious battles. And we've never had to wait to say our goodbyes.

"We'll find a sound for them all," I say. "Tonight. We leave tomorrow, but… we have to do something. We have to find a way to grieve them all, to grieve this whole mess. If we can't find a sound for this, for the Awakening, before we leave, then I guess we know how we'll spend our time aboard the ship."

All around, heads nod. Quiet words of agreement pass over lips, and Kala reaches for Melnara, taking her hand easily. Krona rests his hand on my knee, and I wrap my fingers around his.

Resolution fills me, thankful for some promise of relief, if only a small amount.

Clearing my throat, I say, "Now, onto the matter that we brought you here for. There will be some… discomfort. Aboard the ship, during transit."

"Adjustments in speed at the beginning and end of our journey will be unpleasant," Krona adds. "Apparently far worse than the jolts of flights between this station and Termana."

Apprehension clouds the eyes of all those before me, pulling their lips into frowns.

"We need to warn everyone. No one should go into this unprepared. Divide Rysenia's and Skelvan's subordinates amongst yourselves and spread the word," I say, hating the sad necessity of rearranging our ranks.

My voice softens, and I say, "Let them all know to assemble in the cafeteria this evening to begin searching for a sound for the Awakening. This tragedy, everything we've learned since coming here, has shaped us. It can't be allowed to pass unsought or unmarked. We've spoken with the Memory Markers about a new Mark for this, one that will be administered at the funeral. We'll inform them that the sound should be considered when designing the Mark."

Chapter Fifteen
Novay

Reginald

The sweetest voice I've ever known wakes me, whispering my name. I smile, opening my eyes to find Rone lying beside me.

"Mm…" I mumble, wrapping my arms around her. "When did you sneak in here?"

"Just now," she says, planting a kiss on my lips.

I seek her out, hungry for more, but she gives me only a small kiss back. Pulling in a deep breath, I nestle in closer, planting my lips on her forehead instead.

"I made my decision," she whispers, voice too low for me to pick out any underlying tones.

The message from Olivia careens back into my mind, and sleep falls away in an instant. I wait, terrified to breathe, to blink. I swallow hard, and a single second stretches into an eon.

But Rone doesn't make me wait any longer than that. She nods, and galaxies explode within my chest.

"Really?" I ask, incredulous.

"Of course," she says, as if no other outcome had even occurred to her. "I knew last night, but you insisted that I think about it. So, I did. I thought about how to make it work."

She smiles, and my heart leaps into my throat.

"Thank you!"

I press my lips to hers, and this time, she kisses back. A smile parts her lips against mine, making way for a gentle laugh.

"How could you have doubted?" she teases.

But I don't spoil the moment by telling her all the ways I've broken over the years, don't ruin this blissful peace with all the times hope has abandoned me.

I slip my hands into her hair, pulling her against me. I ache to roll her onto her back, to move between her legs, but her wings…

She nips at my bottom lip, and heat rockets through me. Moaning against her lips, I press myself to her.

Soft hands slide beneath my shirt, trailing over the sensitive skin of my waist. Her fingers dance, dipping lower, slipping beneath the waist band of my pants to tease me.

My body aches, straining with need.

I kiss her neck as I untie the little string between her wings, letting her top fall free. Her breasts wait, taut and ready when my mouth finds them. She moans, arching her back and pressing herself against me.

Gripping her buttocks, I squeeze, burning alive for her.

She slides her pants down, turning onto her stomach, and I don't hesitate. I tear my clothes away, kneeling between her legs. She spreads her wings, sliding up onto hands and knees as she moves back against me.

My hands trail up her thighs, over her hips.

And I take the plunge.

Waves of ecstasy sweep through me, aching and sweet.

But she isn't close enough.

Leaning forward, I wrap an arm around her waist, pulling her up to press her back against my chest. My hand roams over her stomach, rises to cup her breast.

And we move together.

She tips her head back, resting it on my shoulder. I slow myself, trying to draw this out, but she squirms against me, urging me onward. My hand dips lower, moving over her, pushing her to new heights.

She calls out my name, voice sweet and breaking. Her legs quake, and her hand grips my hip, pulling me deeper, holding me in place.

When her body relents, she moves away from me, just enough to turn to face me. Pushing me back, she straddles me, kissing my neck as my back hits the mattress. She settles over me, taking me in, and the world falls away.

All I see is her.

All I *feel* is her.

Rone bows to kiss me, moving her hips in delicate little swirls. My body burns for her, and my heart ignites as our lips meet. Her wings spread out behind her, blocking the cold grey ceiling from my view.

My breath comes in gasps as she moves, faster and faster. I grip her hips, holding on for dear life. She sits up, back arching and giving me a perfect view. Her head falls back as she cries out, body quaking around me.

My fingers dig into the soft flesh of her backside, pulling her down hard. She cries out once more, and I find my release, splintering into a million pieces as stars explode in my head. Her breasts rise and fall with sharp, quick breaths, and my heart gallops.

Leaning down over me, she showers my face, my neck, my chest with kisses. A smile tugs at the corners of my lips, pulling a soft sound of contentment free of me.

Reaching up, I caress Rone's cheek, relishing her supple skin, the smooth locks of hair hanging loose about her face everywhere save where the braid holds them back. She's worn that braid ever since her surgery, a mark of her change.

As if anyone would ever need reminded.

I rake my gaze over her face, over her piercing green eyes and the blue striations moving within them, over her plump lips and upturned nose. My heart swells, and my smile deepens.

She tumbles onto her side, wings landing with a swish upon my pillow. Turning to face her, I sweep one arm under her head and wrap the other around her waist, pulling her close.

We lie there quietly, hearts racing and lungs trying desperately to catch up. A soft warmth falls over me, threatening to pull me back down into dreams.

But the wall hisses open, and Lustran walks in, followed by two normal Drennar. Their placid expressions make the dark fear on his face stand out, all the more.

My stomach sours as I sit up, brows furrowing as I hold the blanket over myself.

Chapter Sixteen

Venice Space Research Station

Olivia

"Are you sure we should be there?" I ask.

Again, Tenna and Krona brook no argument.

"You were there that night. You learned and lost. You felt the Awakening," Tenna says.

Krona's eyes soften, and he says again, "You should be there."

They lead us on, taking Ricardo, Dr. Sullivan, and I toward the center of the station. As we draw near, we find more and more Regonians, all lingering, waiting for us. Tenna takes my hand, pulling me forward. Her urgency forces me to walk at a pace too fast to be called a walk, but not fast enough to be running.

She tugs at my hand, pulling me onward. I take a deep breath, preparing myself. My nerves tie themselves into tight little knots, and my mind fills with worries of blame finding me, of guilt reaching into my chest to rip my heart out yet again.

But I'd be lying if I said I wasn't excited, curious.

She said this is the first mourning ceremony of this magnitude since the Drennar left them on Regonia, supposedly to die in space. She compared it to the smaller ceremonies held behind closed doors and tapestries, in any available private space, just after the Awakening.

My heart clenches at the word, at the thought. So many dead, so many terrible truths revealed.

My mother's cold eyes flash in my mind, staring heartlessly as she condemned me to death alongside them. My heart floods with her tears at our last meeting, when she finally said she loved me and she wished she could make it better…

And I told her it was too late.

But even now, I don't regret the words.

I should regret it.

For the moment, I shove away my doubts of my character, focusing instead on the path Tenna carves through the gathered Regonians, bustling in the hall outside the cafeteria. Bodies fill the space, packed shoulder to shoulder.

I cling to Tenna's hand, staring at elbows and biceps in every direction, only seeing faces if I crane my head or pass a child. Turning, I see Krona following behind me with Ricardo and Doctor Sullivan forming a chain behind him.

Squeezing through, we reach a barely open circle in the middle of the cafeteria. We fill the space, standing close, bodies touching. Tenna and Krona position us, three tiny Humans, in the center. I take one of Ricardo's hands and one of Dr. Sullivan's. They join hands, completing our little triangle.

Krona and Tenna join hands, resting their arms on ours. Then, circles form around us, carving order out of the chaos of so many bodies.

I glance around us, watching Tenna's sister place one hand on her partner's shoulder, then her other on Dr. Sullivan's shoulder. Melnara places a hand on the shoulder of a Regonian that I've never seen before, and her other hand lands upon Ricardo's shoulder.

All around the room, the others follow suit. Right hands go out to the side, finding the shoulder of the person next to them. Left hands reach forward, in toward the center, toward us.

A heavy hand falls upon my shoulder, resting easily. Warmth seeps into me, and I fight the urge to turn and look, to see whose grief will be so close.

Am I ready for this?

I cast my mind back over what Krona and Tenna told me of this ceremony, all the while trying to loosen up. But I know I'm not ready. Grief is rarely so public on Termana or any of the stations.

Can I do this?

Will they regret having me here?

Will I mess it up? I know it sounds somewhat simple, but… it likely isn't.

But as the people around me grow restless with chatter, the prospect of new things, of seeing a grief ceremony from a different world, of being a part of such a close community, learning and participating in things I never could have dreamed of, surges within me.

Tenna and Krona raise their joined hands, and silence moves like a wave, rippling outward. Their arms come back down to rest upon ours, and I know what comes next, recalling the description Tenna gave me of the ceremony.

Now, we think of all we lost, all we learned. All we still have and must protect.

I close my eyes.

The attack on Odyssey oozes into my mind, slimy with my mother's betrayal. Her words chill my veins, and horror slithers through me as I remember the Soldiers bursting into the lab. Again, I see two thousand sleeping Regonians perish, convulsing as electricity coursed through them.

Fear grips me anew as the sight of Krona taking Tenna's barely conscious body into the laundry chute flashes over the backs of my eyelids.

The guilt comes back, cutting holes in my heart. My eyes well up, pricking at the corners. My hand tightens on Ricardo's, and I hold back a sob.

Behind me, a keening wail pierces the silence, and I jump. My eyes fly open, and I turn my head, searching for the source of such a sound, the source of such pain.

But all around me, faces contort with anguish. Tears flow freely over the cheeks of seasoned warriors, and frowns drag lips downward. Hands squeeze shoulders, gripping for support.

I look up at Krona and Tenna, at the tears shining on their skin. They lean forward, bowing their heads together.

Shaken by the ferocity of the sorrow around me, my own tears fall. I remember my night in Sparrow, my attempt to take my own life, and my lips quiver.

When my shoulders begin to shake, the hand upon my shoulder squeezes lightly, tenderly, careful not to break me.

But it breaks me wide open.

I let loose a horrendous sob, shattering the too-still air that followed that singular wail. And a melody of agony answers my cry, ebbing and flowing as the remnants of Daen Tribe grieve their Lost Ones.

I know that slowly, our voices will come together. Someone will feel an echo of their own loss in someone else's voice, and they'll match them, repeating and harmonizing. I know that eventually, we'll find a single sound to remember this terrible event.

But right now, that doesn't matter.

All the guilt and pain, all the broken pieces of me pour out through my lips, far louder and far more open than I ever thought to be.

Chapter Seventeen

Novay

Rone

Lustran opens his mouth, but nothing comes out. He stares at the floor, unable to meet my gaze. Pulling in a long, slow breath, he finally says, "I didn't know."

My heart jumps into my throat, but I force words past it. "Didn't know what?" I ask, voice straining against the fear that chokes me.

A sick, slimy feeling slithers through me.

What have they kept from me?

My mind spins, a chaotic maelstrom of all the terrible things they've done to Humans and Leey and Daen Tribe and all the rest in the name of knowledge.

What have they done?

My hands shake, and my mouth goes dry.

The Drennar standing behind Lustran steps around him, breaching Reginald's room, our safe space. I jolt, hating her presence here.

"Clothe yourself appropriately for the temperature of the non-Human sectors," she states, voice a perfect monotone.

I swallow, rising to my feet. My skin warms as the sheet slides away, staying on the bed with Reginald. Lustran turns around, allowing me privacy.

The two Drennar who came with him permit no such courtesy. Their unfeeling eyes watch, sweeping fans of blue light over my modified body, analyzing the parts of me made to be more Human. I shudder before their gazes, hating the touch of that light. My skin crawls, and I hurry to dress, pulling garments on haphazardly just to block their view.

My hands shake, fingers trembling as I tie my top behind my back, securing it between my wings. A single tear streaks over my cheek, and I swipe it away quickly. But those blue fans of light miss nothing. They weigh and measure every heartbeat, every stuttered breath.

The only thing they miss… is the cause.

Drennar have never had a reason to hide their bodies from each other, wearing clothes only if our particular body chemistry disagreed with the average temperature of the facility. We've never had need to be shy. After all, why hide what isn't truly yours? If it belongs only to the pursuit of knowledge, shouldn't it be accessible when necessary?

But my lip trembles, and my throat tightens.

The thought of my body never having been my own claws at my heart, and I nearly buckle beneath the weight of it. My arms wrap around my chest, desperate to shield me from their analyses.

Because I don't want to share myself with them.

Reginald pulls undergarments on beneath the sheet and rises, putting a tender hand to the small of my back. I step closer to him, moving into the embrace of someone who values me, someone who sees me as more than an experiment.

"What's going on?" I ask. My voice wavers just a bit too much for my liking.

"The emotion and reproductive modifications may be affecting your ability to remain impartial. As a Drennar, you were expected to behave rationally despite these things, thus maintaining your ability to oversee experiments."

The woman before me speaks so flatly, so coldly, that I can barely bring myself to think of her as my peer.

She's a Drennar, nothing more than a drone in the hive.

"Your experiment is still valid, as are those that you were overseeing. There has been no lasting harm done," she says.

"Then, what is this?" My brows furrow, and I shake my head. Yet, I know I won't like her answer. My stomach drops before she ever opens her mouth, a product of Human intuition.

"You are to be relocated to another facility immediately to prevent harmful ramifications to your experiments."

My jaw drops, and my shoulders fall.

Reginald gasps.

"What?" I squeak.

"You are to be relocated to another facility immediately to prevent harmful rami–"

Her repetition, her blank eyes, the horrid flat tone of her voice, all join together to taunt me, and my fists clench.

"No! NO! Why wasn't I informed of this?"

"It was pertinent for your experiment and his that you remained unaware until a decision was reached."

Fury rolls through me, narrowing my eyes and boiling my blood. "You can't do this!" I shout.

"We have taken all the proper steps. The new facility is prepared for your arrival. This is fully within our current capabilities," she says.

But her blatant misunderstanding of my true meaning only makes my nails dig into my palms, makes my teeth grind together.

"That isn't what I meant," I hiss.

"It is preferred that you speak the words best suited to your meaning," she says with a single blink. "We must leave. Your departure is set for seven minutes from now. This delay was not accounted for and further illustrates the need to relocate you. Your experiments will be redistributed to uncompromised Drennar. You will now be tasked with the exploration of your modifications in the new facility."

The man who came with them steps into the room, and I step back. He towers over me, bristling with modifications of his own. Sharpened bones stick outward from his arms, running the length of them. They line his cheekbones, hardening his face, making it look so much more alien than the other Drennar.

"No further delay can be tolerated," he says, surveying me. "I extend comfort," he reaches out to touch my shoulder, but the gesture is flat and strange from him. This is no Drennar custom, merely an attempt to placate me.

Another experiment.

"Don't touch me!" I command, swatting his arm away hard enough to smack it against the alonarium wall behind him with a loud thud. The sharpened bone punctures the wall. He doesn't flinch, doesn't blink. He merely transmits a pulse to the wall, ears flashing once, and a burst of static electricity reshapes the wall.

"There is no time for further delay."

Stepping forward, he grabs me by my upper arms and lifts me off the ground. I thrash in his grip, demanding that he release me. One foot finds purchase on his thigh, but he doesn't wince or even tighten his grip.

"Put her down!" Reginald screams.

The pain in his voice stirs a fire within me, and I twist, throwing an elbow into this Drennar's face. The sharpened bone of his cheeks cuts my arm open, sending pain rioting through me. Rivulets of blood drip over my skin.

Lustran rushes forward, grabbing me, pulling me from this stranger's grasp. "I'll bring her along!" he shouts. "I'll do it! Just let her go!"

The Drennar's arms go slack, and I let Lustran pull me away, unwilling to injure him in the process with an errant thrash. But inside, I seethe. My face contorts into a scowl, brows carving lines into my skin.

I guess I shouldn't have gotten used to being valued.

The words hiss through my mind, burning like acid.

But I am more than data, now. I am more than information to be manipulated and gathered.

I am more *than* that.

Chapter Eighteen

Novay

Reginald

Lustran pulls Rone away from the other Drennar, and her swinging arms stop. The scowl on her face deepens as she glares at the unfeeling beasts that would pull us apart, the monsters that watched her as she dressed.

I shudder even thinking of their blank stares, their unflinching analyses. My heart shrivels within me at the prospect of losing her.

They've taken so much from me, already. Are they really going to take her too?

"We must leave," the female Drennar says. "We can afford no further delay."

Pulling a page from Human history, Rone spits, "Fuck your delays."

It almost makes me smile.

But Lustran looks at me, eyes full of sorrow. "I'm sorry," he says, then shakes his head. "For everything."

Shock forces a deep breath down my throat, and a memory strikes me, the reason he looked familiar. I see him as he was twelve years ago, standing over me in my home on Termana, carrying Olivia from her room despite her flailing.

I still feel the weight of his fans of analysis, sweeping over me as he assessed my suitability as a substitute, feel his arms wrapped around me as he carried me away from my family.

I flinch before the onslaught of memories, of Eva's depravity and Olivia's depression.

I open my mouth to speak, but nothing comes out. My eyes fall to the floor for a split second, and I nod, accepting his apology.

Just as Rone isn't the same guard that led me from this room to the testing room for years, he isn't the same man that pulled me from Termana. They aren't the same as the Drennar standing before me, trying to rip my heart to shreds for the millionth time.

I turn to them, only letting my eyes skim over Rone for an instant.

"Please, don't take her away."

The man blinks once, at least willing to hear me out even if only out of curiosity, and I forge ahead.

"Wouldn't you gain more information from this novel experience, from her interactions with me, than you would from separating us? Surely Human history gave you enough heartbreak to study."

Silence falls over us, and my nerves coil tightly within me. I bite the inside of my lip, waiting, aching, desperate for them to answer, to say anything at all. Time stretches before me, though I know their consideration lasts but a fraction of a second.

"Your experiment is in jeopardy if she stays here," the woman says. Her eyes glow with an unusual green light, but it only serves to make them colder, somehow.

The lights on her ears flicker as she continues. "It is true that Humans perfected heartbreak, offering a plentitude of situations to analyze, but there were never any controls. Too many variables were allowed in your societies and your daily lives. We must analyze sorrow alone, separating it from all other variables, to measure its effect on Human intelligence."

And with that, she and the man with bone blades shove Lustran and Rone from my room. The wall hisses shut behind them before I can speak another word.

A private message pops up on my Link, and it plays Rone's words through my head immediately.

"I will fix this." Her tone is acid, dripping over those four little words.

"I will fix this," she says again as the message replays in my mind.

But she shouldn't have to fix this.

My hands ball into fists at my side, and my teeth grind together.

She shouldn't have to fix any of this.

My eyes fall to the floor, locking on a drop of her blood. The red seems to spread, coating itself over my vision, surrounding everything and expanding to fill every corner of my mind.

I slam my fists against the wall, screaming at the top of my lungs. Fury roils within me, and I let it all out, funneling the rage into wordless shrieks. I pound the wall, and my heart hammers behind my ears, beating itself against my ribs.

My lungs struggle, pulling in short gasps of breath between screams as agony burns through me, searing my veins.

"No!" I scream.

A lonely life of empty afternoons and cold nights spreads out before me, and the weight of it buckles my knees. I drop to the floor and scream again, voice breaking.

Because I can't do anything.

I can't bring her back. I can't help Olivia. I can't help Daen Tribe.

I'll just be here, alone, doing absolutely nothing, saying *absolutely nothing.*

For the rest of my life.

The red fades from my sight, and my arms fall to rest in my lap, limp and useless.

Helplessness settles over me, and my heart contracts.

I can't do anything.

My mouth goes dry, and my eyes prick with the promise of tears.

I'm alone again.

My chest tightens, and a lump in my throat chokes me. Crumpling into a ball, I collapse against the cold grey wall, hands cradling my head as I weep.

Chapter Nineteen
Venice Space Research Station

Olivia

Alarms sound in my mind, barely audible in the din of the searching ceremony. They urge me to go to bed, to prepare for tomorrow. We have so much ahead of us, and there is still so much to do.

But I turn the alarms off, squeezing Ricardo's and Dr. Sullivan's hands.

All around me, Daen Tribe mourns, and my lungs work with them. All the pain of the attack on Odyssey, of my mother's betrayal, of the Awakening, sweeps through me, quickly followed by the guilt that led me to pills and a bottle on Sparrow.

But I might need a sound of my own for that last part.

My heart clenches, and hoarse screams rage through me, fighting to be heard through the cacophony of agony and fury swirling through the air around me.

But somewhere close by, a Regonian echoes my cry of pain and anger, matching my scream. A ripple of repetition branches out from there as more and more pick up the battle cry.

Voice breaking, I scream with them, feeding every ounce of disgust and helplessness and violent sorrow into it. The hand on my shoulder squeezes gently, and the Regonian behind me picks up the cry. My bones shake with the noise, vibrating as these giants roar with the same pain that haunts me.

Our voices join together, repeating the scream over and over, and more people join in. The sound morphs, just a little, becoming more visceral, and as I match it, the sound resonates within my heart. The riotous noise builds, echoing back at us from the cold metal walls.

Breathless, I pant with the exertion, lungs trying desperately to keep up. I draw a breath, preparing for the next scream, but something in the air changes.

And I just know.

I don't scream. Just breathe.

Two frantic beats of my heart pass, and then, Tenna and Krona lift their voices in a shriek of fury and pain, matching the sounds that rumbled through Daen Tribe just seconds ago. Their voices move together, reverberating in my chest.

They scream once, twice.

I pull in a deep breath and join in as the entire Tribe joins them on their third scream, forcing all the pain out.

As our voices fall away, silence descends, but it doesn't hurt. It doesn't weigh on me as silence always has, doesn't make me flinch before my own thoughts.

Bodies press inward, and I do my part. Stepping forward, compressing, I move into Krona and Tenna, into Ricardo and Dr. Sullivan. Regonians press against my back, moving closer.

I bow my head forward, resting it against Tenna and Krona's sides. All around, heads incline, joining together. Lips pull ragged breaths inward, inflating battered lungs. I focus on Tenna and Krona and the rate of their breaths, trying desperately to match them.

In…

Out…

Slow and smooth, they control their breathing.

In…

Out…

My heart hammers unsteadily in my chest, punctuating each breath. But I hear the heartbeats of the Regonians around me doing the same to their breaths. Slowly, we all center, breathing in time. The air around us moves in strange waves, ebbing and flowing.

Voice surprisingly steady, if a little hoarse, Tenna says, "We have found it. We can go home with at least that comfort."

Heads lift, and people spread out. Our breathing becomes our own, and somehow, that feels a little lonely. On all sides, Regonians group up into families and friends and lovers, dispersing to their quarters.

But I feel them in my heart, in my lungs. For the first time in my life, I feel like part of a community, like I was part of something real, something bigger than me.

When Krona and Tenna look down at Ricardo, Dr. Sullivan, and me with warmth in their gazes, it even feels like I'm wanted here.

Ricardo moves closer, putting a hand to the small of my back, and I smile.

Chapter Twenty

Novay

Rone

I pace through my new quarters. If it weren't for the resilience of alonarium, I'd worry about wearing a path through the floor, breaking it down beneath me with repeated steps.

My hands curl and unfurl at my sides. I chew at the inside of my cheek.

What am I going to say?

My mind whirls, a riot of betrayal and hurt and anxiety.

How can I send a message to Olivia without Reginald?

But how can I not tell her?

My eyes trace over the new room, sparsely furnished, just like his. For half a breath, I wonder if she would even notice that it wasn't the same room.

But she'd notice his absence.

What am I going to do? How can I tell her they separated us? She's going to think something happened to him.

Or that I betrayed him.

A lance of pain shoots through me at even the thought of turning on him.

No. I have to do this.

Being separated doesn't mean I stop trying. It's just one more reason to do this.

Stomping over to my bed, I plop down on it. I transform the wall with a single pulse of static, letting it record me, but I set it to private. A thing I shouldn't have figured out how to do. A thing inspired by Olivia.

I take a deep breath, trying to shove the nerves away, stuffing them down deep.

"Hi, Olivia. I know you're probably wondering where your dad is, and I want you to know before I say anything else that he's safe. They just separated us…"

A sigh eases past my lips, and my eyes fall to my hands, balled on my lap.

"Apparently our relationship was jeopardizing the experiments they're performing on us and the ones I was meant to watch over."

I shake my head.

"But I can't do it. I can't perform experiments now. Not now that I have emotions, not now that I know what it's like to feel. I can't…"

Lifting my gaze, I face the wall, watching my image shift over it. I analyze the lines in my forehead, the downward curve of my lips.

"I'm in. I know your father wants to help, and I wish I could still reach him. I wish I could see him. I wish…"

A lump forms in my throat, choking me. I close my eyes as my heart breaks, reaching out for him. Pulling in a deep breath, I steady myself.

"I'm not the only one with emotion now. I convinced them to modify a few others. We're all in, but we'll have to be careful. They've separated us from everyone else, and they're watching us. But I took a page out of your book."

A smile lifts the corners of my lips. "I've been doing a bit of hacking."

Chapter Twenty One
Venice Space Research Station

Olivia

After packing away the remaining items that will traverse the galaxy with me, I sit back on my bed. Beyond the open door, Tenna's family bustles about, preparing themselves. The door to the hall lies open as well, letting in the sounds of songs and movement.

Half a smile lifts my lips, but they don't rise further.

How much louder would it have been if they hadn't lost so many?

Sighing, I stare at the things around me, sorted and stuffed into boxes to be stored while I'm gone. Ricardo's boxes sit in neat stacks near the foot of the bed, and I find myself wishing he were here. But more meetings pull him away.

I check the time, knowing I'll have another meeting of my own soon, another training session with the new tech team. And though I know I'll have fun talking specifics with them, I'm just not ready.

My heart hangs low, drifting through memories of those jerking limbs on Washington Station.

What did their voices sound like?

What roles did they play in the Tribe?

I know the answer in one case. Tenna's brother, Efsi, was among those lost in what Tenna refers to as the Descent of Man. His partner, another warrior, died on Washington. My mind drifts over the meal we all shared in these rooms last night, and I see the holes in the conversation that they would have filled. I felt every lull.

And every time, Tenna, Krona, their parents, Kala, and Melnara made the same sound, a soft purr.

Efsi's sound.

They filled the gaps that he would have filled. They did it for his partner, too, keeping them close.

A tear slides down my cheek, and I wonder if I should find a sound for my mother, despite everything she did, despite all the ways she hurt me. The ways she hurt Daen Tribe and the people of Bolivia Station.

But she wouldn't have filled any gaps in my life, even if she were alive.

Laughter draws nearer as Tenna approaches the door, and I wipe my tears away, hastily scrubbing at them with the end of my sleeve. I leave it stretched over my hand, curling my fist into the damp fabric, tucking it between fingers and palm to hide the tear stains. Blinking rapidly, I try to clear my vision before she enters the room, but it doesn't work.

The smile vanishes from her face as soon as she sees me, and fresh tears threaten to fall.

No. Don't do this. She deserves to be happy for a change.

But my eyes don't listen.

Tenna rushes forward, sitting beside me as waves of tears cascade over my cheeks. Her arms wrap around me, pulling me close.

"What's wrong?"

I shake my head. "It's nothing," I say. Habit. Reflex.

"It's clearly something," Tenna says, tightening her embrace.

Be better.

Don't hide.

I grit my teeth, hating how easy it is to pull away from people. But I can't live that way anymore.

"I'm just thinking of all the people you lost… people that should be going with…" My lungs catch, and my breathing hitches, cutting me off.

I guess they'll still be going with. But only their bodies.

Tears fall in earnest, and my face scrunches in on itself. Tenna rubs my back gently, letting me weep. She doesn't judge me, doesn't call me weak.

When she finally speaks, she says, "We find these sounds for a reason. The one we found last night? You should use it."

For a moment, it feels too sacred for me to utter, too much a part of their world. But the feeling of the ceremony, of everyone including me, of my voice joining theirs, is too tempting.

So, despite the humiliation of grieving so openly now that no one else can join me, I draw in a deep breath. I let my lungs shape the sound, screaming the desperate, furious sorrow of the Awakening. It burns through me, shattering the too-quiet room.

Before I finish, a voice beyond the door echoes the scream.

Then, another. Out in the hall, more voices join, commiserating, surrounding me with support and understanding.

Finally, Tenna screams, that same guttural agony, the rage and the pain bursting from her. Then, she turns to me, pulling me closer.

"You're not alone," she whispers.

I nod and let my tears fall, knowing this time that no one here will judge me for them, that everyone here understands.

✳✳✳

In the conference room, I sit with half the screens illuminated. Once everyone arrives, blinking their screens to life one by one, I start with the question we left off on last time.

"I know you were curious about the mechanisms that the Drennar use to send and receive data so quickly. I'm not sure how I forgot to mention that sooner," I say, raising my brows in disbelief.

I'm really not cut out to be a trainer…

"They've installed their own transmitters here, and they use light to send messages. It's a lot faster than anything we've come up with."

Sekani Willis jumps in, saying, "They have transmitters here?"

I nod.

"So, why don't we just take them out?"

"The thought crossed my mind, of course," I answer. "But that'd tip them off. They'd know we found them and that we were rebelling. Then, they'd come to fix the transmitters and do God knows what else while they're here."

Shaking my head, I go on. "This way, we control what information they get, and we can still keep the doors locked. If they think the tech issues are on our end, they won't think they need to fix their transmitters. With their outpost so close, and with how fast they can travel, we can't afford to risk bringing them down on us."

"So, the transmitters stay," Willis says with a slow nod.

"Yep. They see us, but only what we want them to see. Everything looks like old TV broadcasts back on Earth, with static and black lines," I say.

They stare at me blankly, but it isn't exactly surprising. No one really pays much mind to the old, discarded tech of Earth. It's glossed over in our history of technology classes, given maybe three sentences. But no one actually pays attention to it.

I'm just… weird.

"Anyway," I say, getting back to the point.

I push through the rest of our training session, but now, even among people who understand technology and its inner workings, I'm on the outside again. The comradery of speaking with other tech people, the sense of belonging that filled our previous meetings has vanished.

As we draw everything to a close, my mind drifts back to the Awakening, and I'm tempted to cry out as I would amongst Daen Tribe. But I don't.

Not here.

Not among Humans.

I keep my grief bottled up, put my anger away, just like we're supposed to.

And even if I brought it out to air, the people on the screens before me wouldn't understand. They weren't on Odyssey when it happened, didn't see the attack firsthand. They were comfortable in their own quarters, possibly asleep.

They were shaken, of course. All of humanity was.

But they don't know the loss as deeply as Daen Tribe. They don't know the guilt and grief as I do.

So, I seal my lips shut, forcing a smile as we move through lessons, and then the screens go blank, one by one. The expression falls from my face the second the last screen goes dark.

Rising from my seat, I step past the empty chairs which huddle up against the massive metal table. The door opens to the security offices, and I move through them as quickly as I can. Out in the hall, I pull in a deep breath, filling my lungs near to bursting.

Then, I let loose the biggest scream I can manage, pouring the anger and agony of the Awakening into it. My voice breaks, crackling over the emotions.

Before my shout ends, before my lungs run out of air, another voice joins me, bellowing into the halls. Then another, much closer.

And this one, I recognize.

As the sound of the Awakening sweeps through Venice, echoing through metal halls, it reminds me that I'm not alone, that there are others here for me, that I'm here for them.

I turn to face Ricardo as his shout dies on his lips.

But he isn't alone.

Beside him, a Guard stares on, eyes wide and jaw slack. Red hair frames her face, telling me exactly who she is. The only redheaded Guard, the only redhead our age in all of humanity.

Francis.

One of Ricardo's friends.

She stares at me like I'm a lunatic, casting bewildered glances at Ricardo and the halls, still echoing with the furiously mournful cries of Daen Tribe. Heat sweeps through me, creeping up my neck and coloring my cheeks.

This isn't exactly the first impression I wanted.

Chapter Twenty Two
Venice Space Research Station

Ricardo

My voice echoes through the halls, resonating with Olivia's voice and those of Daen Tribe. Thoughts of the Awakening filter through me, but the people spread throughout the station feel the same things, lifting my spirits in the face of such an atrocity.

Slowly, our cries die out, and Olivia turns to face me, eyes appraising. A sympathetic smile tugs at my lips, but her gaze drifts to Francis before she can return the expression.

I look at my friend, and a laugh bursts from me at the expression on her face. She stands with her jaw hanging open and her eyes wide, gaze darting back and forth between Olivia and me. Turning to look back over her shoulder, she peers at the empty hall behind her, still echoing with the anguished shouts of Daen Tribe.

I glance at Olivia, at the blush creeping over her skin. Moving forward, I take her hand

and place a gentle kiss on her cheek. "It's okay," I whisper.

Turning around, I make the introductions. Francis still stares, and Olivia still blushes.

"It's a Regonian custom," I say. "A way of mourning. The Awakening was—"

Francis interrupts, "The what?"

"Oh," I say, remembering. "Daen Tribe has named this tragedy the Awakening. I guess I shouldn't have assumed you'd know that."

Sighing, I wonder how much, or how little, the rest of humanity actually knows about Daen Tribe.

Why haven't they been told about them?

We need to let everyone know what they're like, what their lives are like. Our role as ambassadors won't do much good if the Coalition doesn't use the information we gather to make things better.

Taking initiative, I explain the customs we've learned about thus far. We walk together, moving through the security offices toward

Francis' new post. As we step into her office, I say, "So, that's why we were screaming. It's a way for the community to grieve together."

"Oh," Francis says.

"It's surprisingly helpful," I say, gripping Olivia's hand.

She looks at me, sheepish and still blushing. I nudge her elbow gently. Francis looks around the office, pulling in a deep breath. "Are any of the Regonians staying behind?"

"No, they're all going home," Olivia says with a smile. "Finally."

For the first time, Francis meets her gaze, looking her up and down. "Do you not want them here?"

"It's not that," Olivia says, rushing through her words. "My mother never should have brought them here. They shouldn't have had to leave their homes. It's time they got to go back."

Francis nods. Sitting down behind her new desk, falling easily into the role of Head Guard of Venice Space Research Station, she gestures for us to take a seat. We fall into the chairs facing the desk.

"Now, I know you're both technically my superiors now," she says. "But right now, I don't care about that. And Ricardo, so help me, don't you dare interrupt."

"Francis, what are you doing?" I ask, rolling my eyes.

But she only points at me in warning.

Turning her attention to Olivia, Francis grows even more serious. "If I had my choice, you probably wouldn't be who I'd pick for him."

"Francis, seriously," I say. "There's no need for this."

Shushing me, she goes on. "But, he seems to disagree with me on that. So, I have this to say, and then, I'll leave you be."

I ease back, deciding to hear her out.

"Do *not* hurt him," Francis continues.

Her words pull a smile from me, and my head tips downward.

"If you relapse, if you put him through anything even close to what his parents did," she leans forward, strands of red hair falling about her face, "if you hurt him, I will make *sure* you regret it."

"Francis!" I exclaim.

But Olivia squeezes my hand. I glance at her, as she whispers, "It's okay."

"No, it isn't."

"It is," she insists. Turning to Francis, she says, "I know my failures."

"Olivia…" I whisper, shaking my head.

"My… shortcomings," she corrects, choosing a softer, nicer word, but it still rings false.

Obstacles seems more fitting.

Her hands shake as she goes on, "I know I've hurt him already." A single tear rolls down her cheeks, and she looks away from Francis.

"I'm sorry," she whispers, finally looking me in the eye. "I'm really sorry for putting you through so much."

"You don't need to apologize," I whisper. "Things haven't been easy, I understand that."

She shakes her head, dropping her gaze. I reach up to cup her cheek, leaning my forehead against hers as my heart twists.

"I hurt you though…" Olivia whimpers, voice so small I barely hear it.

"We can move past it," I say. "I want to be with you. If you want that too, we'll move past it. We can get through this."

She gnaws at her lip, but I tip her chin up, begging her to meet my eyes. "Olivia, is this what you want?"

She hesitates, and my heart leaps into my throat.

Sparkling hazel meets my gaze, shimmering with tears. Slowly, she nods.

"Then we'll get past this together."

She nods again, and tears pour over her cheeks in earnest. I press my lips to hers, and she threads her hands in my hair.

"Together," she echoes.

Chapter Twenty Three
Venice

Tenna

All around me, excitement buzzes through the air. My people chatter. Hope fills their words, and an undercurrent of curiosity moves through their tones.

Because soon, we'll be on a spaceship, flying through the Realm of Stars for the first time.

Well, the first time that we'll be conscious.

But that little caveat does little to pull down the mood.

A few of our people cast their eyes about nervously, staring out every window we pass with a mixture of wonder and latent fear.

And I feel it, too.

The words we all believed, the stories of disease in deep space killing off our ancestors, still whisper through my mind. Because though I know that isn't what happened, have seen video evidence that the Drennar never died out, I also know space isn't a safe place to be.

Not for us.

Not for the Humans, either.

We need to be on our own planets, far away from the Drennar.

I glance at Olivia, Ricardo, and Dr. Sullivan. They walk among Daen Tribe, tipping their heads back to meet the gazes of all those they speak with. Slowly, they meander toward the edge of the room, toward the cold, metal walls of the station. A pang of dismay twists my heart. Because Termana *is* the Humans' planet, now. They have nowhere else to go.

Facing down the Drennar is their only hope.

And really, isn't that the case for us too?

Clearly, the Drennar can reach Regonia.

***

The hangar door opens before me, and my stomach flips. Where space would normally sit, the interior of a massive ship waits. Too large to fit in the station, its hatch locks it in place, docked with the hangar directly.

I squeeze Krona's hand and turn to face him. Beautiful green eyes hold my gaze. He steps forward, resting his forehead against mine.

Clasping my hand on the back of his neck, I whisper, "Hoo kai voo mai."

"Hoo kai voo mai," he says, and my skin warms.

Our lips meet, soft and tender. We pull back, take a deep breath, and face our people with the ship looming beyond the hangar behind us.

"Loo rein gordeky!" we shout in unison. *We go home.*

A great roar of excitement rumbles through Daen Tribe, reverberating through the hall, bouncing off metal walls. My heart hammers, skipping beats and slamming against my ribs.

A smile lifts my lips and crinkles my eyes. Krona and I turn to the hangar and lead our people aboard the massive ship.

Chapter Twenty Four
The Realm of Stars

Krona

I strap my harness over my chest and crane my neck to see our people. They sit, strapped to the walls of the ship off to my side and across from me. Their faces contort as anxiety rolls through them, and they croon the sounds of their Lost Ones.

The bodies of our fallen lie in crates, fastened securely to the floor of the ship, hidden from view but all too visible.

They should be on Regonia. Their bodies should have rejoined our world by now.

But they lie before us, shoved in boxes for transport.

Somewhere in the back of the cavernous ship, the agonized shout of the Awakening rises from the lips of a child. It echoes, rolling through the crowd, and I throw my head back to join in the scream of furious agony. Beside me, Tenna grips my hand and lends her voice to the cry. The hatch closes, and the ship groans as if joining us.

Olivia's voice rings out over the speakers throughout the ship, walking us through the process of leaving the Human planet and space stations.

"Time for a jolt," she says. "It's completely normal. We're just disembarking from Venice. We'll be moving a short distance to Termana so the Human soldiers can come aboard. There won't be any turbulence on the way there, but when we dock, there might be some shaking."

I take a deep breath, thankful that Olivia is the one guiding us through this process. She knows what will disorient us and what won't. She'll get us there safely.

Briefly, I wonder about the other pilot sitting up front with her, the man that's trained to fly smaller crafts, but is the best option to aid her on the trip. My stomach flips at the thought of putting all our lives in the hands of a stranger.

But Olivia's there.

She'll keep us safe.

Her voice drifts through the hull, counting down for us. "Three... Two..."

I grip my harness with one hand, tightening my grip on Tenna's hand with the other. All through the hull, a collective breath rushes into lungs lining the walls on this level and all along a second level.

"One."

The ship groans as it breaks free of the station. My entire body quakes with the noise of it, slamming to one side of my seat as we move forward. Somewhere in the back, a few screams break free, careening through the air to grate against my eardrums.

"Everything went just as it should have," Olivia says over the speakers. "The thrusters on Venice maintained orbit, and we're officially unlinked from the Station. We'll be docking at Termana soon, so stay buckled up. I'll let you know what to expect."

I swallow, squeezing Tenna's hand. A bit of relief trickles through me.

That wasn't so bad.

Yet again, the tech has proved to be easier to cope with than I ever expected. Star-sickness, while not my favorite thing, no longer elicits the same hatred or bone-chilling fear it once did.

I glance around at the people of Daen Tribe, taking in their expressions. A smile lifts my lips when I see my own thoughts echoed in their eyes. They sit comfortably now, leaning against each other as well as they can in their harnesses.

We're going home.

The thought whispers through me on a breeze of relief.

We can settle our people back into their homes and gather our Vyrtons.

But how far afield have they run?

What condition are our homes in?

And our fields?

Have the Vaerkin moved in? Or Roon Tribe?

Fear slithers into my stomach, something I never thought I'd feel, tainting our homecoming.

What will we find when we get home?

We've been away so long.

Chapter Twenty Five
Termana

Ricardo

Francis walks away from me. Lists of names detailing all the sleeping Humans buzz through her Link. I turn on my heel, staring out at stacks of cryo-beds.

The same beds used to bring Daen Tribe here.

Pulling in a deep breath, I try to shake the association, try to shake the eerie feeling that crept through my bones when I watched the footage of Olivia's mom unloading them, staring at them like objects to be manipulated.

But try as I might, that feeling holds firm, lodged in my brain.

Approaching a lone cryo-bed, one that has yet to be lifted atop a stack, I place a hand on the cool metal. A window shows me a face, motionless and peaceful. The man within knows nothing of his surroundings. He lies there, vulnerable.

But he chose this vulnerability.

Daen Tribe had no say in the matter.

At my command, my Link fills my head with this man's data. Xianyu Giordano, age twenty-four. Male with above average physical competence, combat training, and mental acuity. No adverse medical conditions.

But I don't want data points.

Staring down at his chiseled nose, at his crease-less eyes, I pick out the pieces of his heritage before my Link ever gets to them. His parents named him for his most obvious genetic lineages, Korean and Italian.

But even this information doesn't feel adequate. I want to know the man before me, so that I may never look at these cryo-beds with anything less than the reverence the lives within deserve.

I don't want to look at them like my brother and Olivia's mom looked at the members of Daen Tribe as they poked and prodded and cut them open.

My Link reviews the information he's allowed to be made public and tells me that he loves to dance, that he's good at an old dance called Salsa. It tells me that he likes fast-paced music and scary movies, that he's single, though only recently.

A small part of me wonders if he would've considered this assignment had his relationship not ended.

I stare out at the stacks of cryo-beds, watching as they're stacked and moved aboard.

What brought the rest of you here?

Machinery buzzes around the hangar, driven by experienced warehouse workers. My nerves wind tight, hoping none of the beds fall. When a Lift operator approaches, I cast one last glance at the face behind the little window.

Nodding, I slide my hand clear of the cool, dark-grey metal. I step aside, clearing the path for the operator to slide the prongs of the Lift beneath the cryo-bed.

Xianyu rests, unaware, as the machine lifts his bed three meters into the air, settling him on the top of a stack.

The woman backs the machine up, and a soft beeping emanates from it. She aligns the prongs with the stack, sliding them beneath the beds of five human beings. Additional prongs wrap around the sides of the stack, securing the load, and she speeds away, careening up the ramp into the ship.

Don't be dramatic.

She can't be going that fast.

My Link tells me that she's only going eight kilometers an hour, and somehow, that doesn't sound right. It seems so much faster with so many lives resting on the end of her Lift.

Francis meanders back over to me, red hair gleaming in the bright lights of the hangar. "Everyone present and accounted for," she says. "All cryo-beds are functioning perfectly, and we only have five more stacks to load."

I nod, peering into the cargo bay of the ship at the stacks of people. Soldiers move efficiently through the cargo hold, fastening the stacks into the ship when the Lifts position them. Overhead, great cranes wait in the ceiling of the cargo bay to arrange the beds when it comes time to wake the people within.

Another Lift moves up the ramp to deposit a stack of beds, and I turn to Francis. She smiles at me, but sadness lingers in her eyes. "Be careful."

"I'll try," I tell her.

"Don't try. Do it."

I laugh. "Yes, mom."

She wags a finger at me, arching her brows. "I'm serious. I expect you back in one piece. Don't you dare disappoint me."

But for all her attempts at light-heartedness, tears shine in her eyes.

My lips drop into a frown, and I nod. Pulling her into my arms, I squeeze tight. Our armor makes the hug awkward, but I don't care.

"I expect to be meeting a couple babies when I get back," I say. "Start your family. Don't worry about me."

"I can worry *and* start a family."

Pulling back, I stare into eyes that have softened with compassion and hardened with ire more times than I can count since I met her. I swallow, feeling the time slip away from me. Two more Lifts buzz up the ramp, tugging me toward the Realm of Stars.

And despite all my excitement, all my desperate desires to set things right and return the Regonians to their home, my heart aches.

"I'll send you messages about Regonia," I say, forcing the words past a lump in my throat.

"About Regonia? You better send me messages before then," Francis chides, laughing through a single falling tear.

"Of course," I chuckle. Then, as the last Lift drives clear of the ship, parking in a corner of the hangar to be locked away, I say, "Goodbye."

"Bye," she says. She sucks her lips in and turns away, casting a single glance over her shoulder as she walks away. The lights glare off her dark armor.

I turn toward the ship, ready to climb aboard and leave Termana behind. My Link helps me navigate the many halls of the ship, already synced to the net within the massive beast. It guides me to the upper cargo area, and I pause at the door. I take a deep breath, trying to steady myself for the sight that I know lies beyond this metal hatch.

But nothing could prepare me.

With a signal from my Link, the hatch slides open, showing me a cargo bay with Regonians lining the walls, strapped in on this level and the level above. And in the center, stacks of a very different kind await.

The Lost Ones.

Over two thousand crates hold their bodies, preserving them until we can get them home. Two thousand casualties. Two thousand lives *taken*.

I grit my teeth and try desperately not to relive the attack on Odyssey, but it haunts me, floating through my mind in a million convulsing images. My heart falters.

Closing my eyes, I fill my lungs with as much air as they can hold. Then, I let loose the scream of the Awakening.

It reverberates through the cargo bay, echoing from the lips of every living member of Daen Tribe. I revel in the knowledge that I'm not alone. The loss, the heartache, and the fury all remain.

But my heart is not their only home.

Pulling in a deep breath, I open my eyes upon the coffins before me.

Coffins that my own brother helped to fill.

Stepping forward, I buckle into a seat at the front of the cargo bay. A handful of Humans sit beside me and across from me, the few staying awake the whole time.

Undoubtedly monitoring the sensors in our seats and harnesses, Olivia hails us on the speakers throughout the cargo bay. Her marvelous voice drifts over us, walking the Regonians through the process of disembarking from Termana. She takes care to warn them of every jolt, every shimmy.

A warm smile lifts my lips as I listen to her. I imagine her showing the other pilot, a man experienced with smaller crafts, all the extra control panels and their functions between announcements to the cargo bay, and my smile widens.

Chapter Twenty Six
The Realm of Stars

Olivia

After we break free of the unmined sections of the asteroid belt and the ship reaches optimum speed, I slip the massive beast into autopilot. Turning to Hugo, my new co-pilot, I say, "Go get some rest. I'll stick around and maintain her for now. She's in auto, so it shouldn't be a problem, but better safe than sorry."

"Are you sure?" he asks, inky skin shining pale blue in the light of the controls. "I can stay longer if you'd like."

"You need rest if you're going to watch over us tonight." I smile at him, but my eyes drift away from the warm, dark pools of his irises, called back to the stars beyond our small window.

"I can take a hint," he says, voice soft and melodious. "I'll leave you alone with them." I turn back to him just in time to watch him jerk his chin in the direction of the stars.

Chuckling, I say, "Thanks."

His hand comes to rest on the back of my seat as he passes, landing with a soft thump. He towers over me, and for a moment, my mind shoots back to my room on Odyssey Station, to Lachlan standing so close, too close, just before shoving me, choking me…

Blinking, I take a deep breath and focus on the stars before me.

He's gone.

And I'm here.

I waste no time, dimming the lights of the controls, shutting off the lights overhead. I open myself to the universe, filling my lungs near to bursting.

I'm here.

I'm alive and I'm further from that place than I ever thought I'd be. And I'm going to go further.

I'm going to see so much.

Awe fills me, and my heart soars as the galaxy throws its arms wide in welcome, and the stars reach for me.

If Ricardo hadn't saved me, I never would've seen this.

Tears trickle over my cheeks, and suddenly, despite all the struggles since waking up in the hospital, I'm finally glad I woke up.

***

My Link alerts me that Hugo approaches, and the door opens behind me a few moments later.

"I believe it's my turn to get acquainted with these new stars," he says.

I turn to face him, nodding. "I suppose so."

"Mind if I fix the lighting?"

"*Fix* it?" I say, rising from my seat. "This is the best way to meet the stars."

He turns the lights back up to their full brightness, chuckling softly. "But the stars can't see us if we hide in the dark."

"Shows what you know about the stars. They make their own light. They don't *need* ours."

He laughs, dark eyes twinkling.

I pass by him in the small cockpit, saying, "If you need anything, just call for me. I don't mind getting out of bed if it keeps us all from dying."

Hugo tosses me a look as he settles into his seat. "I'm sure that won't be necessary."

Quiet confidence oozes from him, and I remind myself how quickly he seemed to pick up on everything earlier.

And Nova is in autopilot…

I don't dare ask what could possibly go wrong, knowing the infinite list I could come up with. Instead, I bid him a good night and venture off to the quarters I share with Ricardo.

***

Scrunching a towel in my hair, I signal my Link to transform the screen on the outer wall of our quarters. The glass turns transparent, letting me see the stars again. "Я ищу тебя by Dina. 2020" plays over the speakers, and I whisper the words under my breath, singing along in the old language.

My shoulders lift as my lungs expand between lines. Tiny water droplets fall onto my bare shoulders, running down my back to soak into the towel wrapped around me. I pad across the floor to the window, bare feet slapping the cool metal beneath me.

Behind me, Ricardo's voice drifts through our room, surprising me. "You speak Russian?"

I nod, sparing a glance over my shoulder for him. Holding my hair towel in a heap against my chest, I smile. "I speak a few of the old languages."

Turning back to the stars, I keep singing, somehow comfortable enough to do so with him in the room.

After everything we've been through, after all the lows he's seen me through, all the times he's saved me… I guess I shouldn't be surprised that I can sing in front of him.

The music buries his footsteps beyond the reach of my ears, concealing his approach. But when his arms wrap around my waist and his lips find my shoulder, I don't jump. I smile at the darkness and the stars, sights I never would've seen again if not for him.

He whispers against my neck, "Which languages do you speak?"

"Well, I speak Common," I say. "Obviously."

Ricardo chuckles near my ear. "Obviously."

I slide my hands over his arms, twining our fingers together. He pulls me tighter against him, resting his chin atop my head.

"Mom insisted that I learn English, French, Russian, and Chinese," I say, leaning my head back against Ricardo's shoulder. "Three of the most influential languages involved in bringing us to space and one that she found beautiful."

"Makes sense," Ricardo whispers.

"Dad actually taught me French though. Mom expected me to learn it on my own like the others, but he knew that one, so he taught me. He taught me Dutch and Spanish, too."

The song ends, and I start it over, setting it to repeat and hoping it doesn't annoy Ricardo.

"After he was gone…" My voice falters, but I clear my throat and continue. "I was angry and sad. I started listening to a few death-metal bands, but so much was lost in the translation. So, I learned Norwegian and German."

Ricardo chuckles.

"I found some angry Ukrainian and Russian rap music back then too. It was all in Russian, so I didn't have to learn another language for it. A while later, I found some really nice music in Japanese…"

"So, you learned that language, too?"

I nod, and he laughs again. "How many was that?"

"Including Common…" I say, counting as my eyes roam over the stars. "Ten."

A startled laugh bursts from him. "I thought I was doing good speaking three old languages."

"You are. Most people only speak one of the old languages, if that." I nestle into his embrace, soaking in the warmth of him.

His lips find the top of my head, and he asks, "What's this song about?"

"Going numb," I answer. "Feeling no pain."

He falls silent. The words and sounds of the song crash over us, reverberating through the room and echoing in my bones.

"Are you numb right now?" he asks.

"No. I'm happy," I whisper, bewildered.

I toss my hair towel onto a small table beside the window and spin in the circle of his embrace, facing him with warmth glowing in my eyes. I slide my hands up his chest, wrapping my arms around his neck.

"I don't remember if I've said it, and… even if I have…" I begin. "Thank you. I'm glad you saved me."

Ricardo's face lights up, amber eyes shining beautifully. He leans his forehead against mine and whispers, "Thank you for trusting me enough to call for me. I know it was an automatic thing programmed into your Link, but it wouldn't have sent me the message if you didn't."

My eyes fall to his chest, but I nod. "I trust you."

Three words I never expected to say to anyone. Three words that feel huge, much bigger than me.

But they're right.

Ricardo touches my cheek, thumb moving gently over my skin. "I trust you too. And I'm glad you're happy."

I meet his gaze with a single tear shining in the corner of my vision.

Rising onto tiptoes, I kiss him, soft and tender. My hand slides into his hair, and he kisses me back. Slowly, he pulls away, eyes roaming over my face, drinking me in.

When our lips meet again, I pull him closer. A deep ache burns within me now that I've confessed something so personal, so unbelievably massive and important.

I trust him.

My hands slide down his torso, slipping beneath his shirt to the honed muscles of his stomach and lower back. Pushing his shirt upward, I revel in the feel of him, moving slow.

He tosses the fabric aside, and then, he grasps my waist, pulling me against him. His hands roam, gliding down over my bottom, and his fingertips graze bare skin just below the end of my towel.

Heat builds within me.

He grasps my buttocks, and I burn, aching for him. Sliding his hands up to my hips, he pushes the towel aside, leaving trails of fire on my skin. He tugs the fabric away, freeing me, and I stare up into marvelous golden eyes, waiting for his touch to return.

Soft as feathers, his hands find me, trailing up the sides of my upper thighs, over my hips, up to my ribs. His fingertips glide over my breasts and upward still. With both hands on the back of my neck, he pulls me in for a kiss.

And we collide, suddenly desperate.

Panting, quivering, I press myself against him. He pushes me back against the cool glass of our window, hands roaming freely over my bare flesh. I tip my head back, inviting him in, and his mouth finds my neck, ravaging me.

The ache builds, churning within me, and I unfasten his pants. We don't even bother to push them down.

He lifts me, wrapping my legs around his waist, then finds his home, moving within me, pressing me to the glass. The universe shifts inside me, and a magnificent weight builds as he rocks his hips. I dig my nails into his back, clutching him tight as he pushes me higher.

Curling forward against him, I drop my head onto his shoulder, kissing his neck, his ear. He moans, and I nip lightly at his earlobe, spurring him on.

Picking up his pace, he turns me to jelly, and my head falls back against the window. A moan escapes him as I move my hips in time with his, plunging him deeper and deeper.

Lightning arcs across my skin, and fire burns through me. I wrap one hand in his hair, heart beating faster and faster. Gasping, I arch my back, aching for release.

Pushing me harder against the window, he plunges deeper, and I shatter in his embrace. Stars burst across my eyelids, splintering my vision as I call out his name.

He drives home a few more times, pushing me toward another release. My body quakes, and my legs tremble. And he keeps going.

Our lips meet as I fall to pieces once more, crumbling and tightening around him. I breathe his name against his lips, and he tenses, moaning softly as he erupts within me. He whispers my name, leaning against me, putting our weight on the sturdy window and the stars.

My lungs rattle at high speed, but my mind fills with one thought, one realization.

I trust him.

Chapter Twenty Seven
Novay

Rone

I lie in bed, as still as I can manage. My eyelids don't flutter. My hands rest, limp, upon my bed, imitating their position the exact moment I fell asleep last night. I measure my breathing, keeping it even.

Anticipation builds within me at the prospect of this evening, and my heart jumps into my throat. But excited as I may be, I stuff it down.

Think of measuring blinks and strides.

Think of measuring the exact size of Lustran's eyelashes or the precise pitch of some faceless Drennar's voice at the old facility.

Anything to stay calm.

My heart rate settles down, evening out once more. For several long moments, I wait. In darkness, with my eyes closed and my body as relaxed as I can get it, I listen for the tone.

As minutes stretch to feel like hours, I begin to wonder if something has gone wrong. But then, a soft, low tone resonates within my mind.

I fling my blanket back and spring from bed. A quick message to Reginald finds him unresponsive. His Link sends an automatic reply, informing me that he's asleep. Disappointment wells within me.

I hope he wakes up soon.

Frowning, I leave my room behind, comfortable that Lustran has all our surveillance issues covered and thankful that the Drennar have never had a need to counter tactics like doctored footage.

I meander through our facility, tasting the exhilaration of rebellion, the freedom of making my own choices. My heart races, expanding within my chest.

In the common area, I find all those whose quarters are closest. Lustran, of course, already sits at the large alonarium table we've taken to conjuring for these nightly meetings.

Beside him, his latest beau, a Drennar by the name of Viahna, glows with the light of her most recent pre-emotion experiment. The tiny lights dot her skin like the freckles some Humans possess, emitting a soft blue light from every bit of exposed skin.

Three others sit nearby, all packed to the brim with modifications, some visible, some not. But the most important one shows in the shaved sides of their heads.

I smile as more of us file in. Taking my seat, I wait to plan for the Humans' arrival, Olivia's arrival.

My stomach flips at the prospect of meeting her. We've spoken in a couple messages, but the idea of her not liking me scares me.

Would Reginald still want anything to do with me if she disapproved?

My fingers fidget, worrying at each other. My mouth goes dry as my thoughts turn dark.

Will we even get the chance to have a real meeting?

So many things could go wrong between now and then. The Drennar could find out about our plans, or something could go wrong with the ships, or the Survival Coalition could decide it isn't worth the risk.

A few more of my fellows join us, filtering into the room. I pull my attention away from my thoughts, desperate for anything productive to focus on.

Lustran calls my name, asking my opinion.

But I never heard the dilemma.

Focus.

If they're going to come all this way, if Olivia is ever going to trust you or stand a chance at living through all this, if Reginald is to have half a chance at seeing his daughter, I need to focus.

"Sorry," I whisper. Clearing my throat, I say, "What was the question?"

He sends a private message packed with data and repeats, "Do you think this will be acceptable?"

I review all the numbers, piece together every angle. "Not so drastic that they won't believe it… But it allows us enough time in the night."

I nod, and he smiles.

But I can't quite return it.

Determination pushes me deeper into the numbers, calculating all the exact amounts of static necessary to shape the alonarium, filling the time until everyone else arrives.

For so many reasons, I dive into the numbers, doing cold calculations with a fervent need to be precise. Every day at my podium, every experiment, every number led me here, honing my mind to measure the demise of Drennar society to the trillionth decimal value.

The seats fill up, and we get to work.

Chapter Twenty Eight
Novay

Reginald

The days pass in a blur. I stare at my ceiling, waiting for a Drennar to come for me. Unmodified, they stare at me with blank eyes, and I wither before them.

The spark of life I found in Rone's presence wilts within me as the nightmare of the past twelve years threatens to repeat. No contact. No real interaction.

No warmth.

My surroundings leech it from me, pulling the humanity from my bones, draining me of emotion. The cold metal walls, the sleek surfaces, the same cold, grey color everywhere.

Whether lying alone in my bed, staring at the ceiling, or plodding along behind one of them to my testing room with downcast eyes, my life ticks slowly past, leaving me behind.

My only refuge comes in the form of messages from Rone and the ones she forwards to me from Olivia. But the delay between them threatens to crush me.

After another long day in the testing room, I drag my feet all the way back to my room. The Drennar before me blurs as my eyes drift out of focus.

The world dulls. The numbers on the screens swirled before my eyes all day, and they swim in my head even now, buzzing a little too loud, a little too sharp, reminding me just how much of a rat I am.

A little lab rat, trapped in a maze that goes on forever.

Or at least, until I die.

The wall opens before me, and I step through, letting the blurred shapes of my room wrap around me. Without a word, the Drennar closes the wall, locking me in. Not that it matters.

They could leave my door open, and it wouldn't make a difference.

Rone said a while ago that the air here is filtered, that beyond this hall and throughout

Novay, particles of alonarium float in the air, particles that would destroy my lungs in a matter of hours if I was dumb enough to run.

Fear, sharp and sudden, locks cold hands around my heart. My eyes snap into focus, and my head jerks up.

Does Olivia know about the alonarium?

They can't come here. They'll die.

I send a quick message to Rone through our private channel, pacing as I do. Tension builds within me.

Please, please message me back. Please tell me something.

My heart jumps into my throat, choking me, and my stomach twists into a tight ball.

A message arrives, and I thank my lucky stars that it's a video message. Collapsing on the edge of my bed, I close my eyes, letting it play over the backs of my eyelids, letting my cochlear implant play the sound within my mind.

Rone appears, vivid and smiling, and her voice unfurls within me. "They know about it.

Sort-of. They know it exists and that they can't breathe it. They're going to Regonia One to take the non-Warrior members of Daen Tribe home, and it's in the air there too. They have filters, don't worry."

She smiles, and I let loose a huge breath. Relief washes over me, and I crumple forward, bracing my elbows on my knees. I press my palms to my eyes but pull them away when it sends static over the image of Rone on my eyelids.

Tracing her face, the lines of her cheekbones, the curve of her lips, I wait for her to go on.

She sits there, pensive, with lips pursed. Her eyes drift downward, and her eyebrows scrunch together. "We'll have to get you a filter if this is going to work. I'm just not sure how I'll get it to you…"

Nodding, she says, "I'll figure it out. I have to go for now but try not to worry too much. I know this sucks right now, believe me. I wish I could see you. But we'll be together again."

She smiles, opening her mouth to speak, but she stops. Shaking her head, she laughs, a small, nervous laugh. "I'll talk to you later."

A smile, and the video ends.

But I only have more questions.

What did she mean 'Regonia One?'

Why do I need a filter?

What am I supposed to do?

My hands ball into fists, and this time, I don't pull them away from my eyes. Gritting my teeth, I try to swallow back how helpless I am, how *useless* I am, in the grand scheme of things.

Everything is happening, one of the biggest, potentially catastrophic, moments in Human history, and I'm just barely on the outside of it.

Falling back onto my bed, I stare up at the ceiling and send Rone another message with all my questions, along with the little caveat to get back to me when she can.

She has things to do.

And I have all the time in the worlds.

***

Rone's message wakes me in the middle of the night. I play it over my eyelids, luxuriating in the sight of her lying on her side, short hair splayed over her pillow. I roll onto my side to complete the illusion, wishing she were here. My hands reach out, sliding beneath the sheet, craving her warmth.

The soft glow of the screen she conjured in her wall to record the message reflects in her eyes, illuminating the blue mods within the green irises. Darkness cloaks the room behind her, but I know the layout of it well, know it from all the messages she's sent.

I know that, even now, another Drennar woman sleeps in a bed across the room. I hear her soft breathing in the background.

"Hi, love," Rone whispers.

My breath catches, and my heart skips a beat. The temptation to replay those words, to listen to her gentle tone over and again nearly stops me from playing the rest of the message. But I know there will be time for that later.

She sighs, and a sad smile spreads over her lips. "I miss you…"

I miss you, too.

She ruffles her hair, then says, "I hope they didn't put you through too much today. I wish you could be here. I wish you could be part of this. I'll try to keep you up to date a little better. Where should I start…? I guess I could start with your questions." She laughs, soft and sweet.

"Regonia One is the planet Daen Tribe comes from. There are three planets named Regonia. They just so happen to be on the first one."

My mind goes into a tailspin.

Three planets?

All named Experiment?

What experiment spans three planets?

Even for the Drennar, that seems extensive.

But Rone continues, moving on to the next question I asked her earlier. So, I store my questions away for my reply.

"As for why you need a filter, I think I'll wait to tell you that. It's a surprise," she says with a smile. It spreads wider, encompassing her entire face. "Okay, I can't wait. Never mind, it's not a surprise."

I barely suppress a chuckle.

"I have a little something in the works to get to see you, but you'd have to come here. I don't know if it'll be approved, but I'm trying."

My heart glows, and I take a deep breath.

Please, let it be approved.

"Oh!" Rone says, visibly brightening. "I almost forgot to tell you. The last message from Olivia was aboard the SCBC Nova. They left Termana about a week ago. Things were going well at that point. She was out in the Realm of Stars, as Daen Tribe calls it."

No wonder she looked so much happier.

"Anyway, I'm going to be awake for a little while longer. If you're awake, send me a message back. We could actually talk, for once. If you're asleep and don't get this until you wake up, send me a message anyway, but I don't know if I'll be able to reply quickly. Sweet dreams."

She smiles, and the video ends.

I send a reply immediately, asking if she could work some magic and make my wall a screen for a while, aching to actually talk to her, to see her. But I don't know if she can hide my room for that long.

Within seconds, the wall beside my bed begins to glow, painted the colors of her. My breath leaves me, and I reach out, touching the cool metal. She puts her hand to her wall, touching the image of me.

A rush of heat surges through me.

"I wish I could be there…" I whisper.

Everything in me cries out, hating the distance between us, the distance between me and everything.

Scooting closer, Rone doesn't pull her nightshirt back up when it slides down to reveal the shadow between her breasts. Her hand slides slowly over her bed, and mischief plays in her beautiful eyes.

"What do you think we'd do if you were here?" She pushes her blanket down and drapes her arm over her hip.

I swallow, raking my eyes over the silky fabric of her night shirt and the bit of skin showing above the waistband of her shorts. Heat builds within me. I trace her thighs with my eyes, then drag them up over her body to meet her gaze.

"I'm sure we could think of a few things," I say, voice low and husky.

Chapter Twenty Nine
The Realm of Stars

Tenna

With our Ullavenans and Ullavekyns gathered around, we begin strategizing for the coming war. Normally, my mind would overflow with plans and the nervous excitement of battle.

But today, my nerves wind tight.

Kala sits across from me, bringing forth ideas about approaching Taron Tribe, but this won't go as it would have before. Nor will the war with the Drennar.

Not without Efsi.

His life flashes through my mind in a series of warm smiles and the occasional prank, and a lance of pain shoots through me.

He should be here...

I glance down at my hand where the mark signaling the loss of him should be but isn't yet.

The Memory Markers will be busy when we reach Regonia.

Softly, I utter his sound, aching to remember him, to know I'm not the only one to grieve for him. The lilting purr of his sound rolls over my lips, and Krona squeezes my knee. Across the table, Kala stops midsentence to join me, to offer her support.

And though my heart still aches, it helps.

Nodding slowly, I meet Kala's eyes just as she finishes the soft coo of our lost brother.

"This battle must be different than all those before," I say, voice as gentle as I can manage. "Without Efsi, you must stay behind."

Her jaw falls open, and she stares at me for a moment. "But... I can't."

"You must. We cannot leave Daen Tribe without an Ullavena present. There has to be someone there who can carry on our line if the worst happens."

She glances at her partner, but only briefly. "It isn't as though I'm in a position to produce heirs. I can't stay behind. It should be you and Krona."

All eyes turn to her, and the air grows thick and heavy with the challenge in her last sentence. Even Melnara stares at her.

"There have been others who lived as you do before. There are ways around that which don't require betrayal," I say, but I know she's aware of this.

My fingers curl, carving divots into my palm. My voice hardens as I add, "I cannot send my people to a war I would not fight myself. Not when I am perfectly capable of doing so. I'm not ailing. I'm not pregnant, and we still have one Ullavena. You. I will not send anyone to fight if I'm not willing to go myself."

The thought of such an abuse of power makes my stomach turn.

Her eyes fall to the table, and she mutters an apology.

Working my jaw loose, I say, "What is the real reason you fight me on this?"

The tension goes out of the room as we settle back into our roles.

"This is the most important battle we will ever see, and I'm one of our strongest warriors. Daen Tribe needs me there."

Pride and a need for glory.

She wants to show that she's strong, that she's capable.

The very quality that made her overconfident in the trial to become Tinera, that pushed her for the showy moves instead of the effective ones. The same thing that kept her from defeating me that day.

"You are a strong warrior," I allow, "but Daen Tribe needs an Ullavena to produce heirs in case Krona or I fall in battle. You know this. I wish Efsi were here, believe me, I do. He'd gladly stay in your stead as he used to. But that isn't an option, now."

I hate the words, hate that he's gone and that we must carry on without him. But my people need me to keep moving forward, to feel my loss and yet never stop fighting for them.

My tone softens as I say, "I'm sorry, but… you can't go up the mountain to propose the alliance with Taron Tribe or to the battle on Novay."

Her face falls, but she nods, accepting it with a sigh. Melnara rubs her back, and we carry on. Though not as enthusiastic as she was moments ago, Kala does her best to contribute to our plans.

***

Days pass, and we do our best to educate Olivia and the few Humans awake about what to expect on Regonia. There should be more people awake listening to these tales, yet so many slumber in things called cryo-beds. Bitterness creeps through me, only kept at bay by the wonder and awe that the conscious Humans greet our stories with.

But with every tale of long, blue-green grass swirling in the breeze, of Vyrtons running in the fields, I can't help but wonder what my home will look like when we get there.

Will our keep still stand?

Built of sturdy stone, it should weather the elements easily. But if the Vaerkin came, if they ransacked our homes and stole our things and our crops and our livestock…

My stomach sinks into my boots at the prospect of rebuilding our homes from the ground up. It sinks further at the thought of the bodies that were left behind when the Humans came for us.

***

After a few days, Olivia forwards a message from Rone, a Drennar that's apparently different from the rest, to Krona and me. My heart stutters at the thought of trusting a Drennar after everything we've learned of them.

They lied to us.

They left us on Regonia. And for what?

But this one doesn't act like the ones from our legends, doesn't act like the ones in Human surveillance footage. They move coldly, speak without affect, stare without expression. But the messages I've seen from this one show creased brows and smiles, fidgeting and laughter. Affection for Olivia's father.

She's different. She's not a typical Drennar.

I remind myself, over and again, telling myself that we can trust her, that we have no choice. She's our only hope to get onto Novay safely.

But I don't have to like the arrangement.

Scowling, I paint the message across the window of our room and call Krona. He strides through the door before I finish uttering his name, and I smile.

"You already got it ready," he says, looking at the window. His Link still blinks with the unopened message from Olivia, the same one she sent me.

Another message comes through, and I know it contains her response to the Drennar. We'll watch that next.

We settle in upon our bed, peering up at the Drennar woman before us. Through the magic of the Link, I signal for the video to begin.

The Drennar woman, Rone, takes a deep breath, wings fluttering restlessly behind her. Slowly, she begins, "Hi, Olivia. I was hoping I'd have Reginald here by now so he could talk to you too…"

She sighs, dropping her gaze to her fists, resting on her lap. "They denied my requests though. He's still alone in the other facility. I wish he could be here, wish we'd hidden our relationship better so they'd just leave us alone."

Her voice cracks over the words, and I feel the ache in her voice, the need to be near him. Her eyes scrunch with emotion, with tears, and my heart twists in my chest. I furrow my brows, analyzing the woman before me, the Drennar that doesn't act like a Drennar.

Her last message comes back to me, the one where she told us that she and some other Drennar were modified to have emotions, that they don't want to experiment on anyone anymore. It seems too good to be true, but I can't imagine a Drennar being such a good actor. I purse my lips.

Beside me, Krona whispers, "She's in a relationship with him? Do Drennar have relationships?"

But it's hard to guess at what a race of people we thought extinct might do.

I cast my mind back over all the footage I've seen of the Drennar coming to take Humans, all the times they stood, blank and expressionless, over weeping people. My mind fills with the sight of them standing a precise distance from each other whenever the cameras caught more than two in the same place.

I think back to the legends that told of beings who remained distant to protect us from the disease that ravaged their bodies.

But really, they just didn't feel for us. They didn't care that they were leaving us, that they were lying. They didn't feel a thing.

I shake my head. "I don't think they do."

"Anyway…" Rone whispers. "They're still keeping those of us with emotion contained to one facility, watching over us. Or at least, watching what we let them see." A smile lifts one corner of her lips.

Finally looking up, she says, "I've learned a lot from you, Olivia."

I squirm beneath the personal touch, wondering if Rone knows Olivia isn't the only one to see these messages. She must know, must assume as much.

But beside me, Krona smiles.

"Ever the inspiration," I say. "What would we do without Olivia?"

The words sober me instantly, reminding me just how close we came to finding out the answer to that question. Krona squeezes my knee, and I put my hand over his.

We need to make sure Olivia never doubts herself, again.

We need to make sure she feels wanted.

"We've come up with some plans for when you're done on Regonia," Rone says, drawing my attention outward once more. She tells us of her plan and the work she and the newly emotional Drennar have been up to.

And slowly, I find myself believing her.

Chapter Thirty
The Realm of Stars

Termana fades away, slipping into the darkness of space. The stars wrap around SCBC Nova, pulling her further from home and introducing themselves to the crew.

As a week passes, and then another, people fall into routines, carried along by Nova, the technology of Earth, a world none of them know as more than a legend, a thought, a video stored away from years gone by.

But the lights that twinkle and guide them are only a small portion of the Realm of Stars.

For the darkness is everywhere else.

Chapter Thirty One
The Realm of Stars

Ricardo

Olivia nestles in closer, waking just enough to slide her hand up my chest, and pulls in a deep breath. Her lips find my collarbone, sending shivers of warmth through me. They disappear all too quickly, replaced by the queasy feeling in my stomach, the same dread that's plagued me for hours.

She descends back into sleep quickly, but I lie awake, waiting for something to go wrong.

She assured me earlier that I was just stressed, and I am. But there's something else at work here. I know it. My gut doesn't usually lead me astray.

As the hours tick by, moving toward midnight and then past, I stare into the darkness and listen to the soft sounds of the vents. I try to focus on the gentle breaths easing in and out of Olivia, brushing over my bare skin.

I figure up how much sleep I could get if I fell asleep right now, a measly five and a half hours. My Link marks the passage of another minute.

Five hours and twenty-nine minutes of sleep. If I fell asleep right now.

But clearly, that's not happening.

Taking a deep breath, I try to steady myself, try to shut my brain down. I picture a ball of thoughts and two hands outside it, pushing all the escaping thoughts back into the ball. But there's always one more waiting to jump free and float through my mind.

Sighing, I cock my head to the side, popping my neck.

This is nonsense.

There's nothing wrong. Just go to sleep.

I close my eyes, but a flash of light bursts over the screen of my Link. Olivia's Link glows against my chest, and I nudge her shoulder.

Drowsy sounds ease past her lips, and I want so badly to kiss her, to fall into sleep with her. But the sick feeling in my stomach intensifies.

We glance at our Links to find we each have a message from Hugo. My stomach drops, and I swallow.

"Cargo bay," it reads. "Some of the beds are malfunctioning. The techs have been notified."

"Shit!" Olivia exclaims, throwing the blanket off us.

We jump from the bed, grabbing our clothes from where they fell earlier. My heart hammers in my ears as I pull my pants on, hopping and nearly tripping, never slowing down. The door slides open before we reach it, and we sprint through the halls to the cargo bay. I tug my shirt on as we run.

And all the while, my Link runs calculations.

How many beds are messing up? Are the people inside okay? Can the beds be repaired? How many Humans will come fully awake if we can't fix them?

Do we have enough food to get through the trip if they wake up this early?

My Link digs through the data, turning up answers. Four stacks with five beds each.

Twenty people.

All healthy and safe for now.

Relief and dread war within me.

It could be so much worse. But can we feed that many additional mouths for this much longer? We've only been in transit for a few weeks. We still have so far to go.

"This is what we get for using cryo-beds that haven't been used since we came to fucking Termana…" Olivia curses beneath her breath, lungs laboring beneath the effort of sprinting and speaking simultaneously.

"Though I guess… They have been used once," she adds.

For Daen Tribe.

My stomach sours at the reminder, but I push myself harder. My feet pound the metal floor, and I thank the makers of this ship for the thick walls. No one wakes. No crowd forms, peering out of rooms at the Pilot and the Specialist running in a panic.

Careening around corners, sliding on slick floors, we cross the distance with our hearts in our throats. As we draw closer, alarms echo through metallic halls, sound bending and doubling back, assaulting my ears. My lungs riot within my chest, but I push harder.

Leaping through bulkheads, we land in the cargo bay. Lights flash red throughout the room, casting terrible shadows through rows and rows of stacked cryo-beds. Darkness and crimson light play beneath the catwalks, and the alarms threaten to shatter my eardrums.

"Fuck!" Olivia shouts, covering her ears. But she must override the alarms with her Link quickly for the noise stops, and the lights cease their flashing, returning to a normal white light.

Maintenance techs rush in through a door three rows down.

"Row 43!" Olivia shouts, and they descend upon the proper row.

Rushing forward, I check connections on the beds, looking for loose wires or panels. Technology isn't my thing, and my heart drops at the prospect of this resting on *my* shoulders. But the techs are way ahead of me, working hand in hand with Olivia to see where the problem lies.

What am I supposed to do here?

My mind spirals, desperate for something to do, some way to help. Casting my gaze about the cargo bay, my eyes light on the one thing I can do.

The Lift sits dormant, locked into place to keep it from rolling about during takeoff. "You guys have this, right?" I whisper, taking off for the Lift.

I throw myself into the seat, using my Link to pull up instructions on how to drive the thing. My rank as a Specialist overrides my lack of certification to use it, and the hydraulic locks retreat, releasing the roll cage and the suspension from their grasp.

Moving slowly, desperate not to crash into any stacks, I pull a lever here, push a button there, all prompted by my Link. The machine jerks along, sending my heart racing as I get closer and closer to the stacks of unconscious humans. So many lives lay stacked before me, and my hands grip the steering wheel tight.

Swallowing back the fear, I maneuver down the rows, moving as slowly as I need to.

Panicked voices reach out to me as Olivia and the techs hunt down the problem. "This bank lost power," Olivia says. "It's this one over here."

"But why?" one of the techs, a young man with a ruddy complexion, asks.

Chewing at her lip, lying on her stomach, Olivia peers inside a control panel in the floor between the rows. "I don't know…" she says.

The other tech, a woman with gray streaks in her black hair, climbs the side of a stack, and my heart jumps into my throat.

It's fine, it's fine, it's fine. They're sturdy enough for her weight.

"This one's about to wake up!" she calls out.

Fear slices through me, and I maneuver toward her, thanking my lucky stars that it's the stack closest to me. She pushes buttons on the top, and yellow lights flicker on the sides of the cryo-bed.

"I need this one down, Sir!" she cries.

My heart hammers in my chest, and blood roars behind my ears as I ease a lever forward, raising the forks of the Lift up.

What if I clip it with one? What if I push it off the stack or knock them all over?

"Am I lined up?" I demand.

She jumps down, landing with more grace than expected, and comes to my side of the stack. "Yeah! You're good. Take him down, Sir."

Easing forward, I slide the forks into the tiny space allotted for them. They scrape along the sides of the cavities, metal groaning against metal, and I cringe at the awful noise. Slowly, I lift the bed off the stack, then back up, lowering it to the floor. Pulling forward, I settle it to the ground a few rows down.

"What of the others?"

"Bring the whole stack down," the tech says. "All five are waking up, Sir."

I stare at the stack for half a breath, then set to work. I splay them out before her, listening as Olivia and the young man work to fix something they call an "Eye." By the time I dismantle the first stack, the woman jumps onto the second stack, pressing buttons and analyzing her Link.

And then, they come down, too.

Spread about along the side of the cargo bay, lined up against the wall, she paces from one to another as they drain the fluids from the lungs of the people within. Lids hiss open, and one by one, people sit up, coughing and choking.

"Got it!" Olivia shouts, sitting back before the panel.

The tech beside her climbs atop the stack of cryo-beds, pushing buttons. The lights on the sides of the two remaining stacks glow a soft green, safely restored to stasis.

All the air whooshes out of me.

Silence descends on us, punctuated by the sounds of the second stack's cryo-bed lids sliding open and people coughing up the remnants of the cryo-gel.

Bracing my elbows on my knees, I drop my head into my hands. My fingers sprawl through my hair, and I let out a long breath, exhausted and weary.

I lift my head, meeting Olivia's gaze. She reclines against the stabilized stacks, legs splayed out before her on the floor.

But the techs keep moving. Having been trained in the thawing sequence and the effects of coming out of cryo-sleep, they rush from one bed to another, helping the people within them sit up and clear their lungs.

Slowly, I climb out of the Lift, not even bothering to put it back where it goes just yet. Olivia's eyes never leave mine as I approach, hazel glittering in the bright lights of the cargo bay.

I reach a hand down and pull her to her feet. She throws her arms around me, and I pull her close. Though I wish we could remain in that embrace, we can't.

I touch her face, smoothing a tear away with my thumb. Before I speak, I run a check with my Link and find that all the recently awoken are alive and healthy.

"We got them out," I whisper. "They're okay."

She nods, taking a deep breath. "Doctor Sullivan is on his way. He should be here soon. I might have to relocate him. He's too far from the cargo bay. If this happens again…"

"It won't," I say, trying to convince myself as much as her.

"Just in case. He should be closer."

I nod, relenting, and we approach the beds to brief the still-coughing Soldiers on the situation. All the while, my Link calculates food stores and the rationing necessary to offset these new mouths to feed.

Chapter Thirty Two
Novay

Rone

With my room successfully cloaked in darkness, I busy myself with reports, fabricating data. The backs of my eyelids flicker with numbers, but I tweak them. With a few deft moves, I cover the changes to our sleeping habits.

Our late nights spent planning and scheming are reported as longer recharge times due to the energy expenses associated with emotions. I justify it all emphatically, including many notes on the importance of emotion in understanding the Human race and the emotional mutations of Daen Tribe.

Halfway through my message, I realize that I've included names of people within the Human race, within Daen Tribe. And though I know the names, knew them before I was modified, it's a touch too personal.

I remove their names from my notes, cringing as I replace them with the numbers each individual was assigned in our early assessment of humanity and Daen Tribe to eliminate confusion of people with similar names.

They're more than numbers.

But here, they aren't.

Pursing my lips, I clean up my notes, leaving some emotion, but removing most. Adjectives and adverbs fall from the sentences, erased in favor of more concise speech. I specify minute details, things that the other Drennar will find important, things that would be odd for me not to include.

But they aren't the things that matter.

Respiratory distress doesn't explain sobbing. It doesn't convey the reason Olivia cries. Muscle twitches don't justify the smiles on Ricardo's face when he sees her. Heart palpitations don't quite cover the closeness between Krona and Tenna.

Between Reginald and me.

Again, I emphasize the need for these modifications in order to understand. And then, I set the report to send shortly after I wake.

Rolling onto my side, I send a private message to Reginald, hoping to find him awake.

He's probably asleep.

Don't get your hopes up.

But tension builds within me, and I find myself hoping, regardless. I wait, heart racing. My muscles tense, itching to move, to stretch. Yet, I wait, lying perfectly still.

Time stretches out with no reply, and my nerves fray. A frantic search of the network finds the sounds of his heart beating steadily, slowly.

He's asleep.

My chest collapses, and a tear slides over my cheek.

I just want to talk to him.

My mind fills with our last full conversation, now three days past. Since then, we've been relegated to drawing our conversations out over the course of the day, replying when we can.

And I haven't seen him, even projected over my wall, for three days.

My heart twists within me, shrinking painfully, and I wince before the sensation.

The Drennar do not *understand this.*

With tears streaming over my face, I fill my mind with the sounds of Reginald's heart and imagine myself lying next to him. I listen, pretending that my head rests upon his chest, and slowly, I drift off to sleep.

Chapter Thirty Three
The Realm of Stars

Olivia

Pulling on pants, I run the numbers through my head again, reassuring myself. The food stores play through my mind on a loop, broken up by the number of meals each person aboard Nova will consume before we reach Regonia and then on our trip to Novay and home. The stores to be left on Regonia for Daen Tribe is to remain untouched.

With each round of spiraling thoughts, I calculate what we can reasonably expect from the hydroponic gardens aboard the ship, adding that in to what we brought from Termana.

The total number of rations necessary to get us through our trip climbs above a million. But there, the unknowns begin.

How many will stay behind on Regonia? Will anyone from Taron Tribe join us?

Will we find any useful food there to take with us? Anything for the people who stay there to survive on?

I crunch the numbers again.

We have enough food.

Even with ten more mouths to feed for the rest of our trip, we have enough. Just barely, but enough.

We just can't afford for anyone else to wake up early.

I sigh. My mind spins as I pull a shirt over my head and tug my boots on. Leaning over, I kiss Ricardo on the forehead, intending to slip out, but he rouses, turning over and moaning groggily.

"Where are you going so early?" he asks.

"To the cargo bay. I want to double check the power banks and the photo eyes for the other stacks before I head to the cockpit."

I start to pull away, but my stomach roils. I close my eyes, fighting off the sudden burst of nausea. I beg my body not to hit me with another panic attack and consider sending a message to Cait about it.

Ricardo sits up, concern furrowing his brows. "Are you okay?"

I nod. "I'm just worried. We can't afford for anything else to go wrong. And we're not even to Regonia yet. There's still so much that could fuck up."

"It'll be fine," he whispers, tugging at my arm. "Sit down and breathe."

I do, but only because my legs go weak beneath me. Sweat drips down my spine and rolls down my forehead as the nausea builds, and I cradle my head in my hands.

Ricardo rubs my back, gentle and reassuring. Throwing his legs over the side of the bed, he rises and says, "Let's get you to the bathroom."

I let him pull me up, hating how much I have to lean on him to make it the four steps to our bathroom. He settles me on the floor near the toilet, and I sit, quiet, trying not to puke.

"It's fine. We have plenty. We'll make it there with everyone safe and sound," I say, but the nausea lingers, rolling through me on violent waves.

I curl around the toilet, throwing up the little I ate last night. My body spasms with the motion, and tears streak my cheeks. Ricardo sits in the bottom of our tiny shower, holding my hair back and whispering soft reassurances.

Heaving, I close my eyes. But there's nothing in my stomach.

Minutes tick by, pushing me closer and closer to my time in the cockpit. I'm running out of time.

But I still need to go to the cargo bay.

I need to check the other beds and make sure they won't mess up.

I need to make sure no one else wakes up.

Slowly, the nausea abates, and Ricardo helps me to my feet. I wash up, hating the cramped bathroom with the sink in the tank behind the toilet.

Warm arms wrap around me, and I nestle into Ricardo's embrace. My head rests against his bare chest, and I breathe in the scent of him.

"We have enough," he reminds me. "And the techs will be going through the beds all day, making sure everything is fine. You don't have to stress yourself out over this. We have it taken care of."

"I need to check, though. I need to see for myself."

"I know," Ricardo says. "But you have a lot of responsibilities as the pilot. Not just the beds. You're going to have to delegate. Let them inspect everything and have them send you pictures or reports or whatever you need them to send you for you to feel comfortable. Just sit with the stars today and take it easy."

I relinquish myself to waiting for answers and mumble, "Can I at least go see that they're there?"

A soft chuckle escapes Ricardo. "You don't have to ask my permission. Technically, we're the same rank. Besides, it's not like I'm giving you orders. I just want you to take care of yourself."

Nodding, I nuzzle my face against his chest. "Okay. Want to come with? You don't have to. You can go back to bed if you want."

"I'll go with," he says. "I need to get up anyway. I'll have my hands full today with the Soldiers that woke up. May as well get a jump on it."

I sit on the edge of our bed, stifling the last of the anxiety and nausea as Ricardo pulls clothes on and freshens up. We meander through the many halls, passing through one bulkhead after another, thankfully not at the breakneck speeds of last night.

Glorying in the massive old ship and all its nooks and crannies, I take in the surroundings as we pass an offshoot here, a wall of electrical panels there. Rivets abound, a staple of old-world space construction.

The old girl seems to breathe, to feel. She's seen so much in her years.

At the entrance to the cargo bay, I marvel at the stacks of cryo-beds, but my stomach still turns at the thought of another night like last night.

The now-empty beds are stacked against the wall, and the Lift rests within its cage.

Four techs move through massive open space, settling in at different panels in the floor. Some sit, some lay down, peering closer at the wires and microchips inside the floor.

Pulling in a deep breath, I accept that they'll find and rectify anything they can. But that doesn't stop me from sending each of them a message saying that I want reports of their findings, along with pictures of the panels they inspect, especially if they find a problem.

"Want to get some breakfast before you take over for Hugo?" Ricardo asks.

"I'm not sure I can handle food just yet."

Turning to face him, I wrap my arms around his waist. He puts his arms around me, and his entire body rocks as he nods.

"Want to sit down and watch until you go up front?"

"Kind of," I say.

We settle in along the wall, sitting in the seats that everyone was strapped into for takeoff. The techs sit, mostly motionless, comparing the insides of each panel to its appropriate manual on their Links. I lean against Ricardo, resting my head on his shoulder. His hand comes to rest on my knee, and I slide my hand onto his chest, feeling his heartbeat.

But time ticks away, and I rise from my perch reluctantly not long after having settled in. My nerves wind tight with every step away from the cargo bay. I send messages to all the techs, repeating my request for photos and reports.

But my heart still lurches at the thought of more people waking. Only when I reach the cockpit to take Hugo's place and the stars spread out before me, when reports from the techs start rolling in, does the tension within me begin to ease.

I slip my laptop from the drawer and begin working on my little project, my present for the Drennar.

Chapter Thirty Four
The Realm of Stars

Krona

Tenna paces beside me, waiting for the newly awoken Soldiers to file into the conference room. Her hands ball into fists at her side, and a scowl mars her face.

Rising from my seat, I approach her, but she doesn't stop moving. I reach out, putting my hands on her upper arms and staring into her eyes. The dark green simmers with a frustration I've seen unleashed on battlefields before.

But these people aren't our enemy.

"Tenna," I gentle. "I know you're upset. I'm sure they had a reason for their actions."

She shakes her head but doesn't speak. Slowly, she pulls in a deep breath. "They know my feelings on this," she says, forcing the words past gritted teeth.

"Yes, but we may not know the whole situation."

"Then they should have told us. We're supposed to be allies. We're going into battle with them," she says, piercing me with her gaze. "We're supposed to be open with each other. Unless that isn't common practice among Human allies."

"It might not be." I shake my head, at a loss.

"They make no sense," she says.

Some of the tension eases out of her as she considers a difference in customs. But her shoulders never fall. Her teeth still grind together. Fury burns within her, and it will until she has a suitable answer.

I chuckle. "It's a good thing they put you on Odyssey instead of me."

The change in subject blindsides her, and her face morphs into a mask of confusion. "What are you talking about?"

"Had you been on Ulysses, had they messed with your memories like they did mine, doubt wouldn't have stalled you as it did me. You would've torn the whole station to pieces with your bare hands." I size her up, running my hands over her arms, feeling the strength within them. I stare into her eyes, see the resolve and perseverance scrawled across her face. "It wouldn't even have been hard for you."

She blushes, and a hint of a smile plays over her lips, but she hides it away quickly.

"There will be time for jokes later," she chides, but her tone is light. "This is serious. They shouldn't be keeping secrets. We deserve to know why they didn't just let all four stacks of Soldiers wake up."

"I know. But we need to go into it with a level head."

"Yes, I know," she says with a sigh. "I wasn't going to hurt anyone."

"That's for the best."

A smile reaches over Tenna's face.

Behind her, the door opens, and Ricardo steps through. He falls into the nearest chair with a sigh, rubbing a hand over his face.

Fear trickles down my spine as I take in his posture, and I release Tenna's arms. She spins to face him, ready to launch into a rant, but stops dead on seeing him. Exhaustion pulls his shoulders low, and a frown tugs at the corners of his lips.

"What happened now?" I ask.

He looks over his shoulder, peering out the door. A few of the Soldiers mill about, talking amongst themselves as they wait for his signal to come in. He pushes the door shut, closing them out for the moment. Leaning forward, he braces his arms on the table and drops his face into them.

"I don't know how to help her…" he mumbles, words muffled by his hands.

Tenna's brows furrow, and she asks, "What? Who?"

"Olivia," he says. He slumps back in his chair, arms falling limply to his lap.

A sick feeling creeps into my stomach at the prospect of Olivia needing help. The battle she fights is terrible.

I know that all too well.

"What happened?" I ask.

He looks over his shoulder at the door for an instant, then shakes his head. "She's worried about the food. Ten more mouths to feed doesn't seem like a lot, but it's thirty meals a day. And we have so far to go."

His face falls, and he goes on, "A couple more weeks to Regonia. That's over four hundred meals. How long will we be there? How much will we be able to find to eat while we're there to offset it? Then, there's the return trip after Novay, and if those beds can't be repaired, that's thirty extra meals a day for months. Who knows who we'll still have left, but I'd rather not count on casualties to keep everyone fed."

Panic spreads over my face, and my stomach drops. The practicalities of our trip fall upon me like a lead weight, and I see it echoed in Tenna's posture.

They weren't keeping secrets. We just didn't consider the magnitude of such a journey. None of our wars before required such lengthy travel times or such isolation. If we needed food, we could hunt or gather as necessary while traveling.

But we can't do that in the Realm of Stars. There are no trees to pluck fruits from, no roots to boil over a fire.

Will we have enough food?

What else have we overlooked?

"We have enough," Ricardo says, holding up his hands to reassure us. "Barely, but we have enough. We brought extra just in case something went wrong. Good-fucking-thing we did."

Leaning forward, he raises his brows and scratches at the bridge of his nose. "But Olivia… She had a panic attack over it this morning. Barely got any sleep after everything last night, and then she got up early to go check every single bed, every panel. Because she just had to make sure everything would be alright, because she feels like it's all her responsibility. But ended up puking her guts out."

"I don't know how to help her. My parents always drank, and I know that's how she used to keep herself calm, but… that night on Sparrow…" His throat closes around the words, around the memory of finding her unconscious and dying. "She's trying. But I don't know what to do."

Tenna settles into a chair, one of the ones specially made for us, and takes his hand in hers. "What did you do this morning?"

I sit down and wait.

"I sat with her," he says with a shrug and a shake of his head. "I tried to get her to breathe, held her hair back when she started throwing up. I don't know… It just doesn't feel like enough. She calmed down, but I don't think it was because of anything I did."

His eyes go distant, taking on a haunted air, and guilt twists my heart.

Is this how Tenna felt when I fought the battle within?

"That's all you *can* do," she whispers, tone hollow. "Just be there for her. Make sure she knows you're there to help."

"It doesn't feel like enough," Ricardo repeats, and his voice cracks. A tear falls from his eye, streaks over his cheek. It drops, soaking into the fabric of his dark shirt, but another replaces it, dripping over his tan skin.

"I know," Tenna says, and her voice carves a hollow in my chest. "It never feels like enough."

"But it is," I say.

Ricardo meets my gaze, nodding slowly. He wipes his tears away with his free hand, all the while chewing at the inside of his cheek.

I put a tender hand to Tenna's back, and she looks at me. "Hoo kai voo mai," I whisper.

She smiles, gently crinkling the dusky, grey skin around her eyes. "Hoo kai voo mai."

A sigh rushes free of Ricardo. "Thanks, guys." Tendrils of dark hair hang loose around his face, curling freely and sticking to the tear tracks. He wipes at his face, then says, "We should probably get started. I can deal with this more later. Let's get them in here so you can meet them."

Tenna turns toward the door with a much lighter mood than she would've greeted the soldiers with mere moments ago.

Ricardo dries the last of his tears as he rises to his feet. He pulls the door open and gestures to the Soldiers, ushering them in. Ten Humans file into the conference room, circling around the table to stand near chairs on the other side.

Their eyes dart back and forth, moving nervously from Ricardo to us. One of them bows. Another stiffly raises a flattened hand to his forehead, then moves his hand outward in a sharp jerk.

I furrow my brows, turning my head toward Tenna without taking my eyes off them, but Ricardo laughs. His shoulders shake with it, and tears of mirth roll down his cheeks.

"Thanks, Tanaka. I needed that." He shakes his head, trying to quell his laughter. "You don't need to bow or salute."

"Sorry, sir. I've never met a King or Queen before," Tanaka, a large man with soft eyes, says. "What's the appropriate greeting in their culture?"

A soft laugh eases past my lips. Slipping into the Human tongue to ease their nerves, I say, "Well, traditionally, Tenna would be addressed first, since she's the natural born ruler. As Queen, she's called Kinera. As King, I'm known as Tinera. We don't stand on quite so much ceremony as the monarchs of your ancestors did with all the groveling and tributes. For the purpose of this conversation, a simple 'hello' works just fine. What's your rank?"

The man before me looks to his fellows, then at Tenna, then at me. He mutters 'hello' to us both, making sure to start with Tenna, then answers my question. "I'm a Specialist."

"So, you and Ricardo are the same rank?"

"Only in our military capacities, Sir," Tanaka says. "He and Olivia are our Ambassadors, which ranks them above us. But as I understand it, given our current lack of higher-ranking defense personnel, the two of you will be leading us?"

"That's correct," Tenna says. "Going forward, you may address us as you would your superiors, had they not turned out to be corrupt, Soundless maniacs."

I hear the lightness of her tone, but the Specialists before us miss it, gazes darting to her face. When they see the smile on her face, tension eases out of them on stuttering waves of nervous laughter.

I smile, but for a different reason. They know who the orders must come from, first and foremost. No military can prosper without proper chain of command.

We might stand half a chance.

Chapter Thirty Five
Novay

Rone

I smile and send a message to Reginald. "Seventeen more have requested to 'understand humanity.' They're getting their modifications in a few days."

A sigh of relief puffs out of me, and I plop back down onto my bed. I play a Human song, letting "Eric by Mitski. 2012" reverberate through my room. For a moment, I just listen, just feel the song as the bass echoes in my chest.

I'm supposed to be preparing for my tests, a range of equations and assessments that the Drennar think will quantify the effects that my emotions have on my cognitive abilities.

But I sit, thinking of him, waiting for his reply, which might say something about the effects emotions have on my cognitive abilities, in and of itself.

It's nice and warm in here, anyway. They can just take my lateness as a sign of cognitive disruption.

I lean back on my hands, and my head falls back, hanging in the space between my wings. My mind fills with the allies that may very well join our ranks soon.

But how will we bring them to our side without the risk of them turning us in?

A message from Reginald comes through our private channel, and I smile.

"That's amazing! What's the total after they're modified?"

Then, a second message. "Will they see the experiments the same way that you do?"

An idea forms, prompted by his words, and I tell him, "I think I might have a way to take care of that."

Within an instant, he sends back, "Well, then I'll consider the problem solved."

Another message comes through. "Since that's not a problem anymore… Do you want to actually talk tonight? I want to see you. Even if it is just video."

My heart skips a beat, expanding within my chest. "Of course. I can't wait."

We set a time, and I send out messages to the Drennar seeking modifications. I carefully emphasize the need for them to remain in their current facilities, working within the confines of their normal routines, for the first couple of weeks. I tell them the role that will play in providing them with an objective frame of reference to process the emotions and their effects and warn them that without such a stable backdrop, the emotions can be overwhelming.

But really, I just need them to see.

I need them to see how cold and cruel our species is, how horrible these experiments are. I need them to see it for themselves, because telling them could never be enough.

A quick message to Lustran prompts him to send a similar message to them, urging them to stay in their current facilities for a short time, offering a second opinion to corroborate my suggestion.

I hope that's enough to bring them to our side.

It'd be difficult to hide our activities from those outside our facility and those within it as well.

Chapter Thirty Six
The Realm of Stars

Olivia

"You know what I want?" I say, staring out at the stars.

The edible packing peels away from my dinner easily, revealing the sectioned off tray of food within. Goulash and a brownie. I stare down at it, wrinkling my nose.

"What do you want?" Ricardo asks from the co-pilot's seat, digging into his own food without hesitation.

"Some of Mrs. Ulric's cake."

My stomach gurgles loudly at the prospect of goulash.

"Still not feeling well?" Ricardo asks, brows furrowing.

I shake my head, poking at the goulash with my fork. "I think I might be coming down with something."

I frown thinking of the food I'm wasting every time I throw up. Scooping up a bite, I shovel the food in, knowing I need the nutrients even more considering how little I'm keeping down. The small bite triggers my gag reflex, but I force myself to swallow.

I set my fork down, settling the food on the fold out tray before me, and drop my head into my hands. Ricardo reaches over to rub my back, and I groan.

"I can't be wasting food like this… It's so stupid."

"It's not stupid. People get sick," Ricardo reassures me. "You might need to go see Dr. Sullivan."

"Maybe if this doesn't go away on its own."

Otherwise, I'm just wasting his time.

But I hear the echo of my own anxiety and depression in that thought.

Lifting my head, I look past the goulash and pick up the brownie. I bring it to my nose, testing it out with a quick sniff. My stomach doesn't immediately revolt, so I take a bite.

It goes down easy. I take another bite.

"Hm…"

Tipping my head to the side, I take a risk, knowing I need to get something substantial into my system. I pile a forkful of goulash on top of the brownie.

Here goes nothing.

I take a bite, and somehow, it doesn't make me gag. The odd combination goes down smooth. "Okay, then."

Looking up, I find Ricardo staring at me, openmouthed. "Did you just… dip that?"

"Not quite. Just… piled some on," I say, then repeat the offensive action. "What's the worst that can happen? I throw up? Odds are, that's going to happen anyway."

"But that can't taste good," he says with a laugh.

"It actually isn't that bad," I say. "You should try it."

He shakes his head, laughing. "I don't think so."

***

Days come and go, but the nausea follows closely on my heels. Determined not to waste Dr. Sullivan's time, I try my best to make it through. My surprise for the Drennar occupies my time, distracting me from my ever-present anxiety, from the need to check and recheck our food stores. The stories Tenna and Krona tell of their homeland help too.

Regonia peeks at us from the horizon, growing larger by the day. Swirls of vibrant blue and a peculiar blue green come into focus, stealing my breath each morning when I start my shift in the cockpit.

I sit for hours, staring out, imagining what we'll find when we descend. As we get closer, my excitement grows, slowly overpowering the nausea as it fades into the background.

***

Stepping into the cockpit, my breath deserts me. Regonia perches before us, swallowing the entire window and blocking out almost all the stars. I take a deep breath, luxuriating in the sight of an actual planet.

"Beautiful, isn't it?" Hugo whispers. "I almost don't want to leave."

Inwardly, I lament the possibility of him staying. Staring out at the planet before us, I want to be alone, to study it in privacy, even if only for a moment.

A massive yawn splits his face open. "I guess I'd better get to bed though. We'll have a big day tomorrow."

"That we will. You especially," I say, slipping into my chair.

He pushes himself up to his feet and squeezes between our seats. "One of the few times that I hate the night shift," he says, laughing as he leaves.

I quickly dim the lights to see Regonia better and turn on some music. "Sick by Chelsea Wolfe. 2013" fills the air as I stare out.

And then, I'm alone with her.

Regonia sits before me, resplendent and mesmerizing. A genuine ocean wraps around the globe, bisecting it. Land masses decorate the planet, partially obscured by clouds.

Clouds! There are fucking clouds!

A spiral of white gauze moves slowly across the southern hemisphere, raking over the ocean and heading for land.

Is it raining there?

What's rain like?

My heartrate accelerates, and a giggle erupts from me. "It's so beautiful," I whisper. Breathing out, I settle back into my chair.

I can't believe I almost missed this.

After a few moments of wonder, I send a cluster of messages. Sitting silently, I watch the planet, taking it in. Moons linger in the distance, far larger and far more colorful than I expected. They don't look anything like the pictures I've seen of the Moon of Earth.

Footsteps sound in the hall, echoing toward me. I smile, imagining the expressions that will light up their faces.

Chapter Thirty Seven
The Realm of Stars

Tenna

My pulse races as we navigate the halls of Nova, moving toward the cockpit. I reach for Krona's hand, lacing our fingers together. He gives my hand a squeeze, and my heart skips a beat.

Olivia's message runs through my mind, over and over. "You should come up here. There's something I want you to see."

It doesn't sound like anything bad, but worry still nags at me, dogging my heels with every step. I pull in a deep breath and push onward, footsteps echoing off the metal tube I traverse.

At a junction, Ricardo steps into view, and his hand jumps to his chest. "Oh, god..." he mutters. "You guys scared me."

I smile, and Krona chuckles.

"How did you not hear us coming?" I ask. "Everything in here is so noisy. It's like we're stomping."

"You're a lot quieter than you think," Ricardo says, falling into step with us. "All of you are. It's shocking actually. But thanks for mocking me and my terrible Human hearing." He tosses a teasing grin at us.

"Anytime."

The cockpit looms before us, massive metal door latched into place. My heart skips a beat.

Ricardo reaches for the latch and swings the door outward. Krona and I step aside to accommodate him. He disappears through the door, and we duck to follow.

As I rise back up to my full height, my breath leaves me. Beyond the window, a massive orb of varying shades of blue and teal, brown and grey looks back at us. Soft shrouds of white float around it.

"Is that Regonia?" I breathe.

But I know the answer, for I know the bodies orbiting it, know the moons I've gazed at all my life.

"It's beautiful," Krona whispers beside me.

My jaw hangs open as the majesty of our home washes over me. The corners of my eyes prick, and a single tear slides over my cheek.

It's so much bigger than I ever could have imagined. Our world holds so much more than I thought.

How many of us are there, truly?

There's so much room, so many places we haven't seen.

Of course, I knew there was a whole world out there, but to see it like this...

Ricardo steps forward, falling into the co-pilot's seat. He shakes his head and mumbles something, but I don't catch it.

Krona and I step forward, right up to the backs of the seats, leaning forward to peer at our home. Desperately, I try to pick out any landmarks from my memory, trying to figure out where we belong on this massive planet. But I've never seen our world from so far away, never had to find landmarks visible from this distance.

A span of jagged terrain looks like it might be the Nurahvi Mountains, the land Taron Tribe calls home, but there are so many black and grey streaks across the teal grasslands.

Could that really be the mountains we've lived beneath for so long?

"Where's our home?" I ask.

Olivia taps a few buttons, and a series of numbers appears on a small screen before her. They make no sense to me, but she interprets them in less than a heartbeat.

Pointing at a tiny streak of black south of the massive mountain range I thought to be the Nurahvi, she says, "These are the mountains near your home, so right here, just west of those. Right about… there."

I lean closer, stunned by just how small our portion of the world really is, how small our section of the universe is.

"When can we go down?" Krona asks.

"Tomorrow," Olivia says. "We still have a little ways to go, but I wanted you to see." Her voice cracks, telling me that I'm not the only one tearing up. "I can put this on all the screens throughout the ship if you want everyone else to see."

But I shake my head. "No, just the ones in the cafeteria."

Krona nods, wrapping an arm around me and pulling me against his side.

"We should be together when they see."

I turn to face Krona, leaning my forehead against his. We plant our hands on the sides of each other's necks. I peer into piercing green eyes, eyes the color of my salvation, and whisper, "We're going home…"

Chapter Thirty Eight
The Realm of Stars

Krona

Bodies cram into the cafeteria, standing shoulder to shoulder. Tenna and I climb atop a table to get the attention of our people, and silence falls over the gathered crowd.

I take Tenna's hand in mine, bringing it to my lips for a gentle kiss. She meets my eyes with a smile before turning to face our Tribe.

"We're so close," I whisper. A deep breath fills my lungs, then rushes out on a sigh of relief.

"There's something we want you to see," Tenna says, addressing our Tribe. "We're not there yet, but we're close."

My heart races, and my smile widens. I need this. *Our people* need this.

"Regonia is so much more than we ever thought, and now, we can see it like we've never seen it before," I say, voice hushed by awe.

I hold Tenna's hand as she lowers herself to sit atop the table, legs hanging over the edge. I climb down beside her, staring up at the wall of screens.

Olivia takes her cue, showing us the majesty of our planet. The air in the room shifts as our Tribe gasps. My eyes roam over the curves of the shores we've never seen, the jagged spikes of mountain ranges we never knew existed.

All around, our people reach for each other. I put a hand on the shoulder of the nearest person, and Tenna does the same. Heads lean on shoulders, and people reach out to lay hands upon each other's backs.

I trace the tiny streak that Olivia said was our mountains, the Nurahvi Mountains, and marvel at their size. They've always seemed so massive, so integral to our everyday lives. Our trades with Taron Tribe kept us stocked with weapons and Bellona flowers. The trek up the mountains requires skill and patience. Their shadows outline our pastures as the sun sets, helping us trace the shape of our days.

But the world is so much bigger than we thought, so much more complicated.

And that says nothing of the worlds beyond our own.

Staring up at the screens with our people, I wrap myself in the wonder of seeing our home from such a spectacular vantage. "Olivia," I say, knowing our people will hear me in the reverent hush, "can you mark our home on the screen so everyone can see?"

She places a small marker in the plains between the Nurahvi Mountains and the river that Mourgam dammed, attempting to condemn us. Again, the air shifts around us as 4,000 bodies draw a single, massive breath.

I smile, and my chest grows tight. A tear falls, then another. "We're going home…" I whisper.

And though I know we'll leave again, venturing up into the mountains and then into the Realm of Stars to confront the Drennar, I can't wait to see our land, our village, our keep.

Whatever condition it may be in, we'll fix it. We'll rebuild. We'll make it ours again.

I wipe tears away, gazing higher on the screens as I do. My eyes trace the moons we stared at every night, the moons that marked our sowing days and our harvests.

From our home, they look serene and empty, but from here, they look as varied as Regonia. Swaths of teal and blue dapple the surface of two of them. Dark greys and black mottle the third, and the fourth shines an iridescent pale gray.

And for the first time, I wonder what we would find if we travelled to each.

Our people sway together, whispering their joy. But why, when our hearts are so full, should we only whisper it?

Not daring to pull my eyes from the screens, from the visage of our home, I sing.

But no song we've ever sung fits this new experience. We've never been taken hostage, never been to space. We've never been the subject of vile experiments before or lost so many. We've never met aliens.

And we've never had a homecoming so spectacular or quite so long in the making.

So, no words pass my lips, only sounds, only a flowing vocalization. My low tones echo through the room, reverberating softly among our people. Tenna joins in, offering a sweet, yet husky compliment to my voice.

Within moments, the whole of the cafeteria is a riot of wordless celebration, of voices rising and crashing together at the beauty of our home.

Our spirits rise, and our voices go with them, ascending to heights they haven't reached since we were taken from Regonia. The metal walls of the cafeteria vibrate, resonating with our song, and a smile lifts the corners of my mouth, crinkles the skin around my eyes.

My heart soars, and I turn to face Tenna. My partner. My love. My Kinera.

The only person I would look away from this glory to see.

Her eyes sparkle, and she glows with the warmth of our people's song. Leaning in, I touch her neck, pulling her in for a kiss, pulling our voices from the song for just a few breaths.

A fire burns within me, but I hold it at bay, setting the embers back for our time alone. We sing with our people until well after the sun disappears on the other side of Regonia, casting our home into shadows. Olivia leaves the screens on, letting us gaze upon the nighttime and sing to our hearts' content.

I hope she and Ricardo listen from the cockpit.

And I hope they sing along with us.

Chapter Thirty Nine

Novay

Reginald

One of the Expressionless leads me to my testing room, and I plod along behind him. I don't bother assessing the mods he possesses, don't bother comparing them to the mods of the guard that led me along yesterday. I don't try to fathom why they might have switched places.

It doesn't matter.

No answer I can come up with will do anything. I can't help with the efforts of humanity, can't assist Rone in any meaningful way.

The wall splits open to allow us access, and I drop into the chair in the center of the room. No desk slides up and over my lap.

I must be watching for the moment.

Yet, I don't lift my eyes to the wall before me or to the Expressionless gathered in the corners. I don't have the energy to try until I have to.

The wall bursts to life, sending rays of blinding light into the room. I jolt, moving faster than I have in days just to shield my eyes. Slowly, the light from the wall dims, and I peek through my fingers.

On the wall before me, I find not the scenes of static and catastrophe that I've grown accustomed to seeing. No bodies float through space, jettisoned after the mass execution. Neither Olivia nor Eva cry on the screen, half-hidden by patches of black or streaks of purest white.

I see only lists.

My eyes cycle through the data quickly, assessing what they've put before me. The Human language glares on their screen, clearly translated for ease of comprehension.

Column names stretch across the top, but the print is so small that I must rise from my seat and approach the wall to read it. Name, age, height, a multitude of measurements of Human bodies and health. They seem normal.

Except that the gender column, all the way down through hundreds of Humans, is strictly female.

My brows reach for each other, and I tip my head to the side.

Why would they even include that column?

To draw my attention to it?

Turning to the nearest Drennar, I ask, "What is this?"

But the Drennar doesn't answer.

Shaking my head, I roll my eyes and return to the data set before me. The first name is a woman named Maria, located on Odyssey Space Research Station. A woman Olivia knows. I read through more column names with my lips pursed.

Marital status, orientation, trimester...

Trimester?

Are all these women pregnant? This must be all the pregnant women on Termana... A whole generation.

Number of previous offspring, twins (y/n), date to be collected.

My blood runs cold.

That column reads the same, all the way down. Ten days from now.

They'll steal an entire generation in one fell swoop.

A bottomless chasm opens beneath me. Rage rips through me on a scream, wordless and all-consuming. I pound my fists against the wall, but the words upon it barely ripple with the force.

My voice a hoarse mixture of gravel and fury, I shout, "What is wrong with you?!"

My fists curl tighter, digging my nails into my palms. I slam my fists against the wall, over and over, but it isn't enough. Agony rips through me at the prospect of so many pregnant women being taken, being dragged to this hell.

My throat rips open with another scream as the entire world crumbles beneath me.

We can't lose so many.

Humanity is barely surviving, barely coming back from near extinction.

I slam my foot into the wall, barely noticing the pain.

But it isn't enough.

A change in the words makes me hope that maybe I've done something, maybe I've damaged their stupid technology. But my eyes catch the change.

A single line is highlighted. All the others blur.

Not that they need to blur the others. My eyes see only the name that glows brighter than the rest, tracing the familiar lines.

Olivia...

My jaw falls open, and my heart plummets. A deathly stillness creeps into me, expanding and pushing every thought away as realization dawns, dark and horrible.

Olivia is pregnant…

And they're coming for her.

I swallow thickly, but my throat is too dry to obey. Panic settles in my gut. A lump wedges itself firmly in my airway, and I choke out a sob. Tears roll freely over my cheeks.

Shaking my head, I whisper, "No… You can't take her." My voice grows louder, harder, bordering on a growl, and I repeat, "You can't take her!"

"She is necessary for our next experiment," the nearest Drennar says. "We will collect her in ten days as scheduled."

I stare at the vile creature, the barren void that dares call itself sentient, and my blood boils. My hands ball into fists once more, and I stomp over to the foul thing.

Glaring up at a face the color of dust, eyes the color of putrid mold, I hiss, "You can't take her. You can't experiment on her! We had an agreement. I cooperated. You put me through hell, but I cooperated!"

"We make no agreements with inferior beings. Your substitution was acceptable merely because you promised to cooperate, which made our task easier," this creature says, and my jaw falls open at their duplicity.

"Had there been an agreement, you violated it when you seduced a Drennar, no doubt in an attempt to leverage a more pleasant experiment for yourself."

"I fell in love with her! I didn't seduce her!" I cry.

"Love does not exist," the Drennar dares to say. "It is a hallucination created by your dysfunctional, inferior brain. Your attempts to manipulate Rone violated the agreement you thought we had. Even so, your daughter is necessary for our next experiment. She will be collected in ten days."

The maddening monotone of the Drennar's voice stirs my fury, and I boil over. Launching myself at this beast, this robot in skin, I punch the expressionless thing, one hit after another. My fists land on what should be a soft stomach, but what feels like metal greets them. Each impact forces my nails into the skin of my palms, and a trickle of blood oozes down my wrist. My knuckles split open.

But the beast before me doesn't even flinch.

I scream up at him, driving my fist against his torso yet again. But still, not a single move, not even the batting of an eye. My veins burn as I imagine them taking Olivia, taking my unborn grandchild, and bringing them to this place.

I reach for the gill slits that line the beast's forearm. My fingers slide between them easily, and I grasp them, pulling as hard as I can. The Drennar draws back reflexively, jerking its arm from my grasp.

Momentum carries me forward, and my head slams against the wall. Pain explodes through me, and I stumble backward. The floor tips, and I struggle against gravity.

But I fail.

I fall.

My head hits the chair I sat in moments ago, and my eyes flutter closed.

Everything fades to black.

Chapter Forty
The Realm of Stars

Olivia

Ten days to go

My alarm blares in my ear, waking me far earlier than I've grown accustomed to. I roll out of bed, careful not to wake Ricardo. A smile drifts lazily onto my face at the sight of his sleeping form, his serene expression.

With a sigh, I push myself to prepare for the day, knowing I need to get to the cockpit as soon as I can. Hugo needs some amount of sleep before we descend, after all. He'll need his wits about him for that.

Yet, fatigue dogs my heels as I dress. Yawning incessantly, I yearn to crawl back into bed. Briefly, I consider a supplement to help me wake, but they're all the way in the medbay. I sigh and pull socks on.

I'll just swing through the cafeteria on the way up front. Maybe food will wake me up.

My stomach growls loudly, agreeing with my plan. Leaning over Ricardo, I push loose hair back from his face. I plant a tender kiss on his forehead, letting my lips linger a moment longer than strictly necessary.

He moans softly, asking, "What time is it?"

A smile spreads over his lips, and he reaches for me, pulling me in for a kiss. Our lips meet, but I laugh.

"How can I tell you what time it is like this?" I mumble.

He chuckles but kisses me again.

My body aches to crawl into bed beside him, but the cockpit awaits. "It's time for me to go…" I say.

"Mmm… I guess. I probably shouldn't distract you."

Chuckling, I say, "No, probably not. You should come up later, though. And by later, I mean 8:54am." I smile thinking of the surprise I have in store for him. Then, remembering his busy schedule for the day, I add, "If you have time."

He chuckles, raising his eyebrows. "8:54am, huh? Very specific." Giving me one last kiss, he says, "I'll make time."

I peer into beautiful amber eyes for just a second longer, then force myself to move. My stomach growls again, and I make my way to the kitchen, hoping they have a meal box with pickles ready to go. I don't even care what else is in it.

Weird. I never used to like pickles, but they sound fantastic right now.

***

Morning ticks by, yet darkness still claims Regonia. But not for long. My heart nearly chokes me, jumping into my throat.

Footsteps echo in the hall behind me, and I peer over my shoulder. Ricardo approaches, eyes alight. "Now, what is it that made you set such a weird time for me to be here?" he asks, dropping a kiss on my lips as he squeezes between the seats.

I smile as he drops into Hugo's chair. "There's something I want you to see, but we'll only be in the right position for a short time because we're moving pretty fast."

I check the time, and my heart leaps into my throat.

Only a couple minutes until it starts.

Briefly, I consider playing music, but I want to hear Nova. I want to listen to the beautiful machine that got us here.

Leaning his head back, Ricardo stares at the dark planet before us. "How much longer until we go down?" he asks, tipping his head to look at me.

"A few hours. We're in an almost-orbit, right now. We're getting closer to the surface but maintaining a speed that keeps us above the same continent despite the rotation. Basically like a slowly falling satellite. Which is why we're going to see something amazing here in a minute."

"What are we going to see?"

Laughing, I say, "It's a surprise. All I can say is that, since we were on a pretty direct approach until an hour ago, it's something no Human has seen in a few hundred years. I feel bad for Hugo. If we'd been scheduled to adjust our approach a little sooner, he would've seen it, but we get to see it first."

Ricardo's brows rise, and he looks back to the planet before us. A comfortable silence falls over us, and I reach for his hand. He laces our fingers together as we wait.

And slowly, the first rays of dawn peek around the curve of Regonia. They aren't bright, not yet. But a faint glow reaches out, calling for us.

Ricardo leans forward. Voice falling to a hush, he asks, "Is this… Are we about to watch a sunrise?"

I nod, never taking my eyes off the beams of light shooting off into space, no longer blocked by Regonia. As the planet rotates, we go with it, and the alien star greets us.

Massive rays of pure, glorious sunlight illuminate the world, showing us mountains and oceans and forests. Plains burst to life, and the clouds reflect everything, shining brilliantly.

My jaw falls open, and a tear slips from my eye. I smile, watching the planet before us come to life, waking for a new day. Pulling in a deep breath, I whisper to the new world, "It's nice to meet you."

Ricardo squeezes my hand, leaning back to take it all in.

We watch a sun rise over an alien planet, and all the while, I thank the stars, and Ricardo, that I lived to see it.

***

My heart races. I slide a finger along the edge of the control panel. Beside me, Hugo adjusts our trajectory, turning Nova's engines to compensate for the planet's gravity. I listen as the massive machine works, responding easily to our wishes.

But the hardest part lies ahead.

Staring out at Regonia, at the land masses and the oceans and the clouds, I know there's a chance we may never even make it down there. If anything goes wrong on entry, if any of the machines malfunction or we're even just a little bit off in our calculations, we could burn up or crash.

For the first time, I'm genuinely nervous in the pilot's seat.

Never before have I flown with so many lives aboard. Never before have I entered an atmosphere.

Never before have I landed a spaceship on an actual planet.

Docking with a station or with the ports on Termana is a completely different process. This is a different beast, a whole new world.

Am I up for this?

Am I good enough for this?

My mouth dries out, and I swallow hard. I lean forward, peering to the side to see the stars.

With my heart in my throat, I whisper to them, "Wish me luck…"

To Hugo, I say, "Ready to get this started?"

Chapter Forty One
The Realm of Stars

Ricardo

I buckle in next to Krona and lean my head back. My heart hammers in my chest as I try to ignore all the nightmare scenarios running through my head. I shove aside images of fires and broken heat shields. I close my eyes against the imagined sight of malfunctioning jets failing to lower us safely to the ground.

Olivia will get us down there safely.

I pull in a deep breath, letting it out slowly.

She's got this.

A smile spreads over my face, because even though I know she's never entered an atmosphere outside of simulators, I trust her to do this. I trust her with my life and all the other lives aboard Nova.

Sure, Hugo is there, too, but even if he wasn't...

She'd still pull it off.

Somehow, she'd write a program to act like a co-pilot. She'd build a whole AI just to get it done.

I chuckle, marveling at the determination that pushed her to make a defense program for all of humanity all by herself.

Turning to Krona, my smile widens as his hand laces with Tenna's. I glance out at the Regonians across from me, peering at them between the stacks of cryo-beds. They look back and forth amongst themselves, occasionally glancing at Krona and Tenna, their Inerans.

And when their eyes alight on their Queen and their King, when they take in the love and trust their leaders feel for Olivia, their shoulders relax.

Olivia's voice echoes through the massive metal bay, explaining the process of landing to the Regonians. Step by step, she walks them through it, even sends simulator footage to all our Links for us to watch as she speaks.

Many people stare at the tiny screens embedded in their arms, listening intently, but a few watch Tenna or Krona or even me.

The atmosphere shifts going from heavy with tension to full of excitement as the prospect of home becomes a reality. I watch the change in them, watch their frowns turn to passionate joy, and my heart expands within my chest.

They'll finally be home.

We'll finally start fixing what my brother and Olivia's mom and all the shitty people they worked with did.

"Here we go," Olivia says over the speakers in the cargo bay, and my heart skips a beat at her jubilant tone.

Chapter Forty Two
The Realm of Stars

Krona

I grasp Tenna's hand, weaving our fingers together. She smiles at me, mossy green eyes glowing. Olivia walks us through the process, but I barely listen after she goes over the safety procedures. I don't question her skills as a pilot, and there's nothing I can do to change the trajectory of this ship even if I did.

Excitement rises within me, and I give Tenna's hand a squeeze. All around us, our people chatter, filling the air with a mixture of anxiety and happiness. Olivia sends us footage of a spaceship entering an atmosphere, and I glance at it briefly.

But our people draw my eye.

They relax as Olivia speaks, trusting her as we do. They meet our gazes, breathing easier when they see our smiles.

"We're going home..." I whisper.

Tenna leans toward me, straining against her harness to kiss me. Her lips part with a smile as they meet mine.

I reach for her, smoothing her dark hair back behind her ear, and her smile widens. She pulls back to gaze at our people, sighing contentedly. "I don't know what we'll find down there," she says, "but we'll make it work."

I nod, heart swelling with the faith she has in us, in our people. "We always do," I say.

She gives my hand a squeeze, and then, she hums. The tune tugs at my heart, perfect for this journey. We've sung it many times before, usually on our way back home after battle.

But it works just as well for this.

So, I sing.

"Joo sein, ullatak." *We return, victorious.*

Olivia warns us of a jolt, and I grip my harness with one hand. Tenna's grasp tightens on my other, and I watch a ripple of tension roll through our Tribe mates.

Our tones shift to a hum between lines. The ship rocks, jostling our voices, but we don't miss a beat, picking up for the next line, right on cue.

"Svevensonlar, so ullarak." *Battered, not beaten.*

Our voices ebb, trailing off on the last word, letting it echo through the cargo bay. Throughout our Tribe, the men pick up the echo, mimicking it, carrying it forward. I join them, raising my voice and letting the music take me.

And the women sing the next line, voices high and haunting.

"UllaCoomlar ar joo vasnens, bin joo minay." *Lost Ones in our hearts, on our lips.*

Olivia warns us of another jolt, but I barely notice it, leaving the music behind to join in for the next line.

"Al joo sve vesne ray." *And we fight another day.*

And so, we descend toward home, with a song in our hearts and our hearts on our lips.

Chapter Forty Three
Regonia

Olivia

Mountains take shape beyond the window, careening into focus. My eyes strain to pick out the details, the rocks and crevices, the peaks and valleys. My heart races at the prospect of climbing them, and blood thunders through my veins.

Grasslands swirl beneath them, waves of teal rippling all the way to the shores of a pristine, pale blue river.

The water's actually blue!

My lungs catch at the sight of it, and butterflies erupt in my stomach. But I need to get a grip on myself, at least for the moment.

Hugo and I flip switches, turning on vertical jets, then powering off the main jets. We hover for just a breath, and I meet Hugo's gaze. The same wonder that buzzes through my veins shines back at me from his eyes.

Blowing out a long breath, I nod, and we slowly descend. Stone structures move into focus, and we shift our trajectory, aiming for a large field outside the village Daen Tribe occupied just over a year ago.

I ache to let my eyes roam over it, to take in the details of their home, but Nova occupies my attention. With my heart in my throat, I warn everyone of the upcoming shifts and jolts over the speakers spread throughout the ship.

We rotate, directing the cargo hatch toward their village. Water rushes downstream, cutting across the field not thirty meters from us. Beautiful, miraculous shades of emerald and sea glass, aquamarine and turquoise, bend and sway with the wind of our jets, whipping about in a frenzy.

Hugo and I work in tandem, easing up on the propulsion system and settling Nova upon solid, natural ground. For a moment, I don't think, don't speak.

My gaze locks on the alien world beyond the window, and tears slip quietly over my cheeks. My eyes roam over the foothills between us and the mountains, tracing every crest. In the distance, a massive animal moves, wide, flat antlers scraping the air, bushy tail swishing behind it. I swallow, recalling the name Tenna and Krona used.

It's a Vyrto.

One of the creatures they ride into battle.

A smile lifts my lips as I watch this wild animal graze on untainted lands, and my heart expands within my chest. A lump forms in my throat, choking me as tears well up.

"We're here..." I whisper. "We're actually here."

Beside me, Hugo breathes out a single laugh, but says nothing.

Falling back into my chair, I press the button to speak with the people on board. "We made it. You're home."

And though I can't imagine the celebration in the cargo bay, though I wish I were down there with them, wish I could see their reaction, I sit still. My hands tremble in my lap, and I stare out at the world beyond our window.

A second, smaller Vyrto crests a hill, joining the first. It prances up to the larger animal, happily nudging it, and I laugh, wondering how happy the mother must be that her child has no antlers yet.

A gentle breeze washes over the grass, moving it in soft waves. Small flowers dot the meter high growth, lending the illusion of blinking blue lights as the grass shifts over them.

I pull in a deep breath, wishing Ricardo was here in the cockpit to see this.

But we'll see it even closer soon enough.

Suddenly, my excitement bubbles up, overpowering the awe that struck me motionless until now. So many steps still stand between us and the beauty of Regonia, and my fingers dance over the controls.

Hugo follows suit, infected by my fervor, and we power down the jets completely. I check in with the techs and find them unbuckled and standing at the ready.

"I wouldn't start the thaw sequence on those beds just yet though," one says.

My brows furrow. With a single command, the video feed from the cargo bay splays across the screen before me, and I see why they want to wait.

Chapter Forty Four
Regonia

Krona

Our people rejoice, and my heart leaps into my throat. Harnesses unbuckled, we leap from our seats, ready to descend the ramp and be one with our home.

For now, our joy echoes off the metal walls of the cargo bay, reverberating in our bones. Deserting language, we sing from our hearts, vocalizing together in a harmony too sweet to be contained by words.

My heart swells, pressing itself against my ribs, my lungs. I gasp with the sheer exaltation of being home.

After everything, after the torment of the experiments, after our immeasurable losses, after so much grief…

"Joo kai gordeky!" I shout. *We're home!*

Tenna echoes my cry, singing it, sending the words aloft to play among the catwalks and beams of the cargo bay.

Techs stand by, waiting among the stacks of cryo-beds, and for half a breath, I consider quelling the raucous joy erupting around the stacks.

But our people need this.

And they watch the stacks, careful not to bump them, careful not to jeopardize the lives inside.

A warm smile spreads over my lips.

Tenna wraps her arms around me, and I stare into luscious green eyes. My hands find the sides of her face, thumbs gently caressing her cheeks.

"Joo kai gordeky," she whispers.

A single tear falls from her eye, but I don't wipe it away. I let it trickle down to my hand, then kiss her, throwing myself into our joining. As our mouths melt together and heat spreads through me, our people celebrate around us.

A groan builds within the metal hull of the ship, and I pull back from Tenna to stare at the hatch. Olivia's voice whispers through my mind, and I see Tenna's eyes drift out of focus as she listens, presumably to the same message.

"I'll wake the Soldiers in a minute. You guys have waited long enough," Olivia says, and the hatch begins to open.

The massive door bemoans its own weight, complaining loudly, but rays of warm light peak in through the open space above it. The light reaches for us, calling us home.

Slowly, the hatch lowers, revealing mountains on the horizon. Already, I feel myself rejoining this land, feel the connection I've missed since being stolen away from here. Fresh air fills my lungs, centering me, and I soak it in.

Lower still, the hatch descends, and the foothills peak into view, dotted by pale pink Juno trees and a meandering pack of Vyrtons. I even recognize my own among the group, picking out the missing tines of his antlers even at this distance. My heart lurches, aching to call him home, to feed him and care for him as I once did.

The hatch lowers further still, and beams of light stretch toward the back wall. I reach up, fingers moving in the warmth of our sun.

In the distance, the roof of a single stone building peeks into view. Then, another, and another. I pick out our home, right in the heart of the village, and my breath catches. Vines twine around the columns which support our balconies. Twisting green covers the whole wall facing us.

The buildings closer to us come into view, revealing wide open doors and overgrown plants. A limb from a Juno tree rests upon the home closest to us, soft pink leaves curled in on themselves in death. Stone lies in heaps around the base of the home, and vines reach into the place.

My heart plummets as the hatch reveals the field in which we've landed. Fertile farmland lies buried beneath common grasses, climbing to their full height. The fences we worked to build around this field hang from their posts, snapped by Vyrto hooves or fallen branches. The faint scent of Bellona flowers wafts toward us on a strong wind, and the grass whips against the ramp.

Not a sound stirs within our village.

Neither Roon Tribe nor the Vaerkin appear to have disturbed our homes since we were taken. The fear of star-sickness, the taint of our star-touched abductors, seems to have kept them at bay. Even the animals seem to have abandoned the area.

So much has changed.

My shoulders droop, crushed by the weight of disappointment. Tenna grasps my hand, taking a tentative step forward. Our people stand, dumbstruck, staring out at the land we once called home. They part for us, and Tenna leads me to the ramp.

Pulling in a deep breath, I rake my eyes over the river, tracing its line to the island we use for partnering ceremonies. That wild place looks unchanged, at least.

Clumps of branches and debris rest against the bridge, refuse from Roon Tribe. Smoke trails rise from the village upriver, shrouded from our view by a small cluster of hills.

Beside me, Tenna whispers, "We have a lot of work to do."

Turning to face me, Tenna wraps her arms around me.

"We got our people home," I say. "If we can do that, we can handle this."

Chapter Forty Five
Regonia

Olivia

I take Ricardo's hand as we walk down the ramp. Fresh air fills my lungs, and I eat it up. Our footsteps ring out, loud and sharp on the metal beneath us, but I crave the feeling of dirt beneath me.

Real dirt!

Not whatever we created for Termana. Not that I got to go into the farms often.

At the edge of the field, Daen Tribe wanders into their village, shoulders slumped as they take in their abandoned homes. But Ricardo squeezes my hand as we take the first step beyond Nova's cold embrace.

Waist-high grass swirls around me in a million shades of teal and turquoise, sea foam and aquamarine. I gaze up at the moons and the clouds. The Nurahvi Mountains pierce the sky, breaking up the horizon with their crystalline majesty.

They're massive! No wonder Tenna and Krona thought they were the other mountain range.

Holy shit, how big are those other mountains?

Humbled by the sheer beauty of Regonia, I raise my arms, slipping my hand free of Ricardo's for the moment. I spin in circles, letting the wonder of this place fill my heart. Everything seems to sparkle in this real, natural light.

My shirt rises as I lift my arms higher, and soft blades of grass tickle the exposed skin of my stomach. Laughing freely, I savor the sensation, luxuriating in the warmth of actual sunlight on my skin.

I trail my hands through the grass, straining my ears to hear the river I know rumble nearby. Holding still, I listen closer, picking out the sounds of animals in the distance, chirping and snorting and calling out to one another.

And there, just barely audible, the rushing of water in the distance.

Turning to Ricardo, I find him awestruck and smiling. A laugh bursts from him, and he reaches for me, wrapping his arms around my waist.

His thumb skims my bare skin, slipping beneath my shirt. Golden eyes stare into mine, and he leans in, brushing soft lips against mine.

I kiss him with renewed fervor, body coming alive as I cling to him, twining my hands in his hair. My heart hammers in my chest, and my breaths come in gasps. I pull back, smiling against his lips as he lifts me up, kissing the soft skin of my neck.

Setting me down, he drops to the ground, sprawling out on his back. With a giggle, I fall beside him.

Soft shades of blue-green grasses sway, caressing us in the breeze. Ricardo touches my cheek. I brace myself on my elbow and put one hand on his chest. Leaning over him, my lips brush his.

Then, I lay down beside him, curling up against his side. His arms wrap around me, and we lie in strange grass on an alien planet, watching clouds drift lazily through a sunny sky.

Chapter Forty Six
Regonia

Tenna

Our people spread out, venturing through our village to find their homes, their belongings. I walk straight through, passing our keep. Krona squeezes my hand as we follow my parents to the field on the other side of the village.

The field where Efsi died.

A few steps behind, my sister and her partner follow in our wake, but they're not the only ones. Everyone who lost someone in the Descent of Man goes with us.

My parents pad through the tall grass, hands clasped together. My mother's shoulders shake with silent sobs, pulling tears to my eyes. Krona squeezes my hand again, and I pull in a deep breath.

Climbing over the shattered remnants of the fence, I try not to remember the ships that crushed it when the Human Soldiers came for us. I try not to picture the shining reflections on their helmets, showing us the drooping of our eyelids as we fell to their Bellona gas.

But it all comes back.

All I see are my people taking refuge from the gas. All I hear are the screams ringing from their lips. The surge of battle, the adrenaline and terror of star-sickness.

Again, I watch my brother die, falling to his knees, eye bloodied by the projectile that shot straight through it. I watch him fall, watch him crumple.

"Tenna?" Krona asks, putting a hand to the small of my back.

I glance at him, heart stumbling along in my chest. My brows reach for each other. Softly, I let my brother's sound pass my lips. The gentle coo gathers momentum, echoing as Kala picks it up, then my parents.

Krona touches my cheek, leaning his forehead against mine, and I draw strength from him, from the sound of my brother flowing around me. Taking a deep breath, I pull back, nodding as I meet his gaze before continuing on.

I search the field for bones, stopping at one set of remains after another. But they don't feel like him, don't have his weapons. My mother and father kneel in the grass, and my heart stops.

Have they found him?

They quickly rise, making the sound of the Awakening. A guttural scream rips through them, agonizing and full of rage. Staring around at the field of bones, at our empty homes and the stars we were taken to, I let my voice shake the earth. The Awakening rattles through me, moves through the Tribe in waves. I scream until my throat goes raw and the tears stop falling.

But it could never be enough.

That day consumes me again, and I see him fall. And this time, I know where to look.

Spinning, I run for the place where he died. It takes only moments before I find a skeleton. White bones shine, sparkling in the sunlight when I part the grass to see them. His sword, a honed bone harvested from a deceased Malakar, rests beside him.

I collapse to my knees as Krona reaches me, purring and cooing the soft sound of my brother. Efsi's smile shines in my memory. I reach out to touch his bones, letting one hand rest gently atop his outstretched arm. Tears stream over my face, and I reach for his sword.

It sits heavy in my hand, far heavier than the lightweight bone ever felt before. My heart twists in my chest.

Closing my eyes, I call out to my parents, to my sister and her partner. "He's here," I say, forcing the words past a lump in my throat.

My hands trace the edges of the bone blade, worn smooth from a year of rain and wind, bleached by the light. I turn it over, gazing at the darker side. Tiny gashes and chips mar its surface, carrying the battles he fought before death.

My family approaches, encircling Efsi's remains. Tears slide easily over my cheeks, and I purr, struggling to force his sound past my lips. My cries strangle it, morphing it into something he was not.

Clamping my lips shut, I let my tears fall, sobbing openly. But Kala carries his sound. My parents echo it back to us. Krona rubs my back, kisses my shoulder gently.

The world spins around me, and I struggle for air as that day clouds my mind, yet again. I watch him fall, watch him give his life fighting for our people, and pain lances my chest.

"Today, we set up our homes." I rise to my feet, gazing at the members of our Tribe as they search for their loved ones in this field of bones. "Tonight, we remember them."

"I'll speak with the Memory Markers," my mother says.

My father laments the prospect of so many rafts on such short notice. "We can't craft so many so soon," he whispers, voice hollow. "We lost so many…"

Staring out over the fields, now overgrown and dotted with wildflowers, I trace the river with my gaze. The dark waters cut a swooping path, curving toward our village, then sweeping away.

The island of our partnering ceremonies perches nearby.

But further south, a barren, rocky island sits in the water.

"We won't use rafts," I say. "Not this time. We can't."

Krona follows my gaze downriver, eyes landing upon the larger island. He nods, and his voice is solemn as he says, "We'll take them there."

***

I carry Efi's sword to our keep, feet tamping down the overgrown foliage clogging our paths through the village. Melnara and Kala stayed behind, gathering his bones for the pyre.

I take a deep breath, rounding one last corner, and our home comes into view. But the only home I've ever known has changed.

Vines cling to stone walls, reaching higher than I've ever seen them, and several of the shutters hang at odd angles.

The Juno trees sway in the yard, soft pink leaves shining vibrantly, gleaming like the metal of Nova. But the bucket for gathering sap lies on its side, and the spile is nowhere to be seen. Our door hangs open, and leaves and debris coat the floor.

Gingerly, I traverse the yard and the steps with Krona at my side. I swallow back my nerves and cross the threshold, cringing as twigs and dried leaves crunch underfoot.

Refuse and animal tracks dapple every surface. The ornately carved wooden chairs near the hearth bear the marks of a Svalica, or perhaps a family of them, with each chair leg having been gnawed to needles. Soot-coated footprints speckle their burgundy cushions.

Krona closes the massive wooden doors, and shadows fall heavier around us, as if trying to hide the devastation of our home.

But I see it all.

The shadows don't hide the nests in our chandelier, tucked into the crook of the Vyrto antlers, between the candles perched atop each tine. Nor do they hide the toppled chairs around the dining table or the tattered rug beneath. Scratches mar the door to the kitchen, and muddy prints track up the stairs to our bedroom.

I trace the steps with my gaze. Efsi's sword hangs heavier in my hand as I picture the Healer coming down those same stairs after delivering him, white robes flowing freely.

My hand rises to my chest, palm flat, and my heart beats steadily beneath it. A deep breath fills my lungs.

Behind me, Krona lights a fire in the hearth, chasing the shadows away. He meanders into view, taking up the chain on the wall and lowering the chandelier. After removing the remnants of empty nests, he fetches a small stick from the hearth and lights each candle within the chandelier.

And finally, I move.

Before he can raise the twined antlers and candles, I reach for the chandelier. I trace the wide plates of the antlers carefully, watching the candle wax run from the tines to the center, pooling in small cavities within the bone.

Turning to Krona, I say, "Don't raise it just yet."

Rushing up the stairs, I find Efsi's old room from our younger years. Closed off and safe from animals, it looks so much the same. I run my free hand over the wooden bed frame, the carved bench in the corner, leaving trails in settled dust.

Approaching the chest which held his clothes, I find the pouch he once used to take treats to baby Gestans. My head fills with his smile as he ran to their dens with this soft pouch tied around his waist.

Nodding, I leave his room, closing the door behind me. My feet thud heavily on the stairs. In my absence, Krona righted the chairs around the table, and I climb atop one, now.

Looping the belt of the pouch around the sword, I let the cross guard keep it steady. I step up onto the table, feeding the belt through a gap in the center of the chandelier. A tine sticks up right where the antlers meet, as if made to hold this.

I hang the belt from the antler, letting it run down between them. The pouch flaps against the bleached side of the blade.

"Ready?" Krona asks.

I nod, and he pulls the chain. It clanks through hoops on the wall and the ceiling, and the chandelier rises, Efsi's sword swaying gently beneath it.

***

With hands linked, Krona and I climb from the canoe onto the craggy island downriver from our village. The moons shine overhead, peeking out among the rays of a setting sun. A knot forms in my chest, but I choke it back. I've done this duty before, lighting the pyre of death, the pyre of parting and searching.

But I've never done this for so many.

Carefully, I retrieve Efsi's bones from the boat and lay them upon the stones near the waterline. He rests near the shore with all the others who fell in The Descent of Man. In the center of the isle, our fallen brethren of The

Awakening lie, wrapped in cloth and reverently stacked.

But his partner's head rests near his skull.

They go together.

Flowers decorate the corpses, and strings of beads drape over them, though not enough to truly celebrate their lives. I settle the final strand of beads, the final blossom, upon Efsi's bones and step back with Krona.

We stand in the water, gentle waves lapping at our knees. He takes my hand, and I pull in a deep breath, trying to push air past the lump in my throat as my gaze rakes over our Lost Ones.

The image burns itself into my memory, and a tear slides over my cheek. My gaze comes to rest on Efsi's bones, the root of all he was.

My stomach clenches, and my heart twists. A deep breath does its level best to steady me.

With trembling hands, I reach for the bone dagger at my hip. Krona digs in his pocket for the fire stick. We kneel at the shore, cool water soaking into our robes, and he holds the fire stick near Efsi's flowers. As I position the blade of my dagger at its top, our Tribe begins a lonesome melody, humming softly.

I take a deep breath, Efsi's smile drifting through my mind, and strike. A spark leaps onto the flowers, settling within them. Pristine blue petals curl inward, wrapping up on themselves. They shrivel as embers form along their edges, glowing bright orange.

Exhaling, I rise to my feet, tugging Krona along with me.

Flames lick the leaves. They reach for the beads, gleaming silver in the dying light. Shadows reach across bones and bodies, but even those shadows can't hide these deaths from our sensitive eyes. The fire spreads, jumping from one bouquet to another, and the humming behind us builds.

I sheath my dagger, but I don't turn away, don't climb into the canoe as I usually would. My eyes trace the edges of Efsi's skull, but my mind fills with his beautiful turquoise eyes. My gaze dips to his teeth as the fire crackles over him, and I hear his laugh, deep and booming. Blue and silver beads melt, dripping over his ribs, but I see the man who cradled injured animals to his chest.

As the fire catches, melting his bones and sending them dripping onto the rocks beneath, I take a step back. But still, I don't turn away.

The water laps at my knees, my thighs, sticking the soft fabric of my robes to my skin, but I watch the smoke as it drifts into the sky. In it, I see Efsi at the edge of our fields as we rode back from battle, see a child he hefted to his shoulders before a harvest to see the fields better.

Tears roll over my cheeks, dripping to join the dark water moving around me. My heart twists in my chest, and my stomach plummets.

I'll never see him again.

And yet, I'll never stop seeing him. Everywhere I look, every time I close my eyes… He's there.

A sob shakes me, bursting from my lips, and I close my eyes. Gritting my teeth, I try to block out the sight of him falling at the hands of Soldiers from the stars.

Heat builds as the fire reaches to claim other bodies, sending tendrils out to the cloth wrappings and the bouquets spread over the island. My skin grows hot with it, but I can't open my eyes to see it, can't move away from it. My eyelids glow a horrendous shade of orange, too bright as the fire reclaims the remnants of my brother.

Our people's voices shift from a hum to a soft susurration, drifting in and out. It reaches for me, begging me to join them.

Krona squeezes my hand, whispering, "We should get back across."

But how can I leave him?

How can I walk away from him?

A blade twists within me, and I shake my head.

But the fire only grows.

The smoke burns my nostrils. On the shore behind us, the Tribe returns to a low hum, and a few people lift their voices, separating from the rest of the Tribe.

"Hoo mai taenruta," they sing. *Your sound will go on.*

I part my lips, aching to issue my brother's sound, but no one will hear me, no one will join my voice in this moment. This night, they offer solidarity in a different way.

The humming intensifies, and a few members of our Tribe take up their instruments. The Saileka players start, sliding sleek metallic rods over the taut, dried vines of Saken plants. Deep, luxurious sounds caress the night air.

I open my eyes, and the pyre before me takes my breath away. It claims the whole island, reaching up into the sky. The mass of bodies flickers in and out of view, hiding behind streaks of orange and red, dancing among vibrant tongues of blue and purple flames.

Dropping my gaze to the dark waters, I watch the reflection of the inferno on shifting waves. My heart shrivels within me, but I step back.

Krona and I climb into our canoe as our people sing, "Joo taeparnam hoo." *We will remember you.*

I stare at the flames, rowing absentmindedly toward shore. Krona's eyes rake over me, laced with concern, but I keep my eyes on the melting bones and burning bodies visible over his shoulders. Ash drifts into the sky, shining a brilliant silver in the moonlight.

Our canoe bumps ashore, scraping up the bank to the tune of gentle humming. Water splashes our ankles as we step out, feet landing upon the slick rocks of the river's edge.

Our people desert the hum, voices coming together to sing the next line, and Krona and I join them. "Joo taeka hoo coom joo." *We will carry you with us.*

Finally, I turn from the pyre, but only because I must. There are so many marks to be given this night, and we must go first.

Rows of soft white clothes lay upon the ground, interspersed with torches that crackle beneath the deep, haunting sound of our people.

My shadow reaches over the nearest cloth, painting it a darker shade than my blood will.

Two Memory Markers approach, white gowns billowing around them. I greet them with a solemn nod, then glance up and down the river.

My parents sit cross-legged upon the massive white cloth to my right. Kala and Melnara sit upon the cloth to my left. Their Memory Markers wait, gazing at the pyre, until our Marks have begun.

More cloths line the riverbank, far more than at any other ceremony to date. Every Memory Marker and every apprentice left alive waits to do their work. Bowls of ink rest on every cloth, nestled beside bowls of needles, the same needles the Humans made from harvested samples of our bones.

As Krona and I step onto our cloth, we sing the last of our lines. "Ar joo maiverns, hoo darten taenruta." *In our voices, your life will go on.*

Our Tribe carries the song forward, but until our Marks are done, we'll sing no more. We settle upon the cloth, facing each other and crossing our legs beneath ourselves. Our knees touch, and our hands join, resting between us.

The Memory Markers approach, settling in at my sides. I take a deep breath, slipping my hands from Krona's when they reach for me. They take up their needles and dip them in ink. With great precision, they begin their work, piercing the skin at my wrists over and again.

They draw a vivid blue line across the circle, denoting a death by battle. I grit my teeth against the pain, concentrating on the soft song of my people, and the feel of Krona's hands on my knees, offering me his strength.

Dipping their needles in a darker ink, the Memory Markers fill in the vivid blue circle of my brother's life with black. Tears fall in earnest, but not for the physical pain. Voice pinched, I breathe out his sound. Its echo flows from my parents' lips, my sister's lips, then Krona's and Melnara's, and I draw comfort from it.

My chest caves in, hollowed by this loss.

The Memory Markers finish these simple Marks, but they're not done with me yet. They rise to their feet. One moves to kneel behind me, the other behind Krona. I meet his gaze, nodding with brows furrowed and lips turned down.

Gently, I unfasten the buttons of my robe, letting it fall to my hips, and Krona does the same. My hands tremble against my skin as I pull my hair forward over my shoulders. The loose strands tickle my collarbones, my breasts.

The Marks of the Awakening will take a long time. To put a black line down our spines with three horizontal lines reaching out over our ribs, all outlined with vivid blue, they'll be working for hours, just on us.

And there are so many Marks to make.

My heart aches at the strain the Memory Markers will face, the days and weeks of work ahead of them, ahead of us all. I take a deep breath, holding Krona's gaze. Deep lines mar his forehead, and the flames flicker in his mint green eyes. One corner of his lips turns up.

The Memory Marker presses a needle to my back. I exhale as she taps the needle, driving ink into my skin.

Chapter Forty Seven

Novay

Rone

Nine days to go

I clamor into bed, fingers twitching and wings fluttering restlessly. Again, I send a message to Reginald. And again, I wait. My heart leaps into my throat, choking me as I beg for a response.

This isn't like him.

He's never gone so long without sending a message back, even if only to say he couldn't talk. My stomach drops, and I wonder if they hurt him.

In the blink of an eye, I seek out the video and audio feeds from his room. The video splays across my wall, and my blood runs cold.

He lies there on the bed, unmoving. His chest rises and falls with steady, even breaths. It almost looks like he's asleep.

But the bandages wrapped around his head tell me the truth.

I raise a hand to my mouth, covering the choked sob that seeps out of me.

What did they do to him?

I rotate the image as I sit up, peering at the image of him. He looks so helpless and broken, so small and fragile. Another sob wracks my body, and I lean my head against the wall.

"What did they do to you?" I whisper, voice hoarse.

But no answer finds me.

Salty tears trickle over my cheeks, onto my lips. I clench my hands into fists, gritting my teeth to stifle the agony sweeping through me, but it's so much bigger than I am.

What did they do?

Desperate for an answer, I check Reginald's experiments for the day, but fear slithers through me. I have to see this, have to know.

But do I want to?

Can I handle it?

Pulling in a shuddering breath, I move the image of Reginald's unconscious form higher on my wall with a thought, the alonarium bending to my commands. Beneath it, I display footage from his testing room.

It appears normal enough. He sits in his chair in the center of the room. Guards stand in each corner.

I brace myself for the scene about to play out on the wall of that room, viewed in miniature right before my eyes. But no broken video footage appears.

Only numbers.

Only data.

I dig a little deeper and access the file they displayed for him. I slide the footage of his day to the side, analyzing the information as he reads it alongside me. Occasionally, my gaze drifts to the current feed from his room, in hopes that he'll move or wake.

The physical profiles of around 500 pregnant women sit before me. My heart lurches.

Why...

Off to the side, Reginald explodes, screaming and punching the wall. The data falls away, no longer able to hold my interest.

I watch him yell at the wall, watch him berate them.

"No… You can't take her," he whispers. His voice hardens, turning gravelly as he repeats, "You can't take her!"

Ignoring the data on my wall, I watch in horror as the Drennar tells him that they need his daughter, they need Olivia, for an experiment. My heart shatters within me, and a violent fury seizes hold of Reginald. It sends him spiraling, charging the beast that looms in the corner.

Fear grips me.

"Please, don't hurt him," I beg, but sobs cut off my words.

Because I've seen the aftermath of this particular experiment. Reginald's unconscious form still lies in his bed, splayed across my wall.

Brave or foolish or desperate, maybe all three, he hisses, "You can't take her. You can't experiment on her! We had an agreement. I cooperated. You put me through hell, but I cooperated!"

"We make no agreements with inferior beings. Your substitution was acceptable merely because you promised to cooperate, which made our task easier. Had there been an agreement, you violated it when you seduced a Drennar, no doubt in an attempt to leverage a more pleasant experiment for yourself."

"I fell in love with her! I didn't seduce her!"

I gasp, and the world spins beneath me. For a brief moment, everything centers on that admission, spoken from the lips of my now-unconscious love.

"Love does not exist," the Drennar says, voice perfectly even.

But I know better. His mechanical attempts to explain love away and all the dismissals of a deal Reginald believed in fall on deaf ears as I search for Olivia's data on the wall.

My blood freezes.

Elevated hormone levels that correspond with early pregnancy…

And a collection date.

Ten days never seemed so soon.

No…

Nine days now.

Beside the data, Reginald attacks one of his guards, ineffective as it may be. But then, he goes for the gills. The Drennar jerks away, knocking Reginald's head against a wall, maybe by accident, maybe not.

My stomach drops, and I let out a cry of anguish. Reginald falls, smashing his head against his chair, and fresh tears cascade over my cheeks.

My world fractures, and my heart implodes.

But the monsters in the corners move slowly, evenly. Fans of blue light sweep over

Reginald's unconscious body, so cold, so unfeeling in their analysis.

"Please help him," I plead, but my words don't matter. I can't change the past. My stomach roils at the idea of begging these heartless things, and my blood boils.

But still, I beg, choking on the words, sobbing and shaking.

His blood stains the floor, drips freely from his head. I bring my fist to my mouth, biting my thumb to stop myself from screaming.

The one who smashed his head against a wall bends to collect him, sending signals to the alonarium walls. A small square opens up, filled with all the trappings of Human medical care.

I want them to use our medicine, to really heal him. Silently, I cry for them to do so.

But I know they won't.

For the sake of the experiment, for the sake of pushing his boundaries further.

Thoroughly sickened, I shut the feed off, unable to watch him bleed any longer. I clear the

data from my sight, refusing to stare at the names
of the condemned, refusing to think of what the
Drennar will find when they try to access
Termana.

They'll know the data we've been sending
back and rerouting throughout the Human world
was forged. Olivia's vitals and Link, those of the
other Soldiers and Daen Tribe, may seem like
they're on Termana and the stations, but if the
Drennar breach Atlantis, they'll know.

I jam my hands into my hair, grabbing
great fistfuls. I squeeze tight, rocking back and
forth with my eyes scrunched shut.

Everything's falling apart…

Tears roll over my cheeks, and sobs rattle
my ribs, shaking my entire body.

I need to send a message to Olivia, to
Lustran and the others, to Croon on Termana. But
the message to Croon will take days to arrive.

And the one to Olivia…

My heart freezes, and another sob
threatens to unravel me. Just days ago, I could

have reached her within hours. But now that they're on Regonia?

Routing the message through the transmitters spread across the planet is too much of a risk. Every transmitter is another chance for the message to be intercepted.

Everything is falling apart…

I take my only option, deciding to bounce the message off the transmitter on Meruna to get it around Regonia.

But it'll take three days.

We don't have time for this.

My breath catches as I realize the full gravity of the situation. Olivia mentioned plans for the transmitters on Regonia.

Please, don't completely disable them.

I search back through the messages we've shared, but all she said was that she planned to block Drennar access to Daen Tribe and the surrounding Tribes.

But how?

I send a quick message, just bare bones, just the most basic details, hoping a small message will sneak past her blocks or reach her faster. My brain tells me I'm being foolish, that it doesn't work that way, but desperation makes me hope for it, regardless.

Scrubbing the tears away, I enlarge the view of Reginald's room. I touch the part of the wall that shows his face, his hand, and my throat grows tight.

Please, wake up.

Please, be okay.

I need you. I need to talk to you.

Swallowing hard, I try to steady my shaking hands.

I love you.

Chapter Forty Eight

Regonia

Ricardo

Eight days to go

Waking with Olivia in my arms, I breathe deeply of the Regonian air. My lungs expand with it, drinking in the smells of an actual planet. Rich, earthy scents fill the home Krona and Tenna invited us into last night, *their* home. The sounds of people settling into the place echo up the stairs, barely audible through the thick door.

Rolling onto my back, I slide one arm out amongst the covers, marveling at the size of the bed, the weight of the furs draped over me. If this is what they were used to, how they ever got a good night's sleep in our tiny beds is beyond me.

Olivia nestles in closer, one hand slipping down my chest and over my waist. She grips my hip, pulling herself tighter against me.

I draw in a contented breath, but sweet smoke drifts in through the window, reminding me that beyond this room, beyond the little world I occupy with Olivia, grief still rules this place. I strain my ears, trying to pick out the crackle of the fire, but the island lies too far from here.

Glancing at my Link, I check the time, and a wave of adrenaline courses through me. I carefully extricate myself from Olivia's embrace and spring from the bed. Gazing out the window, I pull my clothes on.

In the distance, the island smolders, but it doesn't look how I expect it to. No bones or charred cloths, no roasting embers rest upon the rocks. Instead, the craggy piece of land shines in the light, as if coated in melted metal. Char marks scar the surface where flowers burned and cloth scorched, but a layer of silver coats the porous stone, gleaming bright and reflecting the morning light.

Already, a crowd gathers near the blankets, preparing to begin the mourning and marking all over again. Everyone who has yet to be marked, as well as everyone who has been marked and can be spared from the efforts to rebuild, will attend today.

The Memory Markers take their places near their cloths, no longer pristine white.

Droplets of blood decorate them, spattering the once-pure surface with the grief of those already marked. The very robes of the Memory Markers mirror the cloths they stand beside, speckled with vivid crimson.

Drawing a deep breath, I spur myself into action. I have too much to do today to stand around staring out the window.

Moving to the bed, I drop a tender kiss on Olivia's forehead. She stirs, mumbling groggily.

"I'll be back soon," I say. "I have to go to the ship before today's ceremony starts."

"Do you need me to go with?" Olivia asks, wiping long, silky black tresses out of her face.

I touch her cheek, staring into hazel eyes. "No, you can sleep a little longer," I say, adding in a gentle smile and a reminder that the techs brought everyone out of their cryo-beds successfully. "I'm just going for a debriefing with the Specialists."

She nods, mumbling something to the effect of, "Sounds thrilling."

With a gentle laugh, I drop a soft kiss on her bare collarbone and draw back. She smiles at me, offering up a small wave in the form of fluttering fingers.

***

Aboard the ship, I sit with the Specialists, preparing before we address all our Soldiers. With everything decided well in advance, we need only gather our courage. None of us expected our promotions. None of us expected to lead so soon.

Least of all, me.

After years of avoiding the limelight and undue responsibility, my hands tremble at the thought of commanding so many. But the men and women around me look to me with respect in their eyes and smiles on their faces. They offer their support, gladly falling behind me as we leave our conference room.

We arrange ourselves along the catwalk, looking down at the Soldiers assembled in the cargo bay. Every single one of them salutes us, and the weight of this endeavor settles on my shoulders.

Just remember, they follow Tenna and Krona first.

I'm not leading an entire army myself. More qualified people are here.

A steadying breath guides me, and I begin, explaining the ceremony that will pass this day and the beginning phase of it that they missed last night while getting checked out for adverse cryo-symptoms. I remind them that they'll be responsible for helping Daen Tribe rebuild while I go with Olivia, Tenna, Krona, and a few select others up the mountain, and that in our absence, they'll take their commands from Kala.

The woman in question waits on the ramp, and I gesture to her. Not that they could have missed her. She stands, a dark shadow silhouetted by the morning sun. White fabric flows all around her, glowing at its edges as the sunlight burns around it.

Her gown's neckline plunges low from its halter straps to her navel. Many braids pull her black hair back from her face, hanging freely behind her back. Towering over every Human here, she lets her eyes roam over them.

I gesture for her to say what she will, and she wastes no time.

"We have a lot of work to do. We must rebuild, and then, we'll ready you to fight alongside us," she says, voice carrying easily through the large space.

"For rebuilding, there will be a small group of us working hand in hand with you, and those numbers will grow as the days pass and more Marks are administered. But for now, for the sake of our ceremonies, your leaders expressed that you are to handle the bulk of the initial reclamation."

Her voice doesn't waver as she says, "It won't be easy work, especially for you. We're made of tougher things than you and can handle more physical strain." Softening, she adds, "Do your best, but please, don't hurt yourselves in the name of penance. There is nothing for you to atone for. The wrongs we must right were not your doing."

She finds my gaze, and a small smile slips over her lips.

Addressing the Soldiers once more, she adds, "In the interest of eliminating any shock, given the ordeal of cryo-sleep, today will be a day for observation. You'll see our world, our grief. At the ceremony, you'll meet our Inerans. Now, let us waste not. The Memory Markers will begin soon, and your Ambassadors will want to be present."

Kala looks to me and inclines her head. Turning, she descends the ramp with the sunlight sparkling on her dark, grey skin. The Mark of The Awakening practically glows against her back, electric blue shining brilliantly, made all the more striking by the black that it encapsulates.

***

Daen Tribe stands before us, framed by the smoke that still rises from the island. Those still awaiting their Marks wear flowing white robes. Those who were marked last night wear soft white clothes that bare their backs.

Teal grasses swirl around their thighs, reaching to my waist and brushing the fabric of my own robe gently against my skin. Sunlight shimmers on the dark waters rushing behind them, stealing my breath away, bordering on unbelievable.

But the pain shining in the tears that streak their faces is something I never would have painted across this moment, proving this to be reality.

Turning to gaze at Olivia, I take her hand in mine. Her skin glows against the white fabric of her robe, and her dark braid drapes over her shoulder. She steps closer, leaning against me, and warmth spreads through me.

I marvel at the fit of our garments, trying to figure out how and why Krona and Tenna found them for us in the night. But Tenna speaks, drawing my attention outward.

"As you know, our journey here was not without help. Daen Tribe depended so dearly upon the honor of our Ambassadors that it can scarcely be expressed, and they have quickly become family. There are many who helped us, many who *will* help us in the coming battles, but without Ricardo's sense of justice and courage, without Olivia's intellect and refusal to back down, we wouldn't be here," Tenna says.

Beside her, Krona's chest puffs out with pride. They look upon us with warmth in their gazes, and Tenna waves one hand, gesturing for us to step forward.

We're family.

I cast my mind over everything, heart breaking at the thought of being part of a real family, one that doesn't tear itself to pieces at every turn.

I cast a tentative glance at Olivia.

Offering up a slow, barely discernible shrug, she mouths, "What's happening?"

But I have no answer for her.

The grass parts around us as we step forward.

"We would like to welcome you into Daen Tribe. The two of you have suffered alongside us, feeling every loss acutely. If you wish to be Marked as part of our Tribe, if you wish to be Marked for The Awakening, you may."

My jaw falls open.

"It is a painful process," Tenna says. "Getting the Marks of our Tribe, as well as those of the Awakening, will take the better part of a day, and you'll have to take breaks. But the honor is yours if you want it."

My arm shakes as Olivia nods vigorously. "Yes," she says. "Yes. I want to be part of Daen Tribe."

Mind spinning, I try to grasp the potential here.

I can be part of Daen Tribe. I can be part of a real family, part of a society that isn't full of backstabbers and corruption.

Tenna smiles at Olivia. "Since we'll need you to go with us into the mountains, you'll be Marked today."

Tenna and Krona turn their gazes to me.

"Ricardo?" Krona asks. "You can take a couple of days to consider it, but if you decide to take this honor, it must be done within a few suns in order for you to heal before our journey."

Closing my mouth, I swallow. I nod, not quite trusting my voice.

But how can I not speak? How can I not thank them for this?

"Thank you," I croak. Clearing my throat, I repeat, "Thank you. I'd love to be part of Daen Tribe."

All around us, a song of joy erupts, breaking up the sorrow of the ceremony to come. Krona and Tenna smile at us, eyes glowing with pride. Beams of light sparkle on their skin.

"We welcome you," Tenna says. She gestures to the cloth at her feet, stained with flecks and speckles of crimson.

Butterflies fill my stomach, and my heart soars. Squeezing Olivia's hand, I look at her, look at the glow in her hazel eyes. Together, we step forward onto the white cloth, settling in for our Marks.

Chapter Forty Nine
Regonia

Olivia

My shoulders rise and fall as Regonian air sweeps through me. My heart flutters, and my hands tremble.

One of the Memory Markers, a woman with soft grey features and pastel blue hair braided up into a bun, settles on my left. A man with wrinkles carved into skin the shade of dusk kneels on my other side. He reaches for Ricardo's arm as the woman takes mine in her massive hands.

"Remember, Sahveera. Be soft in your Mark. Their skin is not like ours," he says.

A nervous flutter moves within me, but the woman nods sagely. "Yes, Maivala," she answers without hesitation.

To us, the man, Maivala, says, "This will take a long time and is not an easy feat for the body to endure. We will stop as often as you need. We'll take breaks to stretch our hands and backs, but if those are not frequent enough, please, be strong enough to speak for your body."

I nod, and so does Ricardo. We join our free hands on our ankles, knees touching as we sit crisscross applesauce. His thumb moves slowly over mine, and despite the nerves twisting my stomach, I smile.

Grass sways in a gentle breeze, shifting on all sides at eye level. Here in the center of this blood-stained cloth with my hand resting in his, with Regonians poised to Mark my body, I feel… right.

This feels like home.

More so than Termana or Odyssey ever did.

Only the pilot seat of Sparrow ever felt close to this, but this… is still better.

Tears slide over my cheeks, because here, right now, I'm part of something.

I have a family that loves me now.

Briefly, I wonder about my father, about the few messages I've exchanged with him, and I hope to build something there.

But here, right now, I have a family.

Smiling wide I gaze into Ricardo's molten amber eyes. Tears trickle over my lips, and their salt stains my tongue.

All around us, Daen Tribe sings and hums, reminding me so much of a song I heard years ago. My Link digs up the title for me. "Will You Follow Me Into The Dark by Klergy and Mindy Jones. 2021."

But their words are different, speaking instead of carrying someone with them in their voices. A few take up instruments, pulling thin metal rods over vines stretched taut across what might be massive skulls.

The Regonian language fills the air, beautiful and melodic. I shut off my translator, having learned the meaning of these words already. I hum along, closing my eyes as I wait for the Memory Marker to start her work.

Tension builds in my stomach, and I wonder how much the needles will hurt. Tattoos were popular back on Earth, but they're rare on Termana. Without a frame of reference, my mind runs wild, filling the space before the needle bites my skin with a churning stomach.

"Are you ready?" Sahveera asks, soft voice jarring me.

A nervous chuckle escapes me, but I nod.

Draping my arm over her knees, she poises the needle over my wrist. Despite all my resolve not to watch, not to torment myself, I find my eyes drawn to my wrist, to the tiny bone needle pressed against my skin with bright blue ink staining its tip.

Sahveera touches my arm and mumbles in Regonian, and my cochlear implant translates. "Your skin really is soft…" Lifting her gaze to Maivala, she asks, "Should we tap the needles with the stone at all? Or would it be best to just… poke them?"

After a brief inspection of Ricardo's arm, Maivala agrees. "No stones. It would go too deep."

I breathe a sigh of relief as Sahveera nods. She smiles at me and leans over my arm.

A sharp pinch spikes through me as she jabs the needle into my skin, and I gasp. What she calls a simple 'poke' is more than that. Regonian strength drives the needle deep into my skin, planting the ink with a jolt.

She pauses, looking at the tiny blue dot left behind, then up at me, as if asking if I wish to continue.

And though I'm sure this day will be immensely painful, I want this Mark. I want to be part of Daen Tribe.

I want everyone to know that I have a family.

So, I nod.

With her needle poised once more, Sahveera drives it into my wrist, over and over, starting slow but moving faster as she gauges my resolve and the true density of my skin. I grit my teeth against the pain.

But my smile never falters, and my tears never cease, spilling my joy into the world.

***

Pain and adrenaline course through me. My free hand trembles in Ricardo's grasp, smeared with blood from the tattoo adorning that wrist. Another sharp jab in my other wrist, and I squeeze my eyes shut. Ricardo's grasp tightens as another tap of the needle rocks him.

Short, controlled breaths guide me through another stab. Gritting my teeth, I prepare for the next.

But it never comes.

Opening my eyes, I look to Sahveera. Her hand no longer hovers over my wrist, needle poised to strike. She doesn't sit, curled over my arm.

A smile creases the soft grey skin around her eyes. A young Regonian approaches, wet cloth in hand. A sharp, pungent scent emanates from the rag. She takes it from him and reaches for my arm.

My heart pounds in my chest, but I lift my arm for her.

Ricardo's hand jerks one last time, pulling my eyes to him. Pain crinkles the skin around his eyes, and he presses his lips together. A muscle in his jaw works feverishly.

But his Marks for Daen Tribe are finished, too.

Another rag floats toward us in the hands of yet another young Regonian, and my nose wrinkles at the smell. A sharp sting on my wrist makes me jump, and I forget the smell altogether. My poor, broken skin rebels against the abuse, crying out.

"Sorry," Sahveera says. "We must clean the blood, though."

I nod but can't quite manage words. My jaw locks in place, grinding my teeth together as she wipes the cloth over my skin. The sting quickly becomes cold, and my fingers tingle with the odd sensation.

She releases my arm and reaches for the other. I force my hand to open, to release Ricardo's fingers from my grasp. Offering up my bloody wrist, I brace myself. The cloth brushes my skin, light and gentle, but Sahveera may as well be burning me with a hot poker. The strange liquid pricks my skin with a million needles, then shifts to an icy sensation.

Shivering, I thank the stars above when she pulls the rag away. She uses another rag to wipe her own hands clean, but my gaze slips out of focus, stealing her ritual from my sight.

Tension builds within my stomach, and my heart races. The world around me narrows to a tunnel, and my breathing accelerates.

A large hand sprawls over my back, and I turn quickly, too quickly. My head spins with the effort, but slowly, Tenna's face swims into focus. Dark green eyes peer into mine, laced with concern.

Tenna says, "Sahveera will Mark another while you take a break."

My breath comes hot and fast, broken by the hammering of my heart. I nod, pulling my legs out from under myself. They shake as violently as my hands, and panic wells within me at the prospect of putting weight on them.

But Tenna pushes gently on my shoulder, holding me down. "She'll go to them. They already wait for her on another cloth. Take your time getting up."

Relief washes through me on warm waves.

Turning to face Ricardo, I crumble forward, dropping my head onto my knees. A soft chuckle caresses my ears, and his hands rub my back. He hisses out a breath as the skin of his wrists pulls tight, and he resolves to rest his hands on my ankles, instead.

"This is a long, grueling process," Tenna admits.

I wonder at her strength. She had a far larger Mark done just last night, and she moves freely without a hint of pain. The stench of the rags that Sahveera and Maivala used on our wrists hangs on her though, piquing my curiosity.

"What's on the rags?" I ask, desperate for a distraction from the pain still writhing through me.

"Kaelno oil. We consulted with Dr. Sullivan last night to make sure it wouldn't have any adverse effects on the two of you and to see if it will have the same beneficial effects. It prevents infections. If applied to an injury, it has a mild numbing effect," she says.

Krona's voice drifts out of the void around me, alerting me to his presence. "Dr. Sullivan ran a lot of tests. It should have all the same effects. We just don't know how long the numbing effect takes to set in. For us, it takes a while. But your bodies may not require so much exposure."

"Thank fucking goodness…" I mumble into my knees.

My companions chuckle, and Ricardo's hands move up and down my calves. Lifting my head, I see the lines around his eyes have already eased and his jaw no longer clenches. Only then do I realize that my own pain no longer curls my toes or pushes my heart along faster than it should ever beat.

I hold my wrists up, raking my eyes over the fresh Marks. Three electric blue bands encircle my wrists, vibrant against my smooth, tawny skin. A single circle rests atop my wrist, and another marks the underside.

I'm part of Daen Tribe, now.

I smile, marveling at the wonder of having a place in a world. A tear pricks at my eyes.

I belong somewhere.

I lift my eyes to Ricardo, only to find him analyzing his own Marks. A wistful smile decorates his face, shining in eyes that sparkle like liquid gold in the sunlight.

"Your wrists may face a bit more pain still," Krona says.

My eyes find him, brows reaching for each other in concern. I trace the Marks on his wrists, on Tenna's wrists. They possess tattoos near their elbows with lines connecting them to the Marks of Daen Tribe, but we won't get those.

Those denote their rank as Inerans.

"What else is there?" I ask.

But my eyes find the small circle on the back of Tenna's hand. Black with a blue ring around it, pierced by a horizontal blue line.

Krona doesn't have that one…

"We are typically Marked for our losses," Tenna says, nodding at the circle my eyes found.

"If you would like to be Marked for yours, you may. Your mother," she says, looking at me, then looks at Ricardo to add, "and your brother were immoral and far from honorable." She keeps a snarl from her face, though just barely. "But their lives and deaths have affected you."

"Their Mark would be different," Krona adds, pale eyes softening. "It wouldn't look like the one Tenna bears for Efsi. He died an honorable death, fighting to protect our Tribe. A traitor's death is marked with a simple, black ring to show the wound they inflicted upon their loved one."

A deep breath puffs out his bare chest, and he sucks his lips in.

"That Mark doesn't have to be done immediately. Usually, we like to allow our people time to cope before giving those, but…" he looks to Tenna.

"It would be best," she says. "We'll have to journey into the mountains as soon as possible, and you need time to heal."

My eyes fall to my knees, but I reach for Ricardo's hands. I squeeze them gently, nodding as I pull in a deep breath.

This is right.

I should *be Marked for her treachery.*

Tenna puts a tender hand to my back, and I glance at her. She stares into my eyes for a moment, seeing far deeper than I'd like.

"This doesn't blame you for what she did," Tenna says. "It just lets people know you've been hurt, you've been betrayed. It lets them know that you were strong enough not to be like her."

Something rips open within me, and tears well up in my eyes. My throat grows thick, and I try to swallow, try to force words out, but none come.

Desperately, I try to blink the tears away.

Tenna's voice softens, and she touches my cheek. "You don't have to hide, especially not here. Anyone who sees the Mark of her death will understand not only your strength, but your pain and the battle you fight within."

"Which reminds me," Krona says. "You survived the battle within. There's a Mark for that, as well."

He turns his arm, showing a thick blue line on the outside of his bicep with a thin black line contained within it. "You've certainly earned this one."

Tears pour over my cheeks, and sobs shake my body.

"Everyone will know how weak I was…" I mumble, words half-choked by the lump in my throat.

Through blurred vision, I see strands of inky hair move back and forth as Krona shakes his head. "They'll know how strong you are to keep going."

Weeping openly, I fight the urge to fall into myself, to crumble into a heap and block the world out with my arms over my head. But a sudden movement stretches the skin of my wrists, sending a jolt of fresh pain through me.

Yet, it draws my eyes to the Marks on my wrists, to the family I have now. With trembling hands and a stomach churning with fear, I reach for Ricardo, for Tenna and Krona. They all reach back, and my breathing hitches. Fresh sobs rack my body as their arms wrap around me.

***

I stare into Ricardo's eyes, amber sparkling in the light of the moons. Curled on my side, I try not to move, not to disturb the new tattoos. My bicep throbs, and my wrists ache. My back feels stiff and sore. Nose wrinkling at the stinging scent of the Kaelno oil, I wait for it to ease my pain.

But I smile.

Sliding my hand over the sheet, I slip my fingers over Ricardo's, lacing them together on the bed between us. We don't move together tonight, don't wrap arms around each other for fear of brushing sensitive skin.

But we're here. We're together.

And somehow, that means more.

Dark lashes fan out over his cheeks as he chuckles. My breath leaves me when his eyes find mine once more, glowing gold.

"Is this real?" he whispers.

"Dreams don't hurt," I whisper, glancing at the thick line tattooed on my bicep.

Desperate for his golden gaze, my eyes find him again. A deep breath puffs out his chest, and a single lock of dark hair falls over his face. Reluctant to release my hand, he blows at it, laughing when it only falls further, landing over his eye.

My smile widens, and I pull my hand from his. My fingers trace his skin, moving slowly as I brush the hair back behind his ear. I let my hand linger, resting my palm on his cheek. Gentle warmth moves through me as his eyes soften.

He touches my elbow, careful to avoid any tender areas, and my heart burns for him. Oceans of molten rock move through me, and three little words burn behind my lips, searing my tongue and begging me to let them out.

I swallow thickly, trying to push them back.

What if I ruin this?

What if he isn't there, doesn't feel that way yet?

What if he could never feel that way for me?

My mind replays the words his friend, Francis, launched at me. My heart plumbs its darkest depths, pulling forth all the things that make him too good for me, all the ways that I'm bad for him.

My drinking and my suicide attempt. My selfishness. My blindness to what my own mother was capable of, my inability to stop her. My depression and my broken little heart.

But those words weigh heavy on my tongue, hovering somewhere between bitter and sweet. I test them out, weighing them in my mind.

I love you.

He deserves those words… But from someone better.

My heart stutters, and my chest collapses. But Ricardo's eyelids hang heavy, hiding amber and light from my view, hiding my furrowed brows from his gaze.

His breathing slows, and his eyes flutter.

Pulling my hand back from his cheek, I twine our fingers together on the bed once more. He grips my hand, ever careful.

"Goodnight," he whispers.

As his eyes fall shut, I sigh.

"Goodnight, Ricardo."

My eyes trace the lines of his face, roaming in shadows on olive skin. Those three little words play in my mind, begging me to whisper them now that he's asleep, to air them in the dark of the night.

But I clamp my lips shut.

Chapter Fifty
Novay

Reginald

Seven days to go

Darkness and pain consume everything. Silence screams all around me. My eyes flutter open, but bright light splits my skull. Groaning, I slam my eyes shut once more, bringing my hands up to cover them for good measure.

Why...

Why does it hurt so much?

I try desperately to remember, but only bits and pieces float through the darkness toward me. A wall of letters and numbers blurs in my mind, losing all shreds of meaning. Drennar stand over me in my memory, shifting like a reflection on water.

Rage curls my hands into fists, pressing them against my eyes, but I don't know why I'm so angry. My heart hammers violently in my chest, but it makes no sense.

I rub my hands over my face, only to find a bandage on my forehead and lightning bolts of pain waiting beneath it. The bandage shifts as I jerk my hands away, tugging at the back of my skull, and fireworks explode across my eyelids.

And it all comes back.

Olivia's pregnant.

My mouth goes dry. The floor falls out from under me, pushing my heart into my throat.

She's pregnant…

And they're coming for her.

Impotent rage boils within me, and a scream rips its way up my throat. Hoarse from disuse, my voice cracks and shatters as I yell. My fists slam down against the mattress, but the motion shakes me, sending waves of nausea rolling through me.

Turning onto my side, regretting the movement all the while, I heave, but nothing comes up. A needle in my arm jabs deeper, and I roll back, hating the worlds and everything they contain.

"Why is this happening?!" I shout into the void of my room, feeling the words echo back at me in the emptiness.

I can't even do anything!

I can't help her. I can't warn her. I can't even fucking move!

I grit my teeth, grinding them together. My head pounds, and my heart races. Desperation fills me, but I can't assuage it, can't save my baby girl.

I can't help her.

Realization dawns on me.

I can't.

But Rone can.

Sending out a desperate plea, I beg her to help, to warn them. Only at the last second do I remember to use our private channel, and cold waves of fear wash over me at the thought of how badly I almost messed up.

I need to calm down.

I'm only going to make this worse.

Fighting every synapse in my body, I force myself to wait for her reply, to hold still for the love of anything good. My jaw locks against a scream, barely holding it in. My nails carve divots into my palms, so I stretch my fingers out, wiggling them to try to ease the tension.

Only then do I notice the soft, subtle ping of a message from Rone, waiting for me. Or rather, several messages.

I let them all play in order, and her sweet words of a morning spent wishing for some time together don't soothe me quite as well as they would any other time. Updates on the upcoming arrival of some newly emotional Drennar cascade over me in waves of tedium, and I hate myself for feeling that way, hate how much I belittle such an important step in our plan.

Finally, a touch of concern seeps into her voice as she asks if I'm okay. The next message, more urgent, begs me wake up, to live. Tears streak over my cheeks, pooling in my ears as I listen to the strain in her voice, the pain laced throughout her words.

Another message, the last message, plays, telling me that a message has been sent to Olivia, but that it won't reach her for a few days. I check the date, groaning when I see that it hasn't reached her yet.

I need her to know. I need her to be okay, to take steps to protect herself.

They're coming for her. They're probably almost there.

Ice water flows through my veins.

They're almost to Termana.

If they get in, if they breach Atlantis, they'll know Olivia and the Regonians left.

My heart plummets as our careful plan threatens to shatter beneath me, and I scream, hating how helpless I am to stop any of this.

I can't keep them from discovering Atlantis or breaking it. Can't keep them from taking my daughter.

Everything I've done…

Everything I thought I accomplished in coming here…

A breath rushes out of me, caving my chest in as it leaves. Silent tears pour over my cheeks.

Was it a mistake?

They're going to take her anyway. Would she have been happy here if they'd brought her before?

What will they do to her now?

Shame burns me, but my mind unfurls, sending images of a life I could have prevented skittering through my thoughts like dropped marbles.

Olivia splayed out on a table, her baby taken.

Olivia watching them torment the child, crying openly.

The child, my grandchild, isolated as I've been, abandoned to its own devices to grow as a lonely, wild thing.

The idea of a grandchild used to fill me with pride, but now… Dread seeps into me at the thought of a poor, defenseless child falling into the clutches of the Drennar.

What would they do to it?

Ice water rushes through me, and my nails dig into my palms again. Sobs rattle my ribs, shaking me and sending my head swimming with pain.

A soft ping shatters my thoughts, and waves of relief wash through me. I open the message, desperate for any word Rone might spare for me, desperate to hear her voice, to see her face.

The backs of my eyelids light up with her dark hair, her shining eyes. Her wings spread behind her, and her hands steeple at her mouth.

Shaking her head, she whispers, "Reginald…"

Her voice breaks, and my nerves wind tight as I brace for whatever horror may have her so upset. But what more can I take?

Her hands go to the sides of her face, sliding fingertips into her hair.

"I was so worried. I didn't know what to do. They were only using your medicine, not ours, and it's so bad. I didn't know if you'd make it, but you did!" Tears stream over her cheeks, and she says, "I even prayed to the Human gods. All of them. I just…"

She pulls in a deep breath, lungs hitching with a sob. "I'm so happy you're awake. I thought I was going to lose you. I just… I can't lose you."

Heart faltering, I suck my lips in. My chest grows tight as her words remind me of the one good thing that came out of my time here.

Her.

The image of her shifts as she wipes at the tears in her eyes. "Reginald, I…"

Her gaze lowers, and her mouth moves without sound. She lifts her eyes, looking straight ahead, straight at me, even through all the distance between us.

Trying again, she says, "I love you. I can't lose you. I know this probably isn't the right time for that, but I do, I love you. And I promise, I'll do *everything* that I can to keep Olivia safe. I swear."

"Please, send me a message to let me know you're okay, but only text. They're watching you so closely now. I can't shield your room right now." Her brows furrow, and her shoulders fall. "I'm sorry. I want to talk to you. I wish we could. I need to see you."

Rone runs a hand over one side of her face, then leans into her palm. "I'll keep you updated on everything. I promise."

Her face fades from my eyelids as the message ends.

My lungs implode, and I sob wildly. My mind whirls with pain, yet still, I weep.

Because I can't even send her a proper message back.

I can't do a goddamn thing.

Not without her shielding my room.

Gritting my teeth against the chaos and fury roiling within me, I try to compose a message. After too many steadying breaths, after too many times of replaying her message, my mind latches onto one sentence.

Three words.

"I love you."

I replay that part of her message over and again, listening to the way those words feel on her lips, watching the way they shape her face, the way her eyes glisten and glow as she says them. A fire burns within me.

And suddenly, I know what to tell her.

"I love you. Thank you."

Chapter Fifty One

Regonia

Krona

My heart warms as the Soldiers work side by side with our people, rebuilding and gathering our Vyrtons from the hillsides. Slowly, our homes feel like homes again.

The Golans are brought back within freshly prepared pastures. The massive animals lumber through the fields, long necks stretching up to reach the branches of the Juno trees. My eyes rake over them, brows furrowing as I notice the scars on their thick black hides from disputes with another herd. They're normally so friendly and lively, but these gentle beasts have been pushed to defend themselves in our absence.

Another wound that the Humans responsible will never know about.

Would they even care?

But I already know the answer to that question. All the things they did to us, all their experiments and their war crimes made it clear enough that they only cared about themselves.

Rage fills me, but I push it out, rolling my shoulders. Gazing out at the fields, I suck in a deep breath.

They've paid with their lives.

And our home is being repaired.

My mind sets to work, planning out all the things yet undone, all the steps to repair our village and prepare for winter. In the distance, Tenna approaches, hips swaying beautifully. Her flowing white dress ripples in the wind, blowing out into the turquoise strands of grass around her legs.

I swallow hard, eyes locked on my partner, my Kinera.

We can figure this all out.

The wind catches her hair, sending long, dark tresses flying. My heart stutters, and my breath catches. Her eyes sparkle in the midday light, bringing a smile to my face.

Coming in close, she grasps my waist, pulling me against her. Her hands on my bare skin send my insides fluttering. The grass whips against my calves, battering my loose white trousers as I lean in, pressing my lips to hers.

Tenna smiles, and a fire burns within me, aching to take her hand and tug her back to our keep. I groan as I pull back, tamping down my desire.

I stare into her eyes and say, "Time to talk to Olivia."

We walk, hand in hand, through our village. On all sides, people work together, regardless of species. My heart swells with pride at the sight.

Up ahead, two Regonians lift a fallen branch from a Vaila house, while Humans wrangle the tiny creatures that have been reclaimed into the fence that surrounds it. They huff beneath the weight of the beasts, eyes full of surprise that animals whose shoulders only reach their thighs could weigh so much.

A shorter Soldier struggles to heft one of the creatures. A passing Regonian woman settles the boards she'll repair the Vaila house roof with onto the ground and leans down to lift the Vaila into the Soldier's arms before carrying on with her tasks. Carefully, she moves the planks from one side of the fence to the other, then steps over the cobbled stone wall.

"Oh, you forgot these," the man calls out.

Lifting a clay pot of tapered stone spikes, he hands them to her over the stone wall. She smiles, thanking him, and I marvel at the exchange, glad to see such easy cooperation.

This might actually work.

In my head, I figure an approximate length of time for us to make it up the mountain and back, then double that time to account for negotiations with Taron Tribe. Fear coils in my gut at the prospect of that meeting going badly, because I can't ignore the possibility.

Redirecting my mind to the task at hand, I hope that the coming weeks will give our people time to trust the Humans. I hope it will give the Humans time to adjust to their new companions, their new allies.

Tenna and I should be here with them the whole time, letting them get used to us as their commanders, but I know Taron will want us there. If we want even a sliver of hope in persuading them to join our cause, it has to be us. We can't risk Kala, and we can't send anyone of a lower rank. Not with star-born in tow.

And I can't be sure Taron Tribe won't try to kill Olivia and Ricardo.

We need to be there to keep them safe.

Chapter Fifty Two
Regonia

Olivia

I lounge in Nova's pilot seat, staring out the window at the vast planet before me as I take a break to stretch my hands. My laptop sits on my lap, poised to save lives and destroy worlds. It weighs heavily on me, but the sight beyond the window buoys my spirits.

Footsteps echo through the halls behind me, and I turn in my seat to find Tenna and Krona approaching, smiling warmly. But something akin to anxiety tugs at the corners of their eyes, pulling their shoulders rigid.

Well, as rigid as Regonians ever get. Great posture aside, there's always a certain fluidity in their gait, a graceful expressiveness that I've come to admire.

I watch them for a moment, smiling at their joined hands and the way Krona nudges Tenna softly, chuckling about some comment whispered only for her. She glows, leaning into him as they walk, and the strange anxiety falls from them.

My heart melts.

How could my mother have torn them apart? How could she use them against each other and erase them?

She must have watched them, must have seen how they are together before sending people to abduct them. Didn't it remind her of how she used to be with Dad?

How could she ruin that? How could she live with herself?

Taking a deep breath, I push my thoughts into a deep, dark corner of my mind and say, "Hey. What brings you two into my lair?"

"Your lair?" Tenna asks, cocking her head to the side. "Swikans live in lairs. This isn't exactly a damp, musty burrow along the river. This place is far more fitting for you than a lair."

For some reason, this brings heat to my cheeks, and I dip my eyes to the floor, faltering before what really shouldn't be a compliment.

Deserving something better than some muddy hole isn't much.

But somehow, she seems to mean far more than that. As the Inerans of Daen Tribe duck to maneuver through the bulkhead into the cockpit, eyes tracing the panels of switches and buttons with curiosity and awe, my blush deepens.

How highly do they think of me?

My mind doesn't give me much of a chance to ponder, throwing an answer in my face immediately.

Too highly.

But Cait's words in her last message ring in my head. So, I rebuke my thoughts, correcting them in an attempt to think positively.

They see me better than I see myself. They see reasons for me to be alive, reasons to praise me for what I've done.

I trust their judgment in other things. Why not with this?

I cut my thoughts off before my mind can supply reasons, instead forging ahead with our conversation. "Well, anyway... Is everything okay?"

Krona nods. "We just wanted to see how Atlantis 2.0 was coming along."

"It's just about ready. I should be done with it this afternoon."

"You said this version is different from the one on Termana?" Tenna asks.

"Just a little. It'll still do the same thing, but it's meant to spread from one transmitter, the one that was used to find you, and hop to another and another and another, like a virus."

"Will it work as well as the one on Termana?" Krona asks.

I nod. "Yeah. I just modified it to spread to try and make the Drennar think it could spread to them if they stay in contact with us." A small laugh escapes me. "Here's to hoping, right?"

Krona and Tenna laugh, but they cut it short, sharing a look that makes me nervous.

"Would it be easier," Tenna begins, "or even possible, to just shut them all off?"

Internally, I groan, remembering the same question from the team on Termana. But I understand. And it isn't wholly unexpected.

"They're worth more to us right now with them in working condition," I say. "I get it. Having those transmitters there feels... icky. But the ship has to stay here, right? We can't take it up the mountain?"

They nod, having gone over the fear its presence would elicit from Taron Tribe in detail already. It makes our journey considerably longer and more arduous, but provoking their beliefs regarding the stars would end all negotiations for an alliance before they even start.

"Once we get to the mountains, those transmitters will be the only connection we have with Rone," I say.

The only connection I have with my dad...

Forging ahead, I say, "Atlantis is keeping the Drennar at bay on Termana. They haven't taken a single person, despite years of taking at least one person a month, sometimes more. If they think it's spreading, they may pull back even further. At the very least, it'll give your Tribe privacy to live without someone watching. We might be able to shut them off later, but that would sever your communications with the Human world."

With me…

My heart twists at the thought of losing them, and my breath hitches.

"But for now, we need to *use* the transmitters."

I try to focus on the beauty of the technology we discuss, the intricacies and sophistication of it. I try to focus on the things I could learn if I could take one apart.

But my heart lurches in my chest at the mere prospect of losing this family that I've just found.

"If…" Tenna begins, glancing at Krona, "If we shut them off later, if you decided to stay here, would you mind losing the connection to them?"

Tears prick at the corners of my eyes, and I look up at my friends. "Stay?" I ask, voice breaking.

Krona nods, swallowing before saying, "You're part of Daen Tribe now. If you wish to stay, you're welcome here."

The air rushes from me, and I lift a fist to my mouth as my chest implodes. Nodding vigorously, I set my laptop aside and leap from my chair. Throwing my arms around them, I say, "Thank you." The words come out broken, but they wrap their arms around me, all the same.

"You didn't think we'd just send you away, did you?" Tenna says.

But I hadn't thought about it, hadn't even considered the possibility of staying. I'd just assumed I'd have to go back.

If I survive the mess with the Drennar.

"Then, it's settled," Tenna says, pulling back. She wipes an errant tear from my cheek, smiling at me.

Krona's pale green eyes glitter in the soft light of the cockpit and the sunlight streaming through the window. His lips turn up in a smile.

Every bit of me seems to grow lighter, to glow with the fact that I have a family now, a home. I take a deep breath, soaking it in.

But my brain reminds me of the other reason for leaving the transmitters. The one that may not get such a positive reception.

"There is one other reason for leaving the transmitters on," I say. Settling back into my chair, I spin it to face them.

Exchanging a look, Krona and Tenna kneel, then sit back on their feet.

"I don't know if you'd even notice it, but… Do you feel… connected… to the land here?"

Another glance passes between them, but the looks on their faces tells me that they sense it.

"The alonarium here, it's in everything. It's in the air. It's the reason Humans can't breathe the air without a filter. But it's in everything else, too."

I pause, meeting dark green eyes, then light ones. "It's in you too."

Not seeming to know where I'm going with this, Krona asks, "Can you eat our food?"

The question blindsides me, but I answer, "Yeah, our stomach acid breaks the molecules into elements we can handle."

Refocusing with a shake of my head, I say, "But… the alonarium is very conductive. It's sensitive to even the slightest changes in static electricity. That's why lightning storms are so bad here. You all have a sensitive metal as part of your makeup, and the transmitters work with that. That's part of how they keep tabs on all of you. I just wasn't sure if you'd be able to feel it."

I watch their faces carefully, see the way concern and confusion slither over their features, furrowing brows and tugging at the corners of their lips. They don't know much about tech, having seen it as an abhorrent disease for most of their lives, star-sickness.

So, I explain, "If, at some point in the future, we shut the transmitters down… You might not feel so connected."

Their shoulders fall, and breaths rush from them. My heart twists, hating that I must bear such horrendous news.

Rushing to soften the blow, I add, "I don't know for sure, maybe you still will. You might sense the small electrical impulses within the animals or the slight bit of static in the air. I don't know. But it's something to consider."

Tenna and Krona share a look of too many hard decisions coming too swiftly. Tenna's mouth falls slightly open. Krona's chest puffs out with a deep breath, then deflates.

"Is it a risk you're willing to take?" I ask.

"Nothing is ever simple…" Tenna laments.

My lips turn up in a sympathetic smile. "You don't have to decide right now. We need them for the time being. Who knows? If we survive all of this and successfully tell the Drennar to go jet themselves, maybe you'll have thought of new uses for them by the time we get back to Regonia."

Chuckling, Tenna turns to me. "Is that our plan? We're just going to tell them to go jet themselves?"

"I mean… It's a little more complicated than that," I say with a smile, "but that's what it boils down to."

Krona shakes his head, laughing. "I guess we can discuss what to do with the transmitters on the trek up the mountain. Are you ready to go?"

"Yeah. I don't have much to take with, so packing was pretty easy." I pat the bag near my legs, stashed beneath the desk. "I just have a little more to do, and then I'll pack this baby in there, as well."

I gaze at my laptop protectively, hoping the trip won't damage it. Of course, I could use my Link for basic tasks in a pinch, but nothing about this mess has been basic, so far. I don't expect it to get easier.

"Have you gotten any new messages from Rone?" Tenna asks, tone guarded. "Any with your father present?"

I shake my head, trying to shove away the loss of his face, the loss of the bond I missed out on for so long. But my lips turn downward, all the same.

"Nothing yet. Her messages won't go directly to my Link after Atlantis goes up, so I'll just have to check in when I can."

***

"Half Remembered Dream by Aaryan Shah. 2023." plays as my fingers dance over the keys, and I smile, implanting the new version of Atlantis into the transmitter humanity first contacted. I strike a few more keys and let it go. A sigh of relief escapes me, knowing I've done good work today, work that will keep Daen Tribe far safer than all the loops and cleanup I've had to run so far to cover our tracks.

And it's work they wanted. Work that can maybe make up for some of the debts my mother left in her wake. Work that can maybe justify the place they've made for me here.

Lifting my eyes to the world beyond my window, I breathe out, luxuriating in the loose feel of my shoulders, so often given to tension and knots.

Satisfaction wells within me as I stare at the curious, slender animals running in the distance with antlers like tree roots and tails like whips. Their short fur matches the blues and greens of the grasses that swirl about their legs.

Tears prick at the corners of my eyes, and I swipe them away, aching to see the world I'm helping to protect, one of the few good things I've done with my life. My throat grows tight with emotion, and tears spill over, pulling me into depths of remorse and happiness, mingling together in strange concoctions.

"Enjoy this," I whisper.

The pain inflicted upon these people was not *my doing.*

I say the words in my head, reminding myself that their losses, their suffering, it was all caused by my mother, by Mulvaney, by the corrupt and vicious Soldiers and Techs beneath them.

Not by me.

Choking back a hiccup of grief at the losses of the Awakening and the burden of letting go of self-blame, I smile once more.

Regonia is so beautiful.

I didn't take them away from this place. I helped get them back here.

Nodding slowly, I let my eyes roam over sweeping turquoise plains and the nearly black river. I watch the strange creatures that fly through the sky, marvel at the vibrant oranges and reds of their wing membranes.

I deserve to be here.

A sob chokes me, cutting off my attempts at speaking positively within my mind.

Enjoy this.

Chapter Fifty Three
Regonia

Ricardo

Six days to go

In the soft, grey light of early morning, with the rays of dawn just peeking over the horizon, Olivia and I move about our room, readying ourselves for the journey. She stows her laptop away in her pack, having removed it last night to work on something she and Rone have taken to calling Alexandria.

The logistics of it all go over my head, but I understand enough to hope it can bring the Drennar to heel.

I adjust the straps of my new pack, that of an adolescent member of Daen Tribe. I recall Krona's words about the item being nearly 50 Regonian years old, nearly 75 of our years. My mind fills with the wear and tear it must have endured harvesting that family's small garden over the decades, passing from one generation to the next. I let my hands linger on the soft, durable leather fashioned from the skin of an alien creature.

How can it be so pliable but so sturdy?

It even outlasted the family that used it.

The unnatural end to an entire family, even with members of three generations alive before humanity found them, settles on my shoulders, far heavier than the pack I wear. Taking a deep breath, I resolve to honor them, to care for their belongings, for the house they left behind which has been promised to Olivia and me.

If we survive all of this.

If she wants to share a home with me.

As she shoulders her pack, leaning forward ever so slightly to compensate for the weight on her back, I realize something. We've slept in the same room, in the same bed, nearly every night since we met. Only when one or both of us was hospitalized or at work have we slept separately.

My eyes fall out of focus, and my brows scrunch together as I pick out the individual nights that we didn't share a bed. And one of them was still spent passed out at her side, holding her hand while she was unconscious in the hospital.

It feels like so much time has passed, like we've grown so much since then.

But a part of me wonders if she's happy like this, if she wants this, wants me, or if I'm just a habit, something forced into her new life since waking that morning on Odyssey, still alive.

Or worse still.

Am I an obligation?

Someone she feels she has to keep around because I saved her, because I salvaged her life when she didn't want it anymore?

Now that she's happy to be alive, to be on a new planet, does she think she owes me?

Her voice rings through the fog of deep thought. "Are you okay?" she asks.

I blink, letting my face relax into a smile as the lines vanish from my forehead. "Yeah," I say, shaking my head. "I was just… thinking.

Anxiety creeps into her eyes, casting shadows within them. But she doesn't speak, doesn't ask me anything. She just waits.

My own feelings for her linger, heavy on my tongue, begging me to tell her. But my nerves get the best of me.

"I was just hoping we have enough packed for our trip," I say.

But the words feel wrong, and I wonder if she hears it, hears the note within my voice that says this isn't what I meant to say, what I *should* say.

The words beat themselves against the inside of my skull, desperate for air.

I shake my head.

"That's not it," I say, lowering my gaze and confessing to the lie, immediately.

I take her hands in mine, tracing the scratches that adorn them from little fixes on her ship and from the work done in fields and homes since landing here.

"Krona and Tenna have offered us a home here," I begin. "I just... It doesn't t *have* to be that way."

I look up, just in time to see something break behind her eyes.

"Oh..." she whispers, the sound more breath than sound. "I guess I just..."

She pulls her hands from mine, dropping her eyes to the floor. My heart shatters, collapsing my chest inward, and all the breath rushes from me.

"I thought..." she trails off again. "I thought you wanted this," she whispers as she rushes past me, moving for the door.

"Olivia, wait," I plead, hating the hurt I've put upon her.

But she doesn't stop, moving into the hall. "Olivia," I say, catching her forearm to slow her down, desperate to repair the damage I've done.

"It's fine," she says. "I shouldn't have assumed. It was dumb."

"No, it wasn't. I do want this, I just… I don't want you to think it has to be this way."

Her eyes meet mine, and tears shimmer on her lashes.

"You want this?" she asks, voice small and cracking.

"Of course, I do." But I need to know. So, I ask, "Do you?"

Olivia nods. Searching my face, hazel eyes darting back and forth between mine, she opens her mouth to speak, but nothing comes out.

She steps closer, sliding her arms around my waist. They rest against the small of my back, just beneath the pack, and she lays her head on my chest.

I wrap my arms around her shoulders, careful not to let their weight push down too heavily on her pack. Warmth rushes through me, and I smile at the prospect of sharing a home with her.

"You scared me," she says, but I'm not sure they're the words she would've spoken a moment ago. "I thought I was just that weird girl that makes everyone put up with her."

A chuckle escapes me. "Not even close."

***

I stand in the pink light of early morning as streaks of purple move across the sky in what the people of Earth once called an aurora. Staring at the village of Daen Tribe, at the people near the river still receiving their Marks, my mind fills with the longing in Krona's and Tenna's eyes when I last saw them gaze upon the ceremony. They want to be here, clearly.

But we can't wait.

Taron Tribe awaits us on the mountain, unaware of our approach.

If they knew of the star-born beings coming their way, of the star-touched people they once saw as allies leading us to them, would they blockade the bridge that leads to their home?

Deciding not to dwell on things we already have plans for, I watch the people of Daen Tribe instead. I watch their lips move in song as they mourn their Lost Ones, watch as those already Marked with the pain of the Awakening go about reclaiming their home.

Feet trod across the earth, tall grass swiping across thighs as my companions set off behind me. The sounds of their departure tickle my ears.

"You ready?" Olivia asks, voice soft and sweet.

I nod but don't speak, taking a few backward steps toward her. My eyes trace the rooftops of the village, straying to the plains beyond the river.

Slowly, I turn to face Olivia, smiling when my eyes find her with alien grasses swaying around her and crystalline mountains shining beneath the aurora far behind. I reach for her hand, and her hazel eyes glow as our fingers lace together.

Krona, Tenna, and two Regonian warriors, a man with pale grey skin and a dark blue braid and a woman with flowing white hair and emerald eyes, trek alongside Vyrtons. Impossibly, the beasts' antlers dwarf even them, and I marvel at the thick necks necessary to support such things. Heavy packs hang from their saddles.

We fall into step, walking slightly quicker than we normally would to keep up with the long strides of our companions.

The mountains rise up, taller with each step we take, and I have to wonder if they're taller than the ones from our long-lost planet. They must be for the Regonians to consider them mountains.

A deep sigh eases through me, filling me with peace and humility, and we trek toward the mountains, toward Taron Tribe, and all the uncertainty the coming days hold.

Chapter Fifty Four
Regonia

Tenna

My spirits soar as we trek across the plains and into the foothills. Grasses swirl against my legs, bending and swaying with the lightest breeze. Even so late in the year, warm air caresses my skin, soft with the scant moisture it holds. I breathe it in, luxuriating in the mild humidity.

Krona's hand wraps around mine as we hike up a small hill, squeezing gently. My muscles stretch and pull, pushing me up the gradual incline, and I savor the feeling of finally moving, finally exerting myself.

The ship and the station were just too small, too cramped to really move, but here?

Here, I could run until my legs threaten to give out beneath me. Here, and very soon, I'll climb steep grades and the occasional cliff face. Here, I can truly exhaust myself as I never could in the Human world.

I glance back at Olivia and Ricardo, and concern etches itself into my heart. Sweat shines on their brows, and they breathe heavily. Wonder sparkles in their eyes as they gaze at this world, at my home, but they move slower than they did just this morning.

I hope this journey isn't too much for them.

Our bodies are hardy, sturdy. But Humans are softer, fragile.

I suppose we could always set them atop the Vyrtons if the trek becomes too much for them.

I decide to keep an eye on them, afraid that their spirit will keep them pushing until their bodies give out. And this trek could well do it.

My eyes drift to the village. From so far away, the rooftops look small. Dots move about by the river, casting long shadows in the evening light. I strain my ears, but their songs no longer reach us.

Despite the agony of the Awakening, despite the loss we still mourn, pride wells within me at the sight of our home. Smiling, I take a deep breath and turn for the mountains once more.

Climbing the hill, I cast my eyes upward, tracing peaks and ravines. And there, near the top, nestled in between two towering peaks, Taron Tribe waits.

But how will they greet us?

***

As the sky turns purple and pink with the dying light, we reach a small stone keep, built especially for journeys to Taron Tribe. But my heart sinks at the sight of it.

Nestled into a copse of Juno trees at the base of the mountain, it waits as it always has. But the remnants of a rock slide lay within, and the wall facing the great stone behemoth litters the ground, a pile of rubble to blend in with its tumbled down brethren.

Beside me, Krona says, "I'll check it out."

But Sevlah, one of our Ullavekyns, volunteers to do so in our stead. His dark blue braid sways against his back as he walks toward the cottage.

We wait, releasing our Vyrtons into the pen nearby, thankful that it still stands. I turn to face Olivia and Ricardo, only to find them slumped on the ground, leaning against their packs. Their eyelids droop.

Did we move too quickly for them?

We'll have to move slower tomorrow.

If the rest of our shelters look like this, it won't really matter if we reach one by day's end anyway.

By the time Sevlah comes out of the house shaking his head, Olivia and Ricardo have fallen asleep against their packs. A smile lifts the corners of my lips.

Briefly, I wonder if Olivia remembered to check if she had a message from Rone. But even if she has one, it'll still be there tomorrow.

Chapter Fifty Five
Novay

Reginald

Five days to go

Days pass with no word from Olivia, no sign that she's even seen the message from Rone.

It should have reached her by now, surely.

My heart aches at the prospect of her coming here, and solitude takes its toll, painting my mind the color of her suffering.

Because why would they be kind to her?

Why would her experiment, the experiment with her unborn child, be a nice, easy one?

Having known only torment at the hands of my experiments, my mind shows no mercy in the things it imagines for her, and I slowly fall apart.

Rone's messages come sporadically, passed along between recruitment efforts and assimilation processes with the newly-emotional. But even her words do little to calm me, to ease the brutality I see the Drennar commit against my little girl every time I close my eyes.

I try my best not to think of the happiness she's so recently found with this man and with Daen Tribe, in the stars and on this new planet. But it creeps into my thoughts, unbidden, twisting the knife.

She finally found a place for herself, a place to be happy. A place to belong.

And they're going to take it away.

I push myself up from my bed, muscles tense and itching to move, to stretch and bend and push the anxiety from me. Pacing my room, I grit my teeth, holding back thoughts of Olivia and the Drennar. My fingers stretch out, then I clench them into fists. I roll my shoulders, stretch my legs.

But nothing helps.

Knots tie themselves tighter in my back, reaching sharp hands up my neck. Lances of pain stab into my skull, adding to the agony of my slowly healing head wounds.

Deep breaths.

I remind myself, over and again, to breathe. I tell myself to stretch, to let it go.

There's nothing I can do.

There's no use getting worked up. It won't help. There's nothing I can do.

There's nothing I can do.

There is absolutely nothing I can do about any of it.

But the thought only crumples my resolve, shattering my last fragile bit of self-restraint. Desperation and despair send my fists pounding against the wall, right where my door should be. Pain rockets up my arm with each impact, but I slam them against the wall anyway.

Screaming at the top of my lungs, I command the Drennar with all the power I don't have, "You can't take her!"

I shout until my lungs threaten to collapse and my throat goes raw. I slam my fists against the wall, one and then the other, until every bone in my hands threatens to break.

But no one answers.

The wall doesn't slide open, doesn't show me some Drennar monstrosity staring down at me with blank eyes. The flat, blue-grey wall stands, unmoved by my plight.

Falling against it, I slide down to curl in on myself at the bottom.

Chapter Fifty Six
Regonia

Olivia

I wake, stiff and sore, in Ricardo's arms. Our blankets lie heavily upon us, made for young Regonians who may have thought them flimsy, but they remind me of the weighted blanket I left behind on Odyssey, one I used when I felt particularly anxious.

Pulling in a deep breath, I marvel at how easy it was to fall asleep last night. Thoroughly exhausted from the long trek, from trying to keep a pace that wouldn't bother our Regonian friends, we passed out against our packs.

Even when they woke us to settle in, we barely got our bedrolls and blankets spread before falling into unconsciousness. With my mind finally at ease, knowing I was doing everything I could, knowing I'd put everything I had into my day's work, I drifted off quickly.

Now, I stretch, reaching up past my head and letting my toes straighten to points. My muscles protest, but only slightly. My eyes roam over the remnants of our fire from last night, tracing the stones that rimmed it and the ash and embers within.

A gentle snort draws my attention, and I turn to look at the massive Vyrto leaning its head over the wooden fence. Krona stands before it, dwarfed by the massive creature. He touches its soft nose gently, and it drops its face down. Massive antlers nearly rake over the roof of the partially collapsed cottage as it rests its forehead against Krona's.

A smile warms my face. My gaze drifts past them to trace Tenna's form, rounding up the Vyrtons with ease.

Briefly, I recall her wondering if she was a rider before, recall her thinking she worked with horses, or their equivalent. They seem to sense her thoughts, to move as she bids them without her having to speak. A whistle here and there, and they tip their heads to her, nuzzling her outstretched hands.

I blow out a soft breath.

Krona casts a glance at us over his shoulder and smiles. "About time, sleep-heads."

Stirring beside me, Ricardo murmurs softly against my ear as he stretches then wraps himself tighter around me. "It's sleepyhead," he says, correcting Krona gently.

"Either way," the Warrior King says with a chuckle. "It's time to be off."

I glance at my Link and seek out the time here on Regonia. With a shock, I realize that we've slept away two hours of daylight already. I jolt upright, exclaiming, "Oh shit... Why didn't anyone wake us?"

My body aches, but I push myself up from the blankets. I kneel in the dirt, scrambling to gather my things and pull on my boots.

Ricardo apparently checks the time, flying into action beside me. He moves in a more organized fashion, making me wonder what sort of drills he may have gone through in his training.

"You needed rest," Tenna says, approaching the fence with Vyrtons following on her heels. She kisses Krona, then puts a hand to his Vyrto's thick neck.

Turning to us, Krona takes in our frenzied appearance. "Relax," he says with a chuckle. "We have a little bit of time."

Only then do I look around, realizing that the other two Regonians are missing. "Where's Sevlah? And…?" I hate that I don't remember her name.

"Sailahti. They're scouting the path," Krona says. "The rockslide may have made some of it impassable. They should be back soon, but you have enough time to pack and eat."

"And stretch," Tenna adds.

I nod, slowing my frantic hands. I glance at my Link. "Is there time for me to check for messages?"

But Sailahti enters camp, smiling wide and laughing over her shoulder as Sevlah comes up behind her.

"We'll keep a pace that won't exhaust you today. That way, you can check tonight," Tenna says.

Shame blooms over my cheeks, and my gaze drops to my pack, to the salvaged comms unit within.

"We were eager yesterday," Tenna says, voice gentle. "We've been cooped up too long. Getting back here, getting to really push ourselves, we moved too quickly. Your legs are shorter than ours. You must have been jogging all day."

"Not quite," Ricardo says with a chuckle.

The tension in my shoulders eases, remembering just how outmatched we are on a physical level.

I'm not weak. They're just... super strong.

Breathing deeply, I glance at the people around me. Each Regonian towers over me. Their mounts loom even taller.

I'll check for messages tonight.

Chapter Fifty Seven

Novay

Rone

Four Drennar stand before me, glancing nervously amongst themselves. I smile, and two of them return the gesture, though it doesn't quite reach their eyes. Tension still lines their foreheads, narrows their gazes.

The wall hisses shut as their escorts leave us to our devices, and my smile deepens. A breath leaves me, and I say, "Thank God."

One of them tips her head to the side, casting confused glances at her compatriots. The lights within her clear skull-plate blink and whir, shifting over her brain.

Turning back to me, she scrunches her brows together and asks, "Did you... Are you... religious now? Did emotion take you so far from logic that you believe in Human gods?"

I chuckle, shaking my head, and the group seems to relax. "No. I just like the expression. Haven't you found any that you like?"

My question seems innocuous. Not at all like I'm testing them to see if they've been sympathizing with the subjects of their experiments.

A man on the end with an extra eye in the center of his forehead and a body like what Humans would call a centaur, if centaurs had scales in place of fur, blushes. A small laugh escapes him.

"I have to hear this one," I say, encouraging him, pulling his name from our databanks. Toorasten.

The girl next to him, a small, winged thing with startlingly-white, glittering skin, elbows him in his front leg. The smile on her face gives me hope.

He meets my gaze for only a second, then stares at the floor as he says, "Wish in one hand, shit in the other. See which one fills up faster."

A riot of giggles descends over us, and he rushes to defend his answer.

"It's not because of poop jokes. I still don't understand why Humans found those funny. It's actually a really deep phrase." Color rises in his cheeks, and he looks from me to his fellows. "It's about the importance of effort. It's about how you can't just wish for things and expect them to happen. You have to try."

I nod, considering his words, and find that I rather like the phrase myself, crude as it may be. When I say as much, the humiliation leaks from his face.

Yes... I think we're off to a good start with these four.

The woman with shimmering clear wings says cheerily, "I like their word 'plucky.' It fits them." Her soft, white hair bounces as her wings flap once, as if agreeing with her words. The smile on her face lights up her eyes, crinkling the skin around them.

"It seems like it fits you too," I say, testing the waters.

She beams, and her wings lift her off the ground, but only just. The ceilings here don't allow for much extra height, even for her small frame. Settling back down to the floor, she thanks me.

"Come," I say. "You have a lot of people to meet."

I turn from them, leading them deeper into our own personal complex. For the first time since learning of the plans to steal Olivia away, hope blossoms in my heart.

Four more on our side may not be a lot, but it's a start. And there are more coming tomorrow and the next day.

Chapter Fifty Eight
Regonia

Krona

We stop for the day as the light sinks in the sky, a little earlier than it did yesterday. The shadows move toward us, galloping at full speed this close to the mountains.

We let our Vyrtons graze on grasses, offering them treats of Vailans, small insects that would otherwise plague our evening with their incessant buzzing. The cottage we'd normally push for on our treks lies far ahead, and with the pace we kept today, we should reach it at the light's highest point tomorrow.

Somewhere to sit when it's time to eat, I suppose.

Yet, I don't mind the delay.

Of course, we need to move quickly, need to gather whatever allies we can muster and push on to Novay, but a slow approach will keep us from exhausting Olivia and Ricardo. And it'll give Taron Tribe some time to push past their fear of star-sickness and greet us with logical distance and wariness rather than the pointed ends of spears.

Hopefully.

As our Ullavekyns tend to the Vyrtons, Tenna and I set up camp. Olivia settles in with all her tech, face alight as her fingers whir over keys. She reclines against the base of a Juno tree, shaded by soft pink leaves, and the grasses sway about her, nearly concealing her.

"Where do you want your bedroll set out?" Ricardo asks, coming up beside me as I kneel to cut away a swath of grass for a fire.

Tenna moves quickly, shearing a ring of grass around me. I stack our kindling, hands moving quickly.

"In the ring Tenna makes," I tell him.

A cool wind blows in from the north, a far cry from the warmth of the day. It's the first time I've felt it since we got here, and I know it doesn't bode well. I cast a glance back at the sky, then at the village, hoping they all make it inside.

"It will be a cold night," I tell Ricardo, suddenly wishing we'd pushed a little harder, just today, just to reach the cottage ahead.

All I can do is hope the change isn't drastic enough to bring us a storm. A shiver runs through me at the prospect of being caught in one, sleeping outside.

Our Skywatchers thought us safe.

But I know they haven't been watching long enough to get a good feel for the winds this season, haven't seen the storms past, haven't felt the changes in the air for more than a few days.

Can they tell already?

They've always had a knack for storms. Skywatchers aren't made, they're born.

But can they tell after being away so long?

Sighing, I try to focus on the task at hand, reassuring myself all the while that we have our Ameeka blankets, have it woven into our bedrolls. The soles of our boots are made of Ameeka sap and fibers.

We'll be fine. It'll keep the lightning at bay if it comes for us.

Swallowing hard, I hope we don't have to test it. Never before have we lain beneath the sky with cold winds coming for us and the threat of lightning hanging over our heads. I cast my eyes to the sky, then force myself to move.

The quicker we can get under those blankets, the better.

After striking a fire stick over the lattice of dried Juno leaves and grasses, twigs and Vaila wings, I rise to fetch more fuel for the fire. A sob catches my attention, pulling my gaze to where Olivia slumps beneath the Juno tree, weeping over her various pieces of tech.

Chapter Fifty Nine
Novay

Rone

Lustran and I walk down the hall, checking on our new recruits. Through Sentrah's open door, we find her kneeling on the floor. She doesn't notice us, doesn't even open her eyes. She brings her hands up in front of her, steepling them and pressing them to her lips.

I tip my head to the side, considering her. The lights within her skull plate spread out through her neurons in a steady wave, slowly undulating. She whispers something and opens her eyes. Color spreads over her cheeks when she sees us.

Words tumble from her lips in a rush. "I was just doing an experiment," she assures us, pushing up to her feet. "I'm done now though."

"It's okay if you were praying," Lustran says.

Her blush deepens, and she turns from us. "I wasn't…"

I nod, accepting her answer, but Lustran's analysis seems accurate. And promising. Odd, considering our roots in logic and knowledge and objectivity, but for our purposes here, it could be good.

Most of the Human religions were pretty staunchly opposed to experimenting on unwilling subjects.

Here's to hoping she hasn't chosen one of the few that endorsed it.

I smile, and we walk on, meandering down the hall. Lustran nudges me, offering up a grin.

Blue-grey halls pass by, monotonous and pale. Without anyone to lay claim to the hall, its surfaces are yet unadorned. But each time we pass by the quarters of one of our compatriots, we see decorations, small accumulations of personality and sentimentality.

Things that the Expressionless see no need for.

A bit of alonarium sculpted to look like an animal here. A flash of color there. A picture where the blank wall once was.

Hope stirs within me, vibrant and real. I can almost taste it, sweet and tangy, though I know it can only be my imagination.

Lustran stands up straighter as we move toward Curata's room, schooling his features into a sly grin. A quick check finds his pulse elevated.

The corners of my lips quirk up.

Music seeps from Curata's room. "Holy Ghost by Legion. 2021." Sounds collide in a mixture of Human cultures, bohemian and electronic, dark trance and piano, all blending into something that stands the hairs up on my arms.

I glance at Lustran, curious.

He tips his head to the side, brows furrowing as we walk. The lights within his brain dance from one synapse to another behind the clear plate in his skull.

We turn a corner and find the hall near her room dark. Lights flash beyond the opening, and something truly magical awaits. My jaw falls open, and my feet pull me to her door.

The music quiets, and a soft voice whispers briefly, sending chills down my spine.

In the middle of her quarters, Curata hovers, spinning slowly in place. The alonarium of her floor reaches up, holding her aloft as vines of alonarium twist and climb her legs, sending flowers and leaves of palest grey reaching out into the space around her.

She tips her head back. Her arms sweep gracefully through the air, coming back to steeple before her chest, then pushing upward, reaching for the ceiling. She pulls her arms back down as the vines twist, slowly rotating her entire frame. Her hands move in delicate waves, fingers seeming to flow like water.

And the ceiling reaches for her, alonarium responding to the static impulses she commands. Thin rods of blue-grey descend from the ceiling, forming shapes at their ends.

My breath catches as I watch, picking out a Vyrto attached to every other rod, massive antlers frozen in place but legs moving as if running. The other rods form only abstract shapes, rippling and undulating.

And the whole assembly rotates, a tiny carousel moving opposite her.

Reginald would love this…

Lights sizzle throughout the abstract shapes, moving in time with the music that swirls through the air around us, heady and disorienting. The flashes and fades illuminate the tiny alonarium Vyrtons and flicker on her pearlescent skin, bare and luxurious. It shines on iridescent wings.

A small gasp escapes me as I marvel at her skill, the intricacy of her work.

Such control over the alonarium…

What's her ranking?

A quick check finds her ranking frozen, suspended for the duration of this experiment, just like all of ours. But it shocks me, just the same.

She's in the top 0.72%…

Lights wick their way up the vines which twirl about her legs, spreading out into the air around her. The flowers bloom as the glow reaches them.

Beside me, Lustran steps forward and reaches out a hand to touch a delicate bud as it moves past us. His wings fall slack, dropping from their tight position at his shoulder blades, and his eyes quickly move to Curata, beholding her with wonder.

"How?" he whispers, voice reverent.

On a whim, I check his ranking, finding him within the top 8%.

The music begins to fade, and Curata snakes her hands upward, melting the carousel back into the ceiling. Graceful and beautiful, she retracts the vines, letting the lights sizzle and flash on the ends as if burning them away.

Surefooted, she steps down from a platform of vines on tiptoes and smiles at us. The music offers one last drum beat, and she lets the remnants of her work seep into the floor.

"That was beautiful," I say.

Her perpetually pink cheeks lend the illusion of a blush, but her neck and chest confirm it. "Thank you," she says.

Her eyes seek Lustran, staring up at him through dark lashes. His mouth moves, but no sound comes out. She takes it for the compliment it is, blushing deeper.

Clearly nervous, she explains, "Humans have people called artists. We could only ever understand those who made their work look like something real. Portrait artists, bust sculptors. People whose work could be evaluated objectively in terms of their skill in reproducing something realistic. But any who strayed, any who interpreted… We couldn't understand them."

Gesturing behind her, she says, "Like this. It matches nothing. But it fits the song. It just… fits. And I understand it now."

She tips her head back, closing her eyes as she lets the song play once more. "I can't explain it, but I feel it, I understand it. It's something the Humans call intuition. The Regonians call it 'daet kvassen ris ahaen kai,' *the sense of what is*. Knowing without explanation… We missed so much."

And she's right.

This strange display, this masterpiece she just created, fits that song. It was beautiful and mysterious and complex, and yet… understood. The intuitive nature of emotions, the concrete ambiguity of them defies all logic.

But it makes sense.

I nod and ask, "Can I show the footage to Reginald?"

Chapter Sixty
Novay

Reginald

Reclining in my bed, I stare at the ceiling, counting down the days. For the past twelve years, they've blurred together here, fading and shifting in shades of pale flint.

But I count the days now, letting my Link guide me.

Five days left.

Five days until they try to breach Atlantis, until they might realize Olivia isn't there.

Five days until they try to take her.

Impotent rage builds within me, curling my hands into fists. I pull in a deep breath, reminding myself that getting upset, again, won't help, but that doesn't undo the knots in my back, doesn't dig my fingernails out of my palms.

Another deep breath.

A message from Rone comes through, trying to rescue me from the fury of Drennar betrayal. Sighing, I open the message. A video pops into my mind, and I pause it for a moment, shutting off the lights in my room and easing down into bed. My head aches as I rest it against my pillow.

I close my eyes, and Rone's smile bursts across my eyelids.

"You have to see this!" she says, chattering excitedly. "I'm not sure how she managed this, but I just had to show you."

She fades from view, leaving me wondering what she could possibly be talking about. Or who.

The video shifts to a pale grey room filled with strange, loud music, dim light, and…

Is that a fairy?

A small woman with creamy, shimmering skin moves delicate arms, lifting, twisting. Soft light shines on wings like a dragonfly, plays on her flowing white hair.

But as she moves, the floor reaches up for her, lifting her, twisting vines and leaves and flowers of pale grey around her legs. It slowly twirls her, and she pulls a carousel from the ceiling with a few delicate moves of her hands.

Creatures with antlers and fluffy tails take shape from the carousel, chasing each other in methodical, never-ending progress.

My jaw drops as I watch real magic.

But it can't be magic. Magic isn't real.

I laugh internally, chiding myself.

There must be some explanation.

Lustran steps forward, reaching out a hand to a delicate bloom as it passes him in its rotation through the room. Rone stands in the doorway, barely in the frame of whatever viewpoint she's sent me footage from.

As the song comes to an end and the fairy woman stops spinning, she approaches the door to her room. She says something about Human artists, about understanding without explanation.

She's a Drennar!

With a start, I marvel at the magic that's just taken place, the technology, the scientific manipulation of material. And an idea takes root in my brain.

She's a Drennar.

But she obviously has emotions.

I watch her blush before Lustran's gaze, wonder at her comprehension of art and music.

The video fades, and Rone appears on the backs of my eyelids once more, words tumbling from her lips. She tells me of this woman, Curata, and her high ranking within Drennar society, her incredible intelligence.

And she might be on our side…

I send a message to Rone as quickly as I can, sparing only enough time to double check the usage of our private channel. I send only text, unable to film properly without her blocking the footage of my room.

"Do you think you can bring her over to our side? And what do Drennar do when confronted with something they don't understand?"

My mind whirls with the potential of this, figuring all the possibilities, making plans. Sudden purpose blossoms within me after so many days languishing like some superfluous piece of baggage. But now, I'm contributing again.

I may not be useless after all.

Chapter Sixty One
Regonia

Olivia

I stare at the screen, but my eyes slip out of focus. Rone still moves there, but I register only blurs. She speaks, and though her voice rings in my mind thanks to the cochlear implant, her words run together.

How...?

I can't be pregnant. I can't be a mom.

My heart twists, filling me with fear. Fear of failing a child. Fear of breaking this tiny person before they ever get a real chance at life. Fear of turning out like my own mom, of spending more time working than with my kid. Fear of falling back into the bottle.

Childbirth looms before me, hanging heavy in my mind.

I'll give birth in space. Aboard a ship that I'm supposed to fly. Hugo can't fly the ship alone all the time. He can't land.

But then, where would the baby be?

I can't expect Ricardo to take care of it all the time.

The blood drains from my face.

Ricardo...

How can I drop this on him?

The world fades around me, narrowing to a single point, a blurred image of Rone on the screen framed by swaying grass. My lungs work faster, and my heart hammers.

But I won't give birth on the ship.

The rest of Rone's words filter in through the rushing sounds of my blood.

They're coming for me.

I'll have the baby on Novay, watched by the Drennar.

A shiver rolls through me.

What will they do to me? To the baby?

My mind whirls as I struggle to assimilate this new threat, *these* new threats, to my life. But dread slips quietly into my mind as a new fear swallows me.

When?

When did I get pregnant? Was it our first time? Was it before I tried to...

Did I ruin our baby on Sparrow?

My Link runs a scan, assessing my current hormone levels, coming up with a rough date.

Relief washes through me, and a sob rattles over my lips.

Oh my god, thank god.

Tears fall freely as I thank whoever might be listening, surprised at myself for doing so, that I got pregnant after I pushed the bottle away, after I took those pills.

I haven't destroyed this kid yet.

My hands tremble, and I press them to my lips, to my eyes. Sobbing, shaking, I barely notice when the comms device is lifted from my lap, when strong arms wrap around me. Ricardo's scent slips into my awareness, and I sink into his embrace.

Everything around me falls away, and reality comes to a pinpoint, just this moment, just me weeping in Ricardo's arms. It crystallizes with sharp edges, jabbing me, slicing me open.

He rubs my back, hand moving in slow circles.

But what would he have done if I'd gotten pregnant before, if I'd hurt the baby that night on Sparrow?

A fresh wave of anguish bowls me over, and I clutch his shirt. My face scrunches up as tears threaten to drown me, to wash us all away.

Gentle sounds whisper over my ears, and Ricardo rocks back and forth slowly. Patience guides his hand in slow, even moves over my back. One hand slides into my hair, holding my head to his chest. My tears slow, and my lungs pull in full breaths.

"Do you want to talk about it?" Ricardo asks.

I scrunch my eyes shut.

I have to tell them.

Trying to calm myself, I focus on the steady beat of his heart beneath my ear, just a bit too fast, thanks to me.

Shame washes over me knowing that I'm falling apart in front of everyone. I try to listen, to hear their efforts to set up camp, hoping they haven't all stopped, aren't all staring at me, but I hear nothing over my own sobbing and the roar of my blood behind my ears.

I have to get myself together. I have to be strong.

They need strength.

But the thought of my own failings only sends me further into despair. Waterfalls of tears pour from my eyes, soaking Ricardo's shirt.

Gritting my teeth, I try to get hold of myself.

You're being stupid. Stop this.

They need you to be strong. They need more than this, better *than this.*

Ricardo tightens his embrace, crushing me to his chest.

But I'm failing them. I'm failing them all.

There's too much to do. I can't just sit here, crying.

I pull away, wiping at my tears. "I need to do something. I can't let you guys make camp without even trying to help."

Tenna's voice comes from behind me, soft and kind, "Your contribution is this." She holds the comms device up. "Feel your way through it so you can tell us what happened. That's your contribution tonight."

I nod, but fresh tears spill over. I open my mouth to tell them, but my voice croaks, catching in my too-tight throat.

With a thought, I switch the audio from my implant to the speakers on the device and let Rone's warning of impending Drennar intervention play for them.

I want to watch Ricardo's face, to see how he reacts to the news of my pregnancy, but I can't bear it. My head hangs low, dripping tears onto my lap.

When the message ends, silence falls over our camp. Tenna reaches for my hand, and Ricardo pulls me against his chest again.

"If they breach Atlantis," Krona says, "they'll know we've left. They'll come here for you. Can they breach it?"

I shrug, suddenly uncertain. Sobs wrack my body, and I shudder against Ricardo.

Chapter Sixty Two
Regonia

Ricardo

I'm going to be a father.

The thought swirls around my head, repeating and turning in on itself. Fear and joy war within me, and I look up at Krona and Tenna, watching carefully, awaiting their turn to comfort Olivia.

I'm going to be a father.

I'm going to… We're going to have a baby.

We're going to have a family, a better family than either of us had growing up.

My jaw hangs slack, but a smile tugs at the corners of my lips. A quick breath leaves me, and I blink a few times, trying to process everything.

We're going to have a baby.

But the Drennar are coming.

And Olivia still cries in my arms.

I tighten my embrace, pulling her against me. But I wonder…

Is she upset about the Drennar? Or about being pregnant?

She mumbles against my chest, words coming out choked and muffled.

I lean back and ask, "What did you say?" Placing my hands gently on the sides of her face, I wait.

She doesn't meet my gaze, hazel eyes hiding behind lids and lashes as she stares at my chest. Tears run over her cheeks, slipping over my hands.

"Olivia, it's okay. What is it? You can talk to me." I steel myself, hoping she wants this baby, wants a family with me, hoping she only fears the Drennar.

Under the circumstances, she'd be eligible for an abortion if she wanted one. She's one of two pilots, one of two ambassadors, heading to war.

No doctor would even bother to submit a request.

And Dr. Sullivan could do it.

She hesitates, chewing at the inside of her cheek and avoiding my eyes. Silence rules her, stretching to an eternity, and my heart twists in my chest.

"Olivia…" I breathe. "Talk to me, please."

Swallowing loudly, she fights against the next sob, pressing her lips into a thin line. She takes a deep breath and whispers, "I didn't hurt our baby, I promise."

"What?" I ask, confusion drawing my brows together.

Finally, she meets my eyes, "I checked. I haven't had any alcohol since. The pills were before. I haven't hurt our baby, I swear!"

I crush her to me, chuckling with relief. "Oh… That's not… I thought you wanted…" I press a kiss to the top of her head and try again. Softening my voice, I say, "I know. If you'd gotten pregnant the first time, we would've known by now. That was ages ago. Hell, we've been in space for months."

"It doesn't feel like it. And I was just... I don't want to ruin this before the baby's even here.

I don't want to hurt it. I don't want to…" Her words trail off, overrun by sobs that shake her against me.

I tighten my arms around her, whispering softly, "I know. You haven't ruined anything. You didn't hurt anyone. The baby's fine."

The words feel foreign, hard to comprehend.

"We're going to raise a baby on an actual planet..." I say, voice hushed by awe.

"Not if the Drennar take me. What if they take the baby? What if they kill me?" She pulls back to stare at me, and her face blanches. Darkness moves within her eyes. "What if they kill the baby? What if they torture it for some stupid experiment?"

"Hey, hey," I say, cradling Olivia's face in my hands. "We're not going to let that happen. Okay? You're pretty good at thwarting their plans, and so is Rone. We'll figure this out."

She nods but doesn't seem convinced.

Leaning against me, she takes a piece of grass into her hands, bending it, folding it. Her eyes drift to the path ahead, to the mountains.

Tenna and Krona each whisper, "Congratulations."

The other Regonians follow, but their eyes all drift to the mountain eventually.

"Will I… Will the baby be alright on the trip up the mountain?" Olivia whispers. "We don't have time to turn back, do we?"

"It's still pretty early on," I say. "As long as you don't get hurt…"

I choke on the words.

"You'll take the paths the Vyrtons take," Krona says. "No cliffs for you."

Chapter Sixty Three
Regonia

Tenna

Dark clouds move through the night sky, blocking the moons as they travel along the mountain range. I lie awake, watching them from beneath my Ameeka blanket, listening to Krona's even breathing beneath my head. A quiet hope whispers within me.

Let the clouds pass without incident.

Let them leave us behind. Let them move south and vanish from sight before they unleash their fury.

I strain my eyes, watching their silent progress through the darkness and hoping to glimpse stars between them. But they layer over one another, far too thick to see the Realm of Stars.

A small part of me misses the beauty of space seen through our windows on the ship, vast and humbling. Free from lightning.

Taking a deep breath, I feel the earth beneath me, feel the blankets atop me. I concentrate on Krona's breathing and the sound of his heart. I close my eyes, making my peace with the danger we face here at home and hoping the storms don't claim anyone in the village.

But we're home.

I take another deep breath, listening to the soft footsteps of Sevlah, pacing on first watch.

And slowly, I drift off to sleep.

***

Four days to go

Morning washes over us, gray and dismal. The light of day struggles to reach through the clouds crowding the sky. I sit up, taking stock of our party, eyes darting from one yawning face to another.

Everyone made it.

I chide myself for my silliness, knowing the thunderous bolts of death would have woken me if one struck near enough to kill any of us. But my eyes turn to the sky, to the northern horizon.

Too many clouds yet linger, stalking toward us.

They hang over us as we pack up camp, as I question our decision to keep moving. They loom as I shake my head. We can't afford the delay of waiting for them to pass, but they darken as we climb atop our Vyrtons and ascend into the Nurahvi Mountains.

Every step my mount takes, every time I jostle upon her back, we get closer to the clouds, closer to the lightning that could strike us down at any moment.

The grasses thin, giving way to stone and Lahrike. Krona stops our procession, dismounting. He kneels, using a knife to gather some of the spongy vegetation. It shimmers, showcasing every shade of purple imaginable. The grey blossoms seem dull by comparison, but they have their uses, too.

He harvests enough to fill three pockets on his pack and four on Sevlah's pack. Satisfied, he climbs back atop his Vyrto's back.

"Will it be enough?" I ask, glancing at the plentiful patches surrounding us.

After some consideration, he nods. "If they haven't taken to harvesting it themselves over the last year, this will last them a while." As we move forward, climbing a slow grade and winding up the side of the mountain, he meets my gaze. "At the very least, it'll show them we haven't fallen so sick as to forget ourselves. Or them."

He gazes up at the black stone mountains, at their crystalline peaks, thoughtful yet again.

"They'll give us a chance to explain," I say. "We aren't dealing with Orlansi anymore."

Krona chuckles, shaking his head. "I can't even express how thankful I am that Relnoc and Dresde are more reasonable than he was."

I hate to bring his mood low, but I have to ask, "Do you think they're still leading?"

"They're no older than us. Unless the Vaerkin learned the paths while we were gone or they fought Roon over hunting grounds, they shouldn't have faced battle," he says. A deep breath lifts his shoulders, rushing out as a sigh. "But nothing is certain."

***

As the grey light dips and shadows begin to consume us, we reach the first cliff. I slide from my Vyrto's back, grateful for the excuse to stretch. Bending and reaching, I ease my muscles from the long day riding.

But a glance at Olivia tells me we did the right thing.

I remind myself that she has to meet Taron Tribe, that we don't have time to turn back, but the anxiety of having a mother-to-be on this journey weighs heavily on my shoulders. The life within her means too much to risk like this. That baby deserves more than death-defying journeys.

But for now, there are no other options.

I look to Krona and drink in the spark of light gleaming in his bright green eyes despite the clouds blocking most of the sunshine. He smiles, vaulting from the back of his Vyrto. Sauntering over, he slides a hand around my waist and plants a soft kiss on my lips.

485

"I've missed this," he whispers.

"Me too."

My hands wrap in his hair, pulling his lips against mine again. Heart pounding in my ears, I force myself to pull back. We still have to climb, still have to set the bridge. There's still a long way to go before we reach a wide enough section of the path to make camp.

Though his hands are tense, dragging over my flesh as if reluctant to let me go, he doesn't stop me when I step back. He stretches as I approach the cliff.

Behind us, I hear Olivia ask Sevlah how we're supposed to get the Vyrtons up it, but I don't hear the answer he gives her. I place my hands on well-worn grips, finding the small stones and crevices I've used to climb this cliff many times in the past. My feet find their marks, and I haul myself up with ease.

My memory guides my hands, but I still watch, still check their placements. Glancing up, I see the top of the cliff far out of reach, but every move brings it closer.

My heart races, and my arms and legs rejoice at the activity. After so long in space, on a ship and a station and a planet not built for my kind, the exertion sends my blood singing through me.

When I'm high enough, Krona joins me on the cliff face, climbing beneath me. We move together, synchronized after years together.

As darkness falls, peeking over the mountains at us, I reach the top of the cliff. Pushing myself atop it with ease, I turn and gaze at the distant village. Plumes of smoke rise from chimneys and from the fire they reignited on the island our dead lay upon.

But they're home.

Finally.

A deep sigh eases out of me, and I step back from the cliff edge. Krona climbs into view, cresting the top and smiling in the darkness. I savor the sight, yet again thankful that our eyes work better than those of the Humans.

"Ready?" I ask.

He nods, and we move to the next cliff edge, forsaking the winding path that promises to lead us up. Our ramp waits, rope still secured and wound through the four pulleys dotting the side of the taller cliff.

We take the rope in hand and pull. Over and over, we heft the weight of the massive ramp, moving it closer to the edge of the cliff. It grates over the stone, sending up small sparks as it goes, but they land on stone and birth no flames.

I push myself, finally able to do so, and the edge of the ramp sticks out into the air beyond our little platform. We pull again, and I feel the moment that the ramp starts to slant downward, the moment of ease as its weight starts to fall, then the sudden jerk as it drops back.

Down below, Sevlah shouts when he secures a rope to it, then signals when he begins pulling it further out to keep it from grinding to a stop on the stone below. By the time we secure it into place, shadows rule, but the Vyrtons know the way. Their dark eyes glow in the night, drinking in every scrap of light and bouncing it back at their surroundings. They climb the ramp, joining us and waiting for Krona and I to mount them once more.

We make slow progress up the path, and the small clearing that we would normally use for a midday break appears before us.

We busy ourselves with fire and bedrolls, provisions and food for our Vyrtons. Olivia settles in to send a message back to Rone.

Chapter Sixty Four
Regonia

Ricardo

Three days to go

Sunlight peeks over the horizon, finding me wide awake. I watch it rise as my heart sinks.

This baby...

I sigh. Olivia's concerns drift through my mind, but I can reason those away easily enough. She hasn't had a drink or taken any pills since getting pregnant. She hasn't hurt our baby. I know that.

But... What if I mess this up?

I had a chance to prove myself raising my brother, and he turned out to be a homicidal scientist with delusions of holding the ethical high ground. He never learned the consequences of his actions or learned to notice the lengths others went to in order to help him.

But how much of that was him?

And how much was my own failure?

Some small part of me begs my mind to give me a break.

I was a kid. I didn't know how to raise a kid.

I didn't have a good situation to work with, didn't have any resources to raise him with.

Maybe our parents hurt him worse than I thought they did. Maybe I wasn't able to save him from them as much as I thought.

But those things just feel like excuses.

I drop my head into my hands, ripping the horizon from view.

I was just a kid.

I shouldn't have had to raise him, shouldn't have had to protect him from our parents. That shouldn't have fallen to me.

With a sigh, I whisper, "I did the best I could."

Lifting my gaze, I stare at streaks of orange and yellow in the sky. "My best is better now. I'll do my best with this baby."

Exhaling, I nod slowly and remind myself, "My best is better now."

***

I walk alongside the Vyrtons, wishing I could gaze up at Olivia. She sits upon one of the massive beasts, resplendent and framed by the late morning light.

But the terrain demands my focus, repeatedly tripping me as small rocks shift underfoot. None of the steady, flat surfaces on Termana or the stations prepared me for this.

The strange purple vegetation coats everything here, thick and oddly spongy. My feet sink into it, but I can never gauge how far I'll sink before hitting solid rock. A centimeter? Five? Every step is a little mystery, and I find myself watching my feet, peering past grey flowers and purple leaves, straining to see the black stone beneath it.

But it just looks like shadows.
Or the shadows look like the stone.

Ahead of me, Krona and Tenna amble easily, muscle memory guiding their feet as surely as if they grew up on these peculiar stones and… moss?

Is this moss?

I bow my head forward, straining my eyes to see it better. My Link runs a brief visual analysis and informs me that it has some qualities of moss and some qualities of actual sponges. I scrunch my brows.

Not exactly helpful.

I nearly barrel into Sevlah's back, stopping short to avoid tripping into him. Krona and Tenna scramble up another cliff face, using ropes and pulleys to slide a ramp over the edge for us. I marvel at their work, at the ingenuity of it all.

Atop her Vyrto, Olivia giggles, catching my attention. My gaze snaps up to her, and I know she saw me nearly plow right into Sevlah. Mirth dances in her hazel eyes.

Gaining control of herself, she asks, "Are you okay?"

I nod, blushing. "Just a bruised ego."

She laughs harder.

"Yeah, yeah. Laugh it up. I can't get pregnant just to get out of hiking," I tease.

"That's a shame. It's a good deal, really." She purses her lips, considering. "All those times I was puking my guts out, all the fun side effects I might get later, childbirth… It's totally worth not having to climb a literal mountain on foot."

We laugh heartily, and for a moment, I think everything is fine.

But as the laughter fades, her features shift. She swallows, takes a deep breath. Her brows reach for each other, and she sucks her lips in as she looks down at her hands, balled before her.

"Olivia?" I ask, voice gentle. "What's wrong?"

But the ramp drops into place with a loud thud, shaking the stone beneath my feet. My eyes jerk over to see the first of our party ascending, leading the Vyrtons upward.

Olivia's mount moves forward, and she shakes her head once.

I'll have to try to get her to talk later.

***

We stop at a small mountain stream for a drink, letting the Vyrtons nibble on leaves and buzzing insects. Olivia smiles with the scout named Sailahti, laughs with Sevlah. But my mind lingers on this morning, on the myriad things that could have struck such fear into her heart.

As we set off for the afternoon, my thoughts fill with the logistics of a pregnancy in space, away from the doctors more accustomed to these things, away from the equipment to properly handle this situation.

After all, no one expected a birth aboard this ship.

We should have been more careful.

But the thought stings me. Guilt tears at my insides at the prospect of wishing my child away.

Yet, I don't wish my child away. I just wish…

I wish the circumstances were better. I wish we could be doing this from the safety of the village or the station. I wish we weren't climbing a mountain in the desperate hope that Taron Tribe might ally themselves with us against the Drennar.

You know what? I wish we weren't going up against the Drennar. I wish they'd just left us the fuck alone.

But then, I never would've met Olivia, at all. Never would have met Krona or Tenna.

Never would've come to this planet.

As my feet plod over the rocks and the purple sponge-moss, I grapple with guilt and the impossible longing to have all the good things in my life with none of the bad. I laugh at myself, derisive and humorless, as we ascend two more ramps to bypass sheer cliffs.

When the fourth cliff of the day looms over us, casting long shadows, we make camp in the flat area before it. I settle in next to Olivia at our fire, and my mind wanders to the life she carries, the life we made. My eyes land on her stomach.

I want to give you everything.

I want to give you so much better than the life I had.

I glance at our companions, at the smiles on their faces despite everything.

If we make it through this, they'll be there. These are the faces, the temperaments, our baby will grow up with.

Their honor and strength, their love and loyalty... These are the lessons our child will grow up with.

And suddenly, despite all the hardships before us, I smile, too.

Chapter Sixty Five
Novay

Rone

Two days to go

"What experiments were you overseeing?" I ask Curata.

Her face dips into a frown, an unusual expression for her. It doesn't fit the strange pink hue that never seems to leave her cheeks. Her milky skin sparkles, iridescent from some prior experiment, further contrasting the sadness that tightens her eyes.

She stares at her hands, fidgeting in her lap, and her bottom lip even trembles.

"Do I have to talk about it?" she asks, her voice a small, hoarse mockery of its usual chipper tone. "Is this part of..." A hiccup interrupts her. "Is this an experiment?"

I shake my head, reaching for her dainty hand. My fingers wrap around hers. "No. I was just curious. You don't have to say it if it hurts too much."

She glances up at me, holding my gaze for the briefest hint of a moment before shying away again. But not quickly enough to hide the tears brimming in her eyes.

"I know I shouldn't... I mean, I know I'm supposed to..."

She shakes her head, dislodges a few tears. They splatter onto the back of my hand, trickling over my skin. When she speaks again, her voice comes out thick, choked by the tightness in her throat. A peculiar effect of emotion that we never believed real.

"It hurt," she forces herself to say. "It hurt to hear them scream."

Chills run down my spine, and I wonder what horrors she bore witness to.

"I know it shouldn't have, and I know I shouldn't say that," she says, voice rising as she prepares to defend herself as I know she must have done outside this compound.

I cut off her explanations, her justifications.

"It hurt me too," I tell her. "I couldn't stand to watch them suffer anymore."

A small admission.

But a treasonous one.

She stares at me, open-mouthed. "Really?"

I nod, watching her carefully. I guard my reaction, but a message from Lustran, viewing our exchange from a distance and analyzing every biological metric within our grasp, tells me to trust her.

"It doesn't have to be that way," I whisper.

She leans in, and all the hope that typically occupies her face falls away, a mask peeling back to reveal a deep hollow within her. "But how? What could we ever hope to do? We're stuck here. Just because we don't see it happening anymore doesn't mean it isn't."

I breathe a sigh of relief. Lustran's judgement of her was accurate. A smile tugs at the corners of my lips, and I say, "I have a few things to tell you."

***

Buoyed by the success with Curata and assured that Lustran will speak with her further to figure out a role for her to play in our plans, I float into the common room. Sentrah sits, staring thoughtfully at the darkened wall and the bright words splayed across it. I scan it quickly and realize it's an old religious text from the Human world.

Odd…

Wasn't she the one who questioned me about god? Wasn't she the one we thought was praying?

I recall the way her synapses lit up beneath her clear skull plate as she wondered if I'd fallen so far from logic as to become religious. Now, the words reflect on her blue-black skin as she peruses the praises of some almighty god.

I tip my head to the side, considering her.

But something alerts her to my presence, and she wipes the words from the screen instantly. She doesn't turn to face me.

"You didn't have to do that," I tell her. "Their religions are interesting. We can read together, if you want."

"That's okay," she answers. "I was done. It's all nonsense anyway."

She pushes up from her chair, one she's shifted to a dark red, emulating leather rather than the pale grey of the world beyond our compound. Rushing from the room, she keeps her gaze on the floor.

Chapter Sixty Six

Regonia

Krona

One day to go

The skies clear above us as we climb, clouds parting to shine brilliant light down upon the mountains. One cliff after another, the world around gleams with hope. I chide myself for doubting our Skywatchers, even if they have been so long away from home.

Our slowed pace will push us beyond the time frame of their predictions, but our only option is to keep moving.

We pass the day with clear, pristine light to guide us, moving beyond the black stone to the clear turquoise of the mountain peak. It shines beneath our feet, showing facets and prisms where its edges meet the dark stone beneath it.

The light fades as the sun tucks itself in for the night. The stars shine overhead. I glance at Olivia and Ricardo, and for the first time in months, I fear the stars again.

Not because of a sickness that doesn't exist, but because of the creatures that told us it did.

The creatures coming for her.

I look up to the stars once more, and my hands curl into fists. Silently, I vow to protect her, to protect the family she and Ricardo deserve to have.

Tenna approaches, steps soft despite the crystalline surface beneath her feet, but I'd know the sound of her, the feel of her proximity, anywhere. She takes my hand, unfurling it and twining her fingers with mine.

"I know," she whispers, eyes drifting to Olivia and Ricardo.

***

Abduction Day

The day moves slowly, filled with the agony of an animal waiting for a predator to strike. I keep a careful eye on the skies, chiding my own derision, knowing that the Drennar will go to Termana first, that we'll have the length of time it takes them to get a message back to Novay, the length of time it takes them to drop soldiers down upon us from their home world.

I remind myself that it doesn't matter how closely I watch the sky. They won't come here first.

Clouds roll in, dark and angry, as afternoon comes and goes. They block out everything, moving down alongside the mountains and roiling as they go.

Evening falls upon us, and the dark clouds part in the distance. As we settle in for the night, I can just make out the Taron settlement on the peak across from us. A massive stone bridge waits, ready to lead us across the ravine that separates us from them.

The sun sets, reaching through the crystalline mountain peak and lending a teal shade to the air around us. The smoke from our campfire sends a clear signal to our once-allies, and I can only hope they'll hear us out.

The clouds close in, blocking the sun and robbing us of the diffuse green light shining through the crystal. Our campfire crackles, and the first peel of thunder rips through the sky.

Panic slams through me, but I didn't see the lightning.

How far was it?

Where did it strike?

I turn quickly, taking stock of our camp.

But I know if lightning struck here, it would have bounced between us.

"We should spread our camp tonight," Tenna says.

My eyes trace the horizon, searching for the village, but the darkness of a stormy night hides the homes below from view.

At least it isn't burning.

Slowly, silently, we move our bedrolls out and apart from each other, spacing ourselves out in a line down the path. With sticks and boulders, anything we can find, we frame our Ameeka blankets like tents and hope the rains don't bring a landslide down upon us. After stowing our Vyrtons beneath an overhang, we bed down.

Tenna and I camp near the bridge, and we sit in the mouth of our tent, watching the guard tower on the other side. The rains move in, heavy and violent, whipped against us by thrashing winds. Our fire goes out, sending plumes of smoke spiraling into the air.

But the fire at the guard tower, the torch safely concealed beyond their open window, burns freely. It silhouettes two Taron warriors peering out at us.

Lightning bursts through the sky, lending them enough light to see our scattered camp, our small numbers. Showing them we mean no harm, harbor no plans of attack.

A year ago, they would have called us across the bridge, beckoning us to safety. No hesitation. No qualms.

But now, fear holds them still.

Fear of star-sickness.

Fear of us.

Chapter Sixty Seven
Regonia

Olivia

Ricardo and I curl up together in our tent, listening to the rain batter the thick Ameeka overhead. My insides coil tightly as the tension that's been dogging my heels all day twists just a little tighter.

Sitting atop a Vyrto, I spent the better part of the day working on Alexandria, but I finished my little present for the Drennar late this afternoon. Ricardo and I worked on our surprise for Taron Tribe after that, rehearsing and working out accents for the remainder of the day.

But now, balled up in our tent with nothing to do, nothing else to think about, my mind fixates on Termana and the stations.

Are they okay?

Did Atlantis hold?

With no way to know, no way for news to reach us for days to come, all I can do is sit and wait and pray to a bunch of gods I don't even believe in. My hands ball into fists, and a helpless, frustrated sob breaks from my lips.

Ricardo slips an arm around my waist, pulling me against him. "I know," he whispers. "I know."

I rest my head on his shoulder, trying not to cry, trying not to worry. I stare out at the darkness, at the valley, flickering into view as lightning flashes across the sky. Thunder roars through the air, beautiful and so very loud. I try to focus on the wonders around us, the miracles of nature.

But my mind spirals.

If only I had some whiskey…

The thought slithers through my mind, soft and small and hideous.

Before the thought even completes itself, I recoil from it, hating myself for its presence.

I can't drink. Even if I had alcohol here, I can't.

For the baby. For Ricardo.

For all the people counting on me not to fuck this up.

Tears fall in earnest as I wither before my own mind. The gravity of the situation falls heavy upon my shoulders, building the desire for a drink, stoking the shame burning in my gut.

Why am I so weak?

Cait's voice doesn't whisper through my mind to answer me, to correct me. It's been too long since we spoke. I don't even know what she sounds like anymore. All I hear now is the rain on the stones, on the Ameeka over our heads.

How can she push me forward from back at the station?

Can I do this alone?

Ricardo plants a kiss on the top of my head, and I close my eyes. My skin raises in goosebumps, spreading in waves over my body. With a deep breath, I remind myself that I'm not alone.

I force myself to speak, pushing myself to trust. "Do you think Atlantis held up? Do you think they got through?"

He rests his head on mine. "I've never seen anyone do the things you can do. I don't know if they got through, but I know that if anyone could keep them out, it's you."

***

One day after Abduction Day

Clouds hang heavy above us, threatening more rain. Morning crawls along, dragging us in its wake. Ricardo escorts me to a nearby crevice in the crystal, and I reach out a hand, running my palm over the smooth stone.

My eyes fall shut, and I listen to the sounds of the world around us. The shrill cry of an animal in the distance, the whistle of wind through ravines and over cliffs. The rumble of thunder, carrying the next storm just a little closer.

Turning from the mountain, I look out at the valley below. The river carves a snaking line through foothills and fertile fields. Smoke rises from chimneys in the village far below, and even now, people sit near the river, taking their marks on once-white sheets in the storm's brief respite.

I cast a glance back at the rest of our camp, at Tenna and Krona, at Sevlah and Sailahti. They sit at the edge of the bridge, almost on it, stripping the now-dried grey blossoms of the Lahrike from the spongy, purple leaves.

Ricardo begins, "Joo taesei—"

"Joo *seilar*," I correct. "They add -lar at the end if it's past tense. Tae- at the beginning means future tense."

"How do I keep mixing those up?" Ricardo asks with a chuckle and a shake of his head. "And how are you so good with languages? Okay, what is it again?"

"Joo seilar kur sein Daen Jooahrn kur loo gordeky," I say with a gentle smile. "Ar daet Skon ris Soons, joo yvelar joo isvens. Valn joo ban daet isve."

We came here to return Daen Tribe to their home. In the Realm of Stars, we made ourselves allies. Yet, we seek an ally in you, as well.

We practice for the rest of the day, taking refuge in our tent when the rains return.

Chapter Sixty Eight

Regonia

Tenna

Two days after Abduction Day

Another day dawns beneath clouded skies. Thunder rumbles in the distance, but the lightning doesn't show its face on this side of the peak.

At least, not yet.

Tension brews as we watch the sky, the bridge, the guard towers. We wait for a lightning strike or a drop of rain. Or an arrow. But the morning passes, uneventful, with our stomachs tied in knots.

Grey light filters through the clouds, casting a hazy teal shine over our camp as it refracts off the crystalline mountain tops. As the light reaches its highest point in the sky, the first drops of today's rain fall. They splatter over us, drenching our camp.

Krona and I take shelter in our tent, and all our compatriots do the same. Our Lahrike bundles come with us, gathered hastily and shoved into

Ameeka bags. The cool raindrops cling to me, to my hair, sending shivers over my skin.

The sky beyond the tent flashes, too bright, and thunder shakes the world. The rumbling continues long after the air goes dark, coming closer, getting louder. The ground shakes beneath us, and a horrifying realization slithers through me.

A rock slide.

My blood runs cold, and my mind races, trying to figure a way out of this. But the cliff and the threat of arrows or spears from Taron Tribe if we set foot on that bridge hold us in place.

Krona grips my hand, and I meet his gaze with panic squeezing my heart, my throat. His piercing green eyes widen, and he whispers, "Hoo kai voo mai."

As we wait for the lightning to bounce from one to another, to claim us here on the mountainside, I say, "Hoo kai voo mai."

Better to die here, serving our Tribe, than unconscious on a lab table in the Realm of Stars.

I close my eyes, leaning my forehead against his. He clasps the side of my neck, thumb tracing my jaw.

At least we got our people home.

I resign myself to death, even as my heart leaps into my throat, but the rumbling stops.

Gulping in sharp breaths, I laugh a short bark of relief. "We're alive..." My voice hitches as hot tears spill over my cheeks.

Slowly, I open my eyes, gazing at Krona.

We made it.

But a scream rips through the air, punctuating the drumming of rain on our tent. My blood runs cold, drains from my face. All the air rushes from my lungs.

In an instant, Krona and I are out of our tent, charging into the rain, but half our camp lies buried beneath tumbled crystalline rocks and boulders. Olivia and Ricardo peek out of their tent, staring in horror at the landslide that almost completely claimed Sevlah's tent and separated us from Sailahti.

A muffled groan seeps out of the rubble, and my stomach lurches.

Light flashes and thunder rumbles in the distance. Moving without thought, I grab the first boulder I come to, rolling it down the mountainside. Krona climbs up beside me, tossing small rocks over the edge with abandon.

We start from the top, careful not to topple anything else down upon Sevlah. From the other side, Sailahti grapples with stones and small boulders, white hair slick with the rain and clinging to her face. Loose stones whisper over the landslide, barely audible over the rain.

Ricardo jumps in, but Olivia stays back, hand over her mouth.

I breathe a sigh of relief that she didn't come closer, but I never stop moving, never stop throwing stones over the cliff. They crash and clatter as they roll further down the mountain. The sky flickers yet again, and my ears struggle beneath the weight of thunder.

Slowly, we uncover Sevlah's tent, and another burst of lightning illuminates the blood spreading beneath the crumpled Ameeka. Dark red coats turquoise crystal.

"Sevlah?" I say, voice cracking as I step forward.

Another groan greets my words, low and broken. Far too quiet.

Slowly, we set to work moving the remaining rocks to free the Ameeka, careful not to disturb the lump that seems to be Sevlah. A moan issues from the tarp, creeping out from where I thought his feet would have been.

Sickness moves through me in waves as a bolt of lightning pierces the sky, showing me another puddle of blood seeping over the stone, shining in the light and barely diluted by the rain.

I meet Krona's gaze in the flickering dark, heart lodged in my throat.

Chapter Sixty Nine
Regonia

Olivia

Lightning flashes, and Sevlah's blood glistens in the night. Rain batters the puddle, splashing and rippling, lending the illusion of life to the crimson liquid as it rushes from Sevlah.

And he lies broken, unmoving.

A moan breaks from his lips, too soft, too quiet.

Sickness moves within me, rising up my throat. Doubling over, I retch, spilling my meal over the stone at my feet, thankful for the thunder that covers my noise.

I can't distract them. Sevlah needs them.

Tenna, Krona, and Sailahti assess him, careful hands moving over limp arms and closed eyes. But they don't touch his legs.

They don't need to.

I try to keep my eyes from tracing the bones which jut out in jagged shards, try to keep myself from puking yet again. But I fold over, knees meeting the rocky ground.

My body contracts in heaving lurches, and I close my eyes, desperate not to see the mess I'm making. My hands grasp wet stone. I focus on the drops of rain sliding over my scalp, dripping down my temples. I listen as it drums against the mountain, listen to the wind whistling through the peaks.

Gentle hands find my back, and Ricardo asks, frantic, "Are you okay?"

I nod. "The baby doesn't like blood..." I say with a groan.

"Can't say I blame it," he says. His hands slip beneath my arms. "Here, let's get you up. You need to rest in the tent where you can't see him."

I shake my head. "I can go. I've got it. Please..." I meet his eyes, careful not to look beyond him, not to stare at the way Sevlah's feet seem twisted backward. "Please, just help him."

Before he can rise to his feet, before I can begin my procession back to the tent, a shout rings through the air. All our gazes jerk toward the bridge to a Regonian man standing in the center of the massive stone structure.

"Svevensonlar is Coomlar?" he calls. *Battered or Lost?*

My Link translates it for me, but I've learned enough Regonian by now not to need the help.

He holds his torch aloft, awaiting our response. The wind whips at the flame, but a plate of some sort shields it from the rain. His dark skin shines in the light, so dark it almost looks blue.

Leaving Sailahti to tend to Sevlah, Krona and Tenna step past us, cautious as they move over wet rock. They may have ridden into battle with this man just last year.

But so much has changed.

My heart leaps into my throat as we watch their silent progress toward the bridge, toward the man that could offer us aid or turn us away.

"Svevensonlar," Tenna answers, and only now do I realize how accustomed I've grown to hearing her speak our language. "Valn too mai kai fein."

Battered. But his spirit is leaving.

Tears spring forth, pricking at the corners of my eyes. I tremble as they fall.

The man on the bridge takes a tentative step forward.

"Sei. Ka too." *Come. Carry him.*

"Hoo kai rahn ahngata? Ris sootvali?" Tenna asks. *You're not afraid? Of star-sickness?*

"Ahn hoo ka sootvali, Regonia kai coomlar," the man answers gravely. *If you carry star-sickness, Regonia is lost.*

Bile rises in my throat as I realize the depth of despair he must dwell in now. I swallow it back, rising to my feet. I draw the Taron man's notice, see his jaw twitch once.

And then he leads us across the bridge with Krona, Tenna, and Sailahti carrying Sevlah's broken body. I barely remember to grab my pack.

Chapter Seventy
Reginald

Novay

Three days after Abduction Day

Some emotionless guard leads me down the dreary, grey hall. I drag my feet, guessing at what I'll see in my testing today. I tell myself to stop thinking about it, to stop dwelling. Again and again, I remind myself that I finally did something worthwhile.

My mind fills with Curata's display, her art.

The way we'll use it.

For a moment, I feel terrible using something so beautiful for such an end, but war doesn't care for things like sentiment.

The guard stops before the same section of bland wall, and it hisses open, just like every day before. The hideous monotony wears on me, yet again, but I follow him in, not even bothering to look at him.

My eyes find the chair in the center of the room, and I follow my feet there. Settling in, I take a deep breath, resigning myself to whatever torture might wait for me on the wall. Slowly, I lift my gaze, not quite ready for the day.

Will they show me their assault on Termana and the stations?

I don't want to see it, but I need news. I need to know how it went.

Did they breach Atlantis?

The dull denim color shifts, showcasing the darkness of space, the gleaming shell of Termana and her stations. The stars shine brilliantly behind my home.

A strange, excited dread fills me, tightening my chest, pushing my heart up into my throat. I try to hide my reaction, but I know they've already noticed. They've recorded and measured it in thousands of different ways, analyzing the oxygen content of my blood, the dilation of my pupils.

They're probably even measuring the speed my fingernails grow at, just on the off chance that might somehow have something to do with anything.

Just go with it.

Leaning forward, I ask, "What have you done now?" And though I know they haven't taken her, know they didn't find her there even if they breached Atlantis, I force the words to come out. "Did you take her?"

My voice breaks at the prospect of it. My heart lurches at the promise of them seeking her out across the galaxy.

A sleek black form takes shape outside the nearest station, materializing before my eyes. My breath hitches. My mind goes back to the night they came for me.

If they get through, I'll see how they did it this time.

I brace my elbows on my knees, steepling my hands and pressing them to my face. I shake my head as small black spheres drop out of the larger ship and move toward Odyssey station. My heart freezes.

The little crafts land on the hull, adjacent to the airlocks. The bottoms flatten out, morphing to fit the shape of the station before spewing three Drennar out onto the surface of the station, one from each craft.

They approach the airlock, sleek suits fitted closely to their bodies, outlining extra limbs and wings. Their face plates gleam in the light of the stars. They stand before the airlock, waiting, patient as ever. The camera zooms in on them, and only now do I realize that there must be a second ship.

Sickness moves within me, churning my stomach.

Will they experiment on them on the ships?

They were taking a lot of people, but... not enough to take two massive ships.

Slowly, the Drennar back away, but the airlock doesn't open.

My breath rushes out of me, and waves of relief wash through me. But I don't get time to hope that they'll leave, that they failed.

That Atlantis held up.

One of the Drennar breaks free from the pack, heading back to the small black ship only to return with a smooth grey block. I narrow my eyes, trying to puzzle out what it could be. A tiny blue light flickers on its surface, blinking with each step that the Drennar takes. Her ears blink in time with it.

She sets it down beside the airlock, and her ears blink twice. The block spreads out, thinning and moving to form a circle around the airlock. The tips of her ears blink three times, and the tiny light on the ring of alonarium flashes three times in answer. It reaches up, forming a dome and encapsulating the airlock.

My heart drops through the floor.

"No…" My voice comes out a hoarse mockery of its normal timbre, trailing off into nothing. "Please, no."

The universe narrows to a single point, that little grey dome. I watch them place another smaller block of alonarium. Without ever lifting a finger, they form it into a smaller dome, attaching it to the larger one.

A new airlock...

My scalp prickles, and my stomach heaves. Ice cold dread rushes through my veins.

The camera view changes in a dizzying instant. Suddenly, I stare out through the visor of one of the Drennar, seeing the domes up close. A section of the smaller one slides away, and the Drennar step within its confines, locking themselves in.

The next dome opens, revealing the airlock of Odyssey station. Through the visor, I watch the Drennar kneel before the large metal contraption, the staple of human life in space. Another Drennar steps into view, releasing gas from a pocket of their suit, white clouds pouring from their upper arm.

Reaching forward, my unwitting host retracts the suit from their hand, revealing a metallic digit in place of an index finger. She slides it around the airlock door, and blinding light burns my retinas. I look away, seeing the sparks fly in my periphery. In seconds, they pull the doors free and slip inside the station.

I bury my face in my hands, stomach churning and heart plummeting. A sob escapes me.

Atlantis worked, but it didn't matter.

Great, heaving breaths shake my shoulders. Tears trickle down my wrists.

They'll know she's not there. They'll know she's gone to Regonia.

My calculations from days ago come back to me, reminding me just how close Olivia is.

A month from here to Regonia in our ships.

Maybe a couple weeks in theirs.

I scramble to think of a scenario where they wouldn't go after her, where they'd let their precious experiment slide, but I come up empty.

They're going to get her.

Continue reading in *Reckoning*, book four of The Regonia Chronicles.

Thank you!

For buying this book. For reading it all the way through.

If you liked it, please leave a review on Amazon, Goodreads, Barnes & Noble, your blog... Anywhere, really. Reviews are the lifeblood of authors, helping books get noticed in the almighty eyes of search engine algorithms. Even if only a few words, a review is incredibly helpful.

Eager to stay up to date on the latest dark fiction from Elexis Bell?

Sign up for her newsletter on her website.

www.elexisbell.com

Other Books by this Author

Literary Fantasy Novels

Soul Bearer

The Gem of Meruna

A Heart of Salt & Silver

Allmother Rising

The Sword and The Savage

Literary Thriller Novellas

Annabelle

Things Left Unsaid

Literary Post-Apocalyptic Novel

World for the Broken

The Regonia Chronicles

Awakening

Faltering

About the Author

Elexis Bell is a quiet nerd with too many hobbies, including everything from gaming to shower-singing and even archery, weather permitting. She specializes in sarcasm and writing stories that make people feel. She's made a home for herself with her husband and a small army of cats.

She writes dark, gritty stories, sprinkling gut-wrenching emotions over high fantasy romance, thrillers, post-apocalyptic romance, and science fiction.

For further information, follow her on Instagram, Twitter, or Facebook, or check out her blog on her website. There, you can sign up for her newsletter to stay up to date on all future book releases, giveaways, and ongoing projects.

www.elexisbell.com